ONE OF HER OWN
A Gemi Kittredge Mystery, Book 1

Shawn McGuire

OTHER BOOKS BY SHAWN MCGUIRE

GEMI KITTREDGE MYSTERIES Series
One of Her Own, book 1
Out of Her League, book 2

WHISPERING PINES Series
Missing & Gone, prequel (novella)
Family Secrets, book 1
Kept Secrets, book 2
Original Secrets, book 3
Hidden Secrets, book 4
Rival Secrets, book 5
Veiled Secrets, book 6
Silent Secrets, book 7
Merciful Secrets, book 8
Justified Secrets, book 9
Secret of Her Own, book 9.5 (novella)
Protected Secrets, book 10
Burning Secrets, book 11
Secret of the Season, book 11.5 (novella)
Blind Secrets, book 12
Secret of the Yuletide Crafter, book 12.5 (novella)

THE WISH MAKERS Series
Sticks and Stones, book 1
Break My Bones, book 2
Never Hurt Me, book 3
Had a Great Fall, book 4
Back Together Again, book 5

Short Stories
The Door
Escaping The Veil

ONE OF HER OWN

A Gemi Kittredge Mystery, Book 1

Shawn McGuire

Brown Bag Books

Copyright © 2021 Shawn McGuire
Published by Brown Bag Books
ISBN: 9798599325321

For information visit:
www.Shawn-McGuire.com

Cover Design by Steven Novak
www.novakillustration.com

First Edition/First Printing February 2021

CHAPTER ONE

My sister was planning to leave again. It wouldn't be for very long this time. I knew because she asked to go for a run with me. A small chunk of time for us to connect before business took her off the island. If the trip would be longer than four days, she would have asked me to block out the entire night. Then we'd crawl into her bed like teenagers having a sleepover and watch whatever was playing on Hallmark. I swear Ashlyn's television was stuck on that channel.

"I'll wait for you outside," I shouted up the condo stairs, running shoes in hand.

"Be right there," she called in reply.

That was fifteen minutes ago. So while I waited . . . and waited, I loosened up. A few gentle squats and quad stretches. Then I balanced on my left leg, right leg straight out behind me parallel to the ground, arms stretched forward. Warrior 3 pose. To maintain balance, I locked my focus on the creamy-white and bluish-purple orchid planted next to the sidewalk. Our gardening-crazy neighbor told me it was called a "Blue Fairy." All I knew was that it was pretty and smelled good.

I was in the middle of doing warrior pose on the other side when the door opened.

"Finally," I groaned. "I could've done two miles by now."

Ashlyn, looking gorgeous as always, pulled the door shut behind her, took one step toward me, then went back inside, returning two seconds later.

"Forgot my water bottle." She went back in again and came out with a baseball cap. "Gotta be careful about the sun. Don't want wrinkles." She patted her cheeks with the tips of her fingers.

I pulled my short hair into a stubby ponytail and added a headband to keep the wisps in place. "You remembered sunscreen?"

"What did I just say about the sun?"

My concern was skin cancer, not wrinkles.

"Where are we going?" Ashlyn asked, pulling her left foot up, heel to her butt for a count of two. Then the right foot. And that was the extent of her warmup.

"Down to Kahului Bay. We'll take Kuikahi Drive to Maui Lani Parkway then to Kamehameha Avenue."

Her jaw went slack. "How far is that?"

"Seven miles." She didn't have to say a word for me to hear her complaint. A fourteen-mile round trip was too much. "That's two miles less than I usually do. You can make it. I'll go slow."

She swatted my shoulder with the back of her hand. "Brat. All right, let's do this."

We took a right out of the driveway, crossed the street, and jogged on the sidewalk. Mrs. Ly, the gardening-crazy neighbor, was on her front porch tending to one of three massive hanging baskets. She waved with both hands and smiled with her whole face.

"Good morning, Kittredge girls."

"Good morning, Mrs. Ly," we answered in unison.

Ash and I had lived on Maui for fifteen years, half my life, and I still didn't know the names of more than a handful of plants. The Blue Fairy orchid being one, thanks to Mrs. Ly. I should let her give me a lesson sometime. We could take a stroll around the neighborhood, and she could share her knowledge. My mind instantly scanned my jam-packed schedule for an empty hour where I could squeeze in a walk. There wasn't one. Not until the schoolyear concluded in about six weeks.

Speaking of schedules, Ashlyn had already put me behind by ten minutes today. After the first mile, I was good and loose and had to stop myself from increasing to my normal speed. Along with shortening the route, running at Ashlyn's pace was okay today too. We were enjoying sister time.

At an intersection, we jogged in place and waited for a car to turn. I looked left and noticed a couple standing by a car a few yards down the street. They were young, high schoolers or possibly college students. The girl had her back to the Corolla. He stood in front of her with his arms on either side of her shoulders. He leaned in, talking close to her face. If I'd looked away at that moment, I would have dismissed the scene as a boyfriend and girlfriend having an intimate discussion. But a blink before I did, the girl turned away from him and looked directly at us. Her eyes went wide, and her back straightened. The boy turned, too, and gave me a grin that made my skin crawl.

"Hang on," I told Ashlyn.

It took two seconds for Ash to know what was coming. "Oh, Gemi. Leave it alone."

"That girl's in trouble."

"Then we'll call the police."

Too late. By the time Ashlyn had pulled her cell phone out of the pocket on the thigh of her capris, I was halfway to the Corolla. Besides, the cops wouldn't handle this right.

"Is there a problem?" I demanded, eyes fixed on the girl. Her mouth opened slightly, revealing a quivering lower lip.

The boy laughed when he saw my clenched fists. "Nothing that concerns you, lady."

"I wasn't talking to you." I softened my gaze on the girl in short canary-yellow shorts and a black floral tank top. With long slightly wavy dark-brown hair, tanned skin, and narrow brown eyes, she looked like an islander, not a tourist. Two more steps forward brought the bruise forming on the girl's right cheekbone into vivid view. "What's your name, sweetie?"

"Nichole. He's Ty."

I couldn't care less what his name was. "Do you need help, Nichole?"

She lifted her chin a minuscule amount, seeming a bit braver now with backup nearby. Good. "I told him last night that I don't want to see him anymore."

"She don't mean that." Ty's tone wasn't that of a broken-hearted beau. He wasn't trying to win back the girl he liked. His posture—looming over her, trapping her inside the cage of his arms—was pure aggression.

My breathing became shallow. My heart rate increased. Anger slithered slowly through my body starting at my toes. I knew, only too well, what that stance meant.

"Gemi." Ashlyn came up behind me. "The police are on the way. Let it go."

Giving the smallest of nods to indicate I'd heard her, I suggested, "Nichole, why don't you come over by us?"

She tried to dip away, but in a flash, Ty hooked an arm around her waist, causing her to cry out in pain or fear.

"Oh, crap," Ashlyn muttered behind me. "Gemi, don't—"

Too late. I lunged forward and wedged my outstretched arms between them. Slamming my forearm hard into Ty's Adam's apple, I pressed gently on Nichole's back, guiding her away from him. As he stepped back, coughing from the blow, I grabbed his arm, pulled it straight behind him, and pressed my forearm against his outer elbow. With enough pressure there, I could break his arm. Instead, in the next blink I swept his leg with mine and dropped him to the ground on his belly. Then I jumped on top of him, pressed my knee into the middle of his upper back, and pulled his left arm up behind him. All of that took two seconds. Maybe three.

"Nichole, I'm Gemi Kittredge. That's my sister, Ashlyn. Go stand by her now, okay?"

Without a word, the girl darted over next to Ash who put a

protective arm around her.

"Let me go, *haole*," Ty cried out. "You gonna break my arm."

"I could, but I won't," I assured as though talking to a small child. I pulled his arm back as far as I could and applied a little more pressure to his elbow. In this position, it wouldn't take much more than an ill-timed sneeze to hyperextend it. "If I wanted to break your arm, it would already be broken. If I want to mess up your shoulder, I can do that too. That could lead to surgery. Extensive physical therapy for sure. So how about you lie still and be quiet?" A little more pressure with my knee silenced his grumbling. I asked Nichole, "Did he hurt you?"

A look of stunned amazement had spread over her face. Ty wasn't going anywhere, yet still, she stuttered an unconvincing, "N-no."

"That bruise on your cheek tells me someone did."

"I, um, I ran into—"

"Don't tell me you ran into a door. Or a wall. Or that you fell. Or that *you* did anything to cause that." I inhaled deeply, trying to control my still hot anger. "Did he do that?"

Nichole's hand went to her cheek, and she gave the smallest of nods.

It took all my self-control to not snap Ty's arm. Fortunately for him, sixteen years of martial arts and MMA training had given me a tremendous amount of self-control. Physically, at least.

Ashlyn leaned close and whispered something to Nichole. Whatever it was, it helped the girl relax. Nichole's shoulders dropped, and she lifted her chin even higher. Good job, Ash.

"He attacked me two nights ago."

As I unconsciously increased the pressure on Ty's elbow, he whined, "Damn, lady. Ease off."

"He raped you?" I clarified.

"He tried to force himself on me, yes." Nichole's jaw set, and she leveled a steely gaze on this piece of gutter trash. "My friend pulled him off me before he could do anything."

I kept my voice as comforting as my hold on Ty was painful. "Sweetie, he did do something. He put his hands on you when you hadn't given him permission to."

The chirp of a squad car's siren cut our discussion short. Rotten timing. I had plenty of other things I wanted to say to her. An officer with his head shaved almost bald got out of the car and stood by his open door.

"I'm Officer Akana. I got a call that there was a physical assault in progress." His dark eyebrows lifted in surprise at the scene before him. "I was told a male was attacking a female."

Ashlyn, smiling big at the uniformed man, explained what had happened. As she spoke, his brows lowered and furrowed in further confusion.

"He's at least twice her size," Akana noted. "You're telling me she pulled him off the victim and has been holding him there for—"

"Almost five minutes now," I called. "I can stay here for another five if you want, but he'll for sure need therapy for his elbow and shoulder if I do."

The officer looked to Nichole for confirmation of Ashlyn's report. She agreed it happened the way Ash said.

"I'll need to get a statement from you," Officer Akana told her as he placed Ty in the back of his squad.

"Can we do that here?" Nichole asked.

A few faces had appeared in windows of nearby houses, but the street was quiet otherwise.

"Let's get out of the middle of the road." He led her to the sidewalk. "I can take your statement here, but you might need to come into the station later."

My adrenaline level decreased, making my previously warm muscles tighten. I swayed side to side, trying to keep my legs a little loose, while Nichole explained what happened. Once she was done, he asked for my version of events which, of course, matched Ashlyn's.

"How did you . . ." Officer Akana once again eyed me in proportion to Ty.

"I'm an MMA fighter."

"Don't downplay it," Ashlyn scolded. "She's the number one female fighter on the island. Number one in the state for her weight class."

My sister could be such a mom sometimes. She went on to brag about my near perfect record and invited him to come watch my fight this weekend.

He blushed, embarrassed by her obvious flirting, but seemed impressed. "Sounds like this young lady was lucky you two came along when you did. Although we don't like to encourage vigilantism."

I gave him a tight smile and held my right foot behind me in a partial standing bow pose. My legs were itching to get back to the run.

"It wasn't vigilantism, Officer Akana," I insisted. "I'd call it Good Samaritanism. I was simply helping a woman in need the best way I know how."

He held my gaze, letting me know with a tilt of his head that I was skirting the line between the two. After noting our contact information, he dismissed Ash and me.

Before we left, I went over to Nichole. "If you want to learn to protect yourself, I teach women's self-defense at No Mercy."

Nichole nodded. "That gym west of Kahului College. I know where it is."

"Tuesday nights at seven and Saturday mornings at nine. Come anytime for a free lesson and see what you think."

Nichole thanked me with a quick hug and promised to stop for a lesson.

After we'd run a few blocks, Ashlyn stated, "You'd think I'd be used to that by now."

"Used to what?" My legs wanted to go faster now, to burn off the rest of the anger still coursing through me, but I held back, letting my sister set the pace.

"You have no idea what you look like from a bystander's point of view. Honestly, Gemi, you're scary. You had that guy on the ground before I even realized you'd moved."

I smiled. Glad I could still impress her. "When do you leave?"

"Tomorrow morning."

"Where are you going this time?"

She chewed her bottom lip as though thinking. "Osaka." She tilted her head to the side. "I think." Tilt the other way. "No, Honolulu."

My sister could be so scattered. She worked for an independent human resources firm that focused on team building. Whatever that meant. Something about in-house workshops and off-site retreats to build camaraderie between co-workers. She regularly jetted off to faraway locales. Many times, it was Japan. Other times Singapore or Taiwan. A few months ago, she was in China for ten days. That was unusual. Normally, she was only gone for long weekends.

"How long will this trip be?"

"Two days." Ashlyn squealed her response. "Well, two days of conference. I'll be back on the third day."

"I'll hardly know you're gone. And you still wanted to go for a run?"

"We haven't seen much of each other lately." She sounded out of breath, so I slowed a little.

"Today is Wednesday. That means you'll be back in time for the fight on Saturday night."

"No way will I miss it. It's the biggest fight of your career."

That was what she said every time she left before a fight. She'd only made it back for about half of them. And every fight was big to me. I hadn't lost in ten years and had only lost twice in the twelve years I'd been fighting. My first loss was my first fight. I was inexperienced and terrified. The second came four fights later. I'd worked my ass off, won three in a row, and got cocky. This weekend I was defending my 14-and-2 bantamweight MMA championship title. A win would give me twelve in a row. A nice even dozen.

"I know you don't like coming—"

"That's not true," Ashlyn insisted. "I don't like watching you get hit."

"Which is why I try to not let that happen very often."

We ran another two blocks before Ashlyn said, "Hang on. My phone's buzzing." I jogged in place, checking my heart rate on my smartwatch, while Ashlyn pulled her phone out of the pocket on her aqua-blue leopard-print capris again. "Dang it."

I knew what was coming. She forgot an appointment. How could my sister hold such a high-level, detailed position with her company and still be so flighty?

"Jeannie is coming to pick me up in an hour." She wiggled her fingers and then tapped a reply. "Getting our nails done."

"Your nails?" I squinted at her hands. Except for two tiny chips, her nails were perfect. "I thought this was a work trip."

Ashlyn finished replying to Jeannie's text and slid the phone back into her pocket. "It is a work trip."

I smirked. "Must be a guy you're anxious to see there if you're so worried about your nails."

"No," she insisted, but the rosy tint coloring her cheeks told me differently. "I have to go shower. We went, what, almost five miles. That's good, right?"

"Five? Ha! We went not quite two."

Ashlyn looked southwest toward home and seemed to be calculating the distance. Then she shrugged. "So I'll get in not quite four miles total. Better than nothing."

I stopped jogging in place long enough to give her a hug.

"Good job with Nichole." She gave me an extra squeeze before letting go. "Who knows what you saved her from. Even though you're scary, I'm proud of you."

"Thanks. I'm just grateful we were there." She turned toward home, and I added, "Choose a pink shade. One the color of your cheeks a second ago. I was right, wasn't I? There is a guy."

Ashlyn pointed a nearly perfect coral-tipped finger at me. "Behave. Enjoy your run. Good luck on your test. I'll see you tonight."

My test. I was ready, but a little more studying never hurt. Fortunately, class wasn't until eleven. Plenty of time to finish my fourteen miles. Since Ashlyn had turned back, I could even add a couple more.

When I finally reached the beach of Kahului Bay, I paused long enough to take my shoes off. I loved running on the beach but hated getting sand in my shoes. With maybe half a mile to go before it was time to turn back and start the return trip home, I saw feet poking out of the foliage about twenty yards away. Probably a homeless person who had slept by the cluster of shrubs—heliotropes, I believed—for the night. There were hundreds of homeless people on Maui, so it was a reasonable assumption.

Except there were also birds. Three of them.

No one would still be sleeping with birds on them like that. Passed out instead of sleeping? There were plenty of alcoholics and drug addicts on the island too. Except, as I got closer and saw the white, pink, and teal running shoes, a sick feeling filled me. They were the exact kind my friend wore.

That was a coincidence. Plenty of people had those shoes. Besides, she lived in Kihei, ten miles from here.

When I was fifteen feet away, the birds—mynahs?—flew off, and small crabs skittered away from the woman. "Hello? Ma'am, are you okay?"

No response.

At ten feet, I saw the woman's face and gasped in horror. I wouldn't be getting a response. Ever.

CHAPTER TWO

The woman had been beaten so severely the features of her face were unrecognizable. Her abdomen, visible between her hot pink jogging shorts and white sports bra, was covered with bruises. I'd seen my share of black-and-blue marks on both fighters at the gym and women at the shelter, but never anything close to this. How long had the attack gone on? Many, many minutes, I guessed, to cause this much damage.

On top of that, the mynahs had been pecking at her.

Bile rose in my throat. I held the back of my hand to my mouth and spun away so I wouldn't vomit on the poor woman. Once my stomach settled, I pulled a small water bottle from the pocket on my running belt. I rinsed my mouth and spit while tugging my cell phone out of the main pocket on the belt. My hands shook so hard I misdialed 911 twice.

"Nine-one-one," a man's voice intoned robotically, "what's your location?"

"Yes, hi, I'm at Kanaha Beach Park. There's a—" My stomach rolled again, and I willed it to cooperate. "There's a body."

"A body? As in a dead body?"

Why would I call 911 to report a live body? Wouldn't I say there was someone unconscious or injured on the beach? The clicking and clacking of the operator typing on a keyboard sounded in my ear. He must have been notifying squads in the area.

"Yes, a dead body."

"You're sure the victim is dead?"

I grimaced and glanced over my shoulder at the woman's face, absently noting the running shoes again. "I'm pretty sure."

"Where in the park are you?"

Good question. Where was I? As I looked up and down the beach for some sort of landmark, a small plane rose above the trees next to me. Kahului Airport. My normal route took me to the other side of the airport where I'd turn back to start the second half of my run. I hadn't made it quite that far.

"I'm on the beach between the harbor and the airport."

"All right. The police are on their way." With a little more compassion, he added, "They'll want to talk with you. Do you feel safe staying where you are?"

He wanted me to stay here? I closed my eyes, took in a slow breath, letting the salty smell of the ocean soothe me, and blew it out again. Of course I had to stay. The birds and crabs would come back if I left. This woman had been through enough.

"I'm fine. I'll stay with her. I can't tell them anything though. I mean, I only found her. I don't know what happened."

"I understand. I'll stay on the line with you until the police get there."

There wasn't much I couldn't handle when it came to a physical confrontation. I was Hawaii's bantamweight champ, after all. As Ashlyn regularly bragged.

"Yes, please stay with me."

The dispatcher promised to check in with me every thirty seconds or so, but otherwise went on with his job. The background noise of life going on comforted me but also seemed wrong. Shouldn't life stop when a life stopped?

I took a few steps toward the woman, close enough to keep the birds away, but not too close. On television shows, the cops got upset if people messed up the crime scene. Was that a real thing? Probably.

The closer I got, the more familiar the woman seemed. Did I know her?

Then it struck me. Her hair. When I first saw her, I'd been too distracted by the bruises and the damage the birds had caused to notice her hair. Now, it was like someone had punched me in the gut. I gasped and dropped to my knees. The long ponytail, partially covered with sand, reached to the woman's waist and was colored from scalp to ends in vibrant stripes—bright turquoise, deep purple, coral pink, and sunshine yellow.

First, the shoes. Now, the hair.

"Heleena?"

Heleena Carrere was the number two featherweight fighter at No Mercy. Number three on the island. Fifth in the state. She'd spent eight years learning to fight and garnering all those impressive designations. None of it meant a thing.

"What was that?" the dispatcher asked. "Ma'am, are you all right?"

"Nothing, I'm fine."

"It's called *mermaid*," Heleena had explained to the crowd that had gathered around her at No Mercy last night. She'd been talking about trying something different for weeks. "What do you think?"

The gym rats praised the look, and a few said they might try something like it. I loved it and was envious of her gorgeous long locks, so different from my chin-length yellow-blond waves.

Heleena was like two different people. In the ring, she never held back. In public, she always hid in the shadows. I had talked with her many times about her fear of drawing too much attention to herself while we worked out together, which wasn't often but was always meaningful. Her father refused to accept a lesbian daughter. He kicked her out of their house when she came out at age eighteen, five years ago, and promptly cut off all communication with her. His actions all but destroyed the self-confidence she'd built up. I encouraged her to find a way to express herself. Since she owned a small salon with her girlfriend, coloring her hair to suit her evolving attitude was the method Heleena chose. Before mermaid, it was ocean blue. Before that, sunset red.

"When you go in, you go all in." I wrapped her in a hug. "I'm proud of you. This is so cool."

Heleena beamed as she touched her multi-colored strands. "Thanks, Gemi. I never would have tried it if you hadn't encouraged me."

Remembering her excitement—was it really only yesterday?—I put the crook of my elbow over my mouth to hold in a sob.

As the shock of realizing this was her started to fade a little, and the reality of the situation set in, someone else slammed into my brain. Her little sister Halle. Halle was the star student in my kids' self-defense class. She idolized her big sister. So many times, after Halle's lessons, I'd spot them in the corner of the gym where Heleena would be giving her fighting tips. Or they'd sit in the lobby, drinking juice from the vending machine, and Halle would braid Heleena's hair and tell her all about what was going on at home.

"Halle never got to see your mermaid," I murmured to Heleena. "It would have looked pretty braided."

"What was that?" the 911 dispatcher asked again.

I shook my head. "Nothing."

Heartbroken for Halle, I pushed myself up to stand and looked away. Like a little kid, I told myself when I turned back it wouldn't be Heleena lying there. Or that I'd been wrong, and she was only sleeping. Slowly, I looked. It was still her. She was still dead.

Out of the corner of my eye, I spotted a man ten or twelve feet away kneeling near the heliotrope shrubs and watching me.

I raised a hand in a wave. He mirrored the movement.

"I'm Gemi."

"I'm Harry. Homeless Harry." He wore orange-and-yellow board shorts, a loose-fitting black tank top, gray canvas deck shoes, and had a puka shell necklace at his throat.

"Did you see what happened to her, Harry?"

Just that fast, he leapt up, disappeared into the foliage, and was gone.

"Ma'am?" the dispatcher asked. "Who are you talking to?"

Ignoring the dispatcher, I called after the man running away. It was a wasted effort. I almost took off after him but needed to stay with Heleena.

"A homeless man," I finally answered. "He ran off."

I crossed the span of sand and searched the trees where Harry had just been, making sure there wasn't another victim or someone else who may have seen what had happened to Leena. No one. The beach was empty except for her and me. Suddenly, I couldn't be there anymore. Not unless someone was with me. Ashlyn was the first person to pop into my mind. But she was likely at the salon or on the way by now.

Risa was the second person I thought of. I hung up on the 911 operator and dialed her number. We had met in the cafeteria at Kahului College two years ago. She'd been twenty-two and a senior in the nursing program, and I was a twenty-seven-year-old and in the second year of my junior studies. We'd both been heading for the only vacant table, decided to share, and by the end of lunch, had formed a solid friendship.

"Really?" Risa groaned into her phone in greeting. "I worked a double shift yesterday."

"I know, but something bad happened." My phone buzzed with a text. Then, it indicated I'd received a voicemail.

"What?" Not thirty seconds into my retelling, she blurted, "I'm on my way."

Text of the voicemail showed the 911 dispatcher calling back and assuring me that the police were on the way. I looked at the text next. It was from Ashlyn. She'd sensed something was wrong. The fact she knew probably should have surprised me, but it didn't, not even a little. After so many years of just the two of us, we were so close we barely needed more than strong thoughts to communicate. Like now.

Is everything okay?

I'm fine. Something happened, not to me. I'll tell you later.

You're sure? You're not hurt?

I swear. I'm fine.

Okay. Talk to you later. Followed by a dozen kissy face emojis.

That eased my tension some. The sound of police sirens shattering the silence a few seconds later helped even more. Within two minutes, the beach, normally vacant this early in the day, was a hive of activity.

CHAPTER THREE

Police officers strung tape in a wide square around Heleena to keep people away. A television news crew showed up with cameras. Newspaper reporters held out cellphones with voice recorders running to capture whatever comments they could get. Vloggers took videos of themselves explaining the situation with Heleena's body and the swarm of officers behind them as a gruesome backdrop. I could barely breathe from the crowd suddenly surrounding me.

"How did they all get here so fast?" I murmured to myself.

"Citizens' band radios," a plain-clothes officer explained while pulling me off to the side, away from the throng. "I need to get a statement from you, but not where they can hear."

As we walked, the officer twisted her long straight rich-brown hair into a bun and secured it with a band. She had the tanned skin of an island native and dark almond-shaped eyes. Her dark slacks and open loose-fitting blouse over a snug tank top gave her a laidback yet no-nonsense demeanor that both comforted and impressed me.

"I'm Detective Malia Kalani." She pulled a small notebook from her back pocket. "You are?"

"Gemi Kittredge."

"You found the body?"

Vibrant Heleena was now the body. "I did."

"What were you doing out here, Ms. Kittredge?

"I like to run here in the morning. It's usually quiet."

"Where do you live?"

I pointed southwest. "About seven miles from here in Wailuku."

"You ran all this way?" When I nodded, Detective Kalani's eyebrows lifted with surprise. "Fourteen miles is a standard workout for you?"

"I usually do sixteen, but my sister wanted to run with me today."

"Your sister." The detective looked around. "Is she here too?"

"No." I held my hand up and wiggled my fingers. "She remembered she had a nail appointment two miles in."

The detective smiled and asked, "What exactly did you see when you got here?"

"Heleena." My voice broke as the emotion of this hit me.

"Heleena? Is that who you think the victim is? You know her?"

Get yourself together, Kittredge. This isn't about you.

I pushed my shoulders back and blew out a sharp exhale. "It's a little hard to know for sure considering the condition of her face. But, yes, I'm about ninety-nine percent sure she's Heleena Carrere."

"How do you know her?"

"She fought MMA with me." A new, different wave of sadness threatened. Everyone at the gym loved Heleena. They'd be devastated when they found out what had happened. I stared past the detective at the cluster of police in the now cordoned-off area. "She was the number two fighter in her class."

"MMA?"

"Mixed martial arts. It's like boxing, wrestling, and martial arts all mixed together."

"Were the two of you close?"

The many times Heleena and I had talked flooded my brain like the waves washing up on shore. "She asked for my help with things now and then."

"MMA things?"

"Sometimes. She fought in a different weight class. She was featherweight. I'm bantamweight."

"What's the difference?"

"Ten pounds. Bantam is one hundred twenty-five pounds to one thirty-five. Feather is one thirty-five to one forty-five."

Detective Kalani nodded as she noted that in her little book. "Go on. You helped the victim with fighting?"

Heleena. Her name is Heleena, not the victim.

"I've been at this longer, so it started with her asking for tips. When she got good enough, we'd spar. The best way to learn is to do."

"You said you 'sometimes' helped her with fighting. What else did you help her with?"

"She had some personal issues that she talked to me about." My more professional side emerged, for which I was grateful. It was easier to deal with this as a nursing student than Heleena's friend.

The detective perked up at that. "What kind of personal issues?"

"Heleena was lesbian. Her parents, her father in particular, doesn't approve of that kind of lifestyle. That stressed her a lot. Along that same line, she lived with her girlfriend, Lana Madison, in Kihei. They got harassed by some of the people in their neighborhood." I sighed, remembering some of our tear-filled talks.

"Why you?"

The question took me off guard. It was like she doubted I was worthy of such an honor.

"All my life," I began, "people from close friends to perfect strangers have told me personal things. I work closely with victims of domestic violence as part of my nursing program and teach women's self-defense at my gym. Many of the women I work with at the shelter end up taking my classes because they're tired of being victims or want to make sure they never will be again. It takes a while to get some of them to open up, but after so many years I can tell if someone needs to talk. I listen but never dig for information and never judge. Maybe they talk to me because that's the vibe I give off." I looked her in the eye, knowing what question was coming next. *How did you get so involved with this?* The detective didn't need to know about my background. That had nothing to do with Heleena's death. I nipped the question before it came. "Everyone has a story, Detective. I bet you do too."

She held my gaze, her expression unflinchingly neutral. She was good. "Which gym do you attend?"

I gestured west. "No Mercy, here in Kahului. Best on the island."

She grinned at the name, as many did, and quickly returned to her neutral expression as she scribbled more notes. "Did you see anyone else in the area when you got here?"

"No. The beach was empty." Then I remembered Harry. "Wait. I almost forgot. There was a guy, called himself Homeless Harry." I pointed at the edge of the heliotropes. "He was right over there but ran off when I asked him if he saw what happened."

While Detective Kalani wrote down my physical description of Harry, the thought that took over my brain was, *this can't be real. Stuff like this happens to strangers, not to people you know.*

"Did you touch anything?" Detective Kalani stated in a way that made me think this was the second time she'd asked.

I blinked. "Sorry. No, nothing."

"Anything else you feel I need to know?"

I scanned the scene, avoiding looking at Heleena's battered body, and retraced my steps since arriving. "Oh, I threw up in the trees over there."

She gave an empathetic smile. "Understandable. This is an upsetting discovery made worse by the fact that you know the victim."

I nodded in agreement and scanned the area again. "Those are my running shoes." I pointed at the pair on the ground near Heleena. "I run barefoot on the beach and must've dropped them there. Can I get them back?"

The detective retrieved them for me. "That's all I've got for now, Ms. Kittredge. Can you stay for a while? I might have more questions for you after we're finished investigating here."

"I've got a test at eleven I really need to study for, but I can stay for a little while."

"Thank you." She tucked her notebook into her back pocket. "Don't talk to any of the reporters. 'No comment' should be your only statement."

I nodded and hugged my arms around my torso. Running shorts and a sports bra had been fine while I was moving. I'd worked up a good sweat, but now the ocean breeze was chilling. I'd also stopped running abruptly, no cooldown or stretching. My legs were getting tight.

I put my shoes back on, hoping warm feet might help, and squatted to loosen my thighs while watching Detective Kalani and the other officers methodically search every inch of the cordoned area. Any little clue could lead to something important, I supposed. What did the bruises all over Heleena's body tell them? I propped a heel in the sand, toes up, and leaned forward to ease my hamstring. From the amount of damage the mynas and sand crabs had done to her, I guessed this hadn't happened recently. She must've been here overnight. Poor Lana had to be crazy with worry wondering where Heleena was.

"Miss, can we get a statement?" a reporter asked.

"You were the first one on the scene, correct?" another added.

"No comment," I mumbled again and again as they lobbed question after question at me. Finally, a uniformed officer came over and told them to leave me alone.

"Thank you," I mouthed at him.

I stared blankly at the scene within the yellow tape and thought back to when Heleena had started with us eight years ago. She'd only been fourteen, nearly the same age I was when . . . No. Not thinking about that right now.

Heleena had been clumsy. She constantly tripped over her own feet when she tried to spar with another student. After two years, something in her turned on. I loved that part. The most satisfying thing about teaching was watching awkward and sometimes scared kids in my self-defense class turn into capable little warriors. Leena's self-confidence grew along with her physical ability. Maybe that was when she'd come to accept herself. I never asked. I should have.

Over time, Heleena became a powerhouse. Her style was to lull her opponent into thinking she was a long-distance fighter, one who would wait until the end before letting loose. She started every fight that way, almost mellow. Unless they'd studied her and learned her method, her opponent would assume they were headed for an easy win and would enlist a full-on assault within seconds. Heleena's clumsy feet had turned fast, though, so she could dance away from pretty much every punch or kick. Anything that did connect was usually a glancing blow. Inevitably, her challenger would get tired and slow down to match Leena's rhythm. That was when she'd charge in. It was almost funny. Even those who did study her and knew what to expect got fooled. The only fighter who seemed to have figured her out was Callie Castro, the number one fighter in the featherweight class and also a member at No Mercy.

Whatever happened to Heleena last night, I was certain she'd fought back. Ashlyn yelled at me all the time for being so jumpy. She'd walk into a room with me on her quiet, perfectly pedicured feet, and I'd throw out a block or a kick.

"If you'd make a little noise," I told her once, handing her an icepack for her thigh, "it would help."

Blocking and defending became muscle memory over time. Automatic reactions, not conscious thoughts. During a fight, head shots could mean getting knocked out. Leena's muscle memory meant her hands would've been up, protecting her head and face. Last night, whoever had attacked her made a lot of contact. Both her face and her abdomen were covered in bruises, which meant her hands weren't up. So either her attacker knocked her out quickly and beat her while she was down or two people had done this. One held her arms, surely getting kicked in the shins from Leena's attempt to get away, while the other delivered the blows.

"Gemi!"

I turned to see Risa waving at me from behind the tape. I jogged over to the officer denying her entry. "Please, I called her to come be with me."

It took another bit of begging, but he finally let Risa duck under the tape, warning us to stay clear of the cordoned-off area. As if I wanted to get close again.

"I called you half an hour ago," I snapped and immediately apologized.

"I had to get dressed and consume some caffeine." Risa paled as she glanced past me at the crime scene. "Oh, man."

I dropped to the sand and covered my face with my hands. "It's Heleena, Risa. Someone beat her to death."

"Heleena's the victim? Heleena Carrere?" Risa sat next to me, then put an arm around my shoulders and pulled me close. "Are you okay? This has to hit close."

"The shock is wearing off. Now I'm just heartbroken. Who would do this to her?"

She shrugged. "Someone from No Mercy."

"What? No way." Our goal might have been to take each other out, in the sporting sense, but No Mercy was a safe place. None of us would do something like this.

"You said she was beaten. There are a lot of people in her immediate circle who have that ability. That sort of narrows the field."

"No," I objected again. "We're family. *Ohana*. We may be in competition with each other, and we may sulk a bit if we lose, but I've never witnessed anything anywhere close to this."

"Someone from another gym then?"

I didn't want to believe that either.

"You're looking a little green," Risa stated. "Do you want a ride home?"

"I will, but the detective asked me to stick around in case she has more questions." I observed the crowd of officers. Most of them were standing around staring or talking. Were they doing any actual investigating? Did they ever? Not in my experience. I dismissed that thought before it brought on an onslaught of other memories I didn't want to deal with. Instead, I noted, "They put plastic bags on Heleena's hands."

"That's to preserve evidence. If she scratched her attacker, there could be skin beneath her fingernails they can get DNA from."

"How do you know that?"

"I work in the hospital emergency department. When assault or rape victims come in, we scrape beneath their nails for biological evidence." Risa smiled and nodded at something over my shoulder. "Besides, a friend of mine is a cop, and she told me that once."

"Risa Ohno."

I looked back to see Detective Kalani walking toward us.

"Hi, Malia."

Malia? Sure that nothing else could surprise me today, my jaw dropped when Risa opened her arms for a hug.

Detective Kalani pulled out of the embrace with a warm smile. "What are you doing here?"

"Gemi and I are friends. She called me." Risa nodded toward Heleena's body. "What did you find out?"

Detective Kalani shook her head slightly. "You know I can't talk about an investigation."

"We already know a woman was beaten to death," Risa pushed, sounding like a reporter.

"We haven't determined cause of death yet." Detective Kalani shot a stern look at me. "I told you not to discuss this with anyone."

"Gemi didn't tell me anything," Risa assured. "I have eyes. I can see the body from here. As can all these fine folks with their cameras."

Kalani mumbled something that sounded like "should've put up a tent or screen."

They should have. Typical bumbling cops.

"I'm going to talk with the owner of my gym," I told the

detective. "I won't give him details, but there's a big fight scheduled this weekend." I paused, getting control over my swelling emotions. "Heleena was expected to win. He needs to know."

"I'll need to talk with him first," Kalani cautioned. "Considering the victim's condition, the gym could be a likely place to find a suspect or two. Who's the owner?"

I wanted to argue that I should do it. Heleena was family, I should break the news. It was more important to catch the killer, though. Besides, if mistakes were made, and I wouldn't be surprised if some were, they wouldn't be due to anything I did. I wasn't sure I could handle seeing Salomon's initial reaction anyway.

"Salomon Kahumoku." Absently, my hand went to my face. "White goatee and hair. Everyone knows him. Just ask."

Detective Kalani took down my address and phone number. "I'll be in touch if I have more questions."

"Does that mean I can go now?"

"You can. I know you were out for a run. Do you need a ride home?"

"I'll take her," Risa assured.

"Will you have someone there for you?" Kalani asked. "Once everything hits you, a support system would be good. Will your parents be there?"

My age was always hard for people to pin down, but no one had mistaken me for a minor in years. I had a baby face. If I ever bothered with makeup, that might add a year or two. My name made me sound like a little kid too. More than once, I thought of legally changing it to Gemma.

I shook my head. "I live with my sister."

"Your sister? How old is she?"

Knowing where this was headed, I let it play out. "Ashlyn is thirty-three." Or would be in a few days.

Detective Kalani pulled out her notebook again. "Is she your legal guardian?"

"I turn thirty next week, Detective," I replied, trying hard to leave out the attitude. "I've been my own guardian for a long time."

Detective Kalani stared, eyes narrowing, searching my face to verify my claim. Same response I got from everyone. "You mentioned you had a test this morning, and you look very young."

"Not to the other college students. They think I'm ancient."

She handed me her card. "All right. Call me if you think of anything that might be important."

I nodded, already wondering the same thing. What was important about this? The timing with this weekend's fight was obvious. The buzz over the upcoming championship fight was growing by the hour. Heleena had been working out twice and sometimes three times a day like a madwoman. It would take a perfect storm of wins and losses for her to reach the number one spot this weekend, but it was possible. Or would have been.

"If I don't win," she'd told me a couple weeks ago, "it won't be because I wasn't prepared."

If preventing her from getting the top spot was the motivation for whoever did this, who would be the likely suspect? Was Risa right and it was one of the other fighters? Did I know this person? No, I couldn't fathom that. The attack had to be unrelated to anything MMA. What were the statistics on random killings? That had to be low. Most likely, it was someone from Heleena's personal life. A homophobe who felt they had the right to tell her how to live her life. Detective Kalani would surely be checking all those boxes. Wouldn't she? Could I trust her to?

Maybe I'd run down to Kihei and talk to Lana myself.

CHAPTER FOUR

Risa pulled to a stop in front of my condo. I got out and slammed the passenger door of her rusty beige Mazda hatchback, stared at a few large bits of metal that had dropped off, and then leaned back in through the window. "Thanks for the ride."

She frowned, worry clear on her face. "Are you okay?"

Good question. All that bruising. Heleena's unrecognizable face. I was guaranteed to have nightmares tonight, but for the moment, I'd never been more grateful for my full schedule.

"I'll be all right."

"Hmm." Risa studied me. "Not so sure. What's on your schedule for today? Other than a lot."

"I've got an exam at eleven. Psychiatric Mental Health. I should study a bit more for that."

"Learning about the crazies," Risa joked.

"It's an interesting class. It's scary what can go wrong in a person's mind."

I wanted to add that our mother would make a great test subject, but Ash and I never told anyone about her. We all drew a certain lot in life. Ashlyn and I got Gabby Kittredge.

She left us thirteen years ago, two years after dragging us to Maui from California. Six months after we arrived, she started complaining about how the island was too low key for her skills. Eventually, she heard about an opportunity to open a nightclub in Honolulu and decided it was perfect for her. That she could barely run our household and had no idea what was involved with operating a club, or any kind of business for that matter, was immaterial.

"How hard can it be?" she scoffed when we asked. "I know people who know people, and they're dying to work with me. It's going to be fabulous!"

I pushed the memories away, not wanting to mix my mother into the hell this day had already become, and returned my attention to Risa. "Second class goes until two. Then I head to the gym for a workout and kids' self-defense at five."

Teaching my little warriors always gave me a sense of accomplishment. If they walked away knowing one more move or having a bit more confidence in their abilities, that was an hour well spent for me as well as them. And considering what had happened to Heleena, making sure they knew how to protect themselves felt doubly important.

"Hopefully, I'll get home early enough to spend time with Ash. She leaves tomorrow."

"Again?" Risa didn't understand why Ashlyn was gone so much. I didn't either, but that was probably because I didn't fully understand what she did. "If people need that much team building, maybe they need to look more closely at who they hire. Anyway, call me if you need someone." She waved a hand in the air as though clearing words from a whiteboard. "Forget that. I'll stop by the gym later to check on you. I've got a couple days off and have some errands to take care of, but I'm here if you need me."

I took my running shoes off outside, a local custom I liked a lot, knocked the sand out of them, and tossed them into the closet just inside the front door. I hadn't checked the garage for Ashlyn's car, so in case she was back already, I called for her. No response. I glanced at the basket on the corner of the kitchen counter where she left her car keys. Empty.

"Aloha," came a scratchy voice from the living room.

"Aloha, Hulu."

Hulu was Ashlyn's African gray parrot. She'd adopted him

from a man who was leaving Hawaii and relocating to Papua New Guinea and didn't want to put the bird through the trauma of the move.

"We need to rename him," Ashlyn had said and then frowned. "I hope that doesn't scar him."

"Why?" I'd asked. "What's his name?"

The man had written down some long Indonesian name neither of us could pronounce, so we changed it to Hulu which meant *feathers* in Hawaiian and seemed to fit him perfectly. A beautiful blend of light and dark gray feathers covered the bird's body and wings while those on his tail were a spectacular vivid red. And he was smart. Not only did he learn his new name in a matter of days, with no apparent emotional scarring, he could also carry on brief conversations. Although that might have been overstating it. Either way, he was fun to have around, especially when Ashlyn was gone for days at a time.

I crossed the living room to the giant six-foot-tall by three-foot-wide white wrought-iron cage in front of the windows. Hulu had the best view in the place. Except for Ashlyn's bedroom balcony view of the ocean. I checked his dishes, one for water and the other for food. Both were full. Ashlyn adored this bird and cared for him like he was her child. Her biggest fear was that one of us would leave a door or window open and he'd fly away.

"Okay, jailbird. Want to break out of there?" I opened the panels at the top of the cage so Hulu could get out and roam around the condo while I studied.

"Thank you," the bird squawked.

"You're welcome. I'm going to take a shower."

As I walked away, Hulu let loose with a cat-call whistle. "Looking good, Peep." Then he growled.

This parrot could mimic like I didn't know was possible. Ashlyn not only taught him that whistle but also the nickname she'd given me years ago because my yellow-blond hair reminded her of a sun-bleached Easter Peep.

I turned and pointed a finger at him. "Behave, dirty bird."

He lowered his head and put a taloned foot to his beak. "Hulu sorry."

As I undressed in my bathroom, grains of sand fell out of my shorts onto the rug. No wonder I was so itchy. And even though I hadn't come close to touching Heleena, I felt like I had her blood on my hands. I shivered, chilled both physically and emotionally from all that had happened this morning. The shower couldn't heat up fast enough.

Minutes later, as water pounded my tight muscles, tears for Heleena joined the stream.

"I'm so sorry, Leena," I moaned into the washcloth I held over my face.

Out of nowhere, someone else popped into my mind. The little girl who had been attacked in a dark parking lot one night seventeen years ago. She'd been thirteen at the time so maybe not *little*, but in my eyes, that was very young. She was okay now, for the most part, but it had taken her years to get to that point. I gently pushed her aside. Much as I wanted to check in with her, right now wasn't the time.

After ten minutes of hot water and hotter tears, my muscles felt less tense and I was warm again. What I really wanted was to talk to Ashlyn. Getting a manicure also meant getting a facial and her hair done, so she was probably still in the middle of her pampering. How did we grow up in the same house, sharing the same tiny bedroom, and turn out so different from each other? The thought of someone pawing at me like that—holding my hands, touching my face—made me claustrophobic. And for Ashlyn, running sixteen miles every day held no appeal.

"I prefer being barefoot in a yoga studio to being barefoot on a beach," she'd insisted the first time I asked her to run along the bay with me. "The sand messes up my pedicure."

And strapping on a pair of boxing gloves and sparring or fighting with someone was far too violent for her. Could she protect herself? Probably, if she had a can of pepper spray in hand as the attack began. Although Ash was more likely to wield a can of hairspray. Fortunately, I was happy to take on the role of her protector. Yet another reason I hated that she was gone so often. I couldn't protect her if she wasn't here.

I got dressed and was about to settle in and study for the exam when my phone buzzed with a text from my sister.

Checking on you.

She mentally heard the hairspray crack, didn't she? *I told you, I'm fine. Promise. You'll be home tonight, right?*

Yep, gotta pack.

I'll tell you about the thing that happened then.

Is it bad?

Something happening to a friend was at the top of my bad list. The only thing that could take the number one spot was something happening to my sister.

It's pretty bad. It can wait, though.

You're sure? Are you okay?

I swear. Pinkie swear. Enjoy your pampering.

Okie-kay. Good luck on your test.

Smiling at her mashup of okie-dokie and okay, I gathered my notes, a bowl of mixed nuts and dried fruit, and a big glass of water, then went out to the lanai. Our condo had the most amazing view. All these years here, and I never tired of seeing the turquoise and blue shades of the ocean, the frothy whitecaps like little surfers. The tiny house we first lived in was awful and not just because it had no view. Since there was no way to come house hunting before the move, our mother had to take it sight unseen.

"Had to put down a three-month deposit," she'd grumbled. "Fortunately they're ready for me to start at that job I told you about. Otherwise we'd have to make do with a tent on the beach until I got one."

Ashlyn and I shared a bedroom that had just enough room for twin bunk beds and a dresser. The kitchen had only four cupboards. That wasn't a problem, because we didn't have enough to fill even that many.

This current job of Ashlyn's had made all the difference for us. When she showed me this condo for the first time and assured me that it really was ours, I felt like a princess, shocked that we each got our own bedroom *and* bathroom. The living room was spacious enough to hold that monster birdcage and still allow us plenty of room for nice furniture. In comparison to the house's kitchen, this one was massive with three times the number of cupboards, although we still didn't fill them all. Neither of us was a gourmet chef, so basic supplies were all we needed. I wasn't sure how we could afford the place, but Ashlyn insisted we were fine.

"Don't worry about things like that," she assured. "I'm the big sister. It's my job to take care of us."

While she might lean toward flighty, my sister truly was one of the most responsible people I knew.

"Speaking of being responsible"—I scrubbed my hands over my face—"study!" I picked a few macadamias and pieces of dried pineapple and mango out of the bowl, propped up my feet, and opened my notes.

I stared at the words on the page and wondered how Ashlyn's previous position as a hostess for a high-end restaurant led to this job. After years of working her butt off to keep the bills paid, she landed it eighteen months ago and quickly worked her way up from grunt to project coordinator and most recently to assistant director. Or assistant to the director. I wasn't clear on that. Despite never giving me solid answers about what she did, my sister was successful and happier than I'd ever seen her. That was all that mattered to me. It didn't hurt that we had a much better lifestyle now too. Instead of having to spend most of my paycheck on living expenses, I could finally finish my nursing degree.

My mind had wandered again. "What does Ashlyn's job have to do with mental health?" I leapt to my feet and paced the length of the lanai. "Not a thing, other than to reveal that you might have some issues yourself."

This was unusual. Focusing on the task at hand was never a

problem for me. I took a big sip of water, inhaled deeply, and returned to the loveseat and my notes.

After finals next month, I had only one semester to go. I'd maintained nothing less than a 3.8 GPA and needed to push all the way to the finish line if I was going to get a decent nursing position after graduation. Then Ashlyn could get a job that didn't require her to be gone all the time. It had taken me six years to get to senior status. At thirty years of age, I was the oldest student in every class. The thing I hadn't admitted to anyone yet, barely even to myself, was that after all these years, I wasn't sure I even wanted to be a nurse anymore.

"Good lord, will you focus!" My brain was all over the place today. Not surprising, I guess, considering my morning.

"Focus," Hulu echoed from the other side of the screen door.

I plugged in my earbuds and turned on loud classic rock. That was the only way I could silence my brain when it wandered. After half an hour of trying, I gave myself permission to quit studying. Not even rock was working today.

"It's okay," I told myself, adopting the tone Salomon used to motivate me before a fight. "You know this stuff cold. And cramming never works anyway. It only stresses you out."

Instead, I rearranged the toys hanging from Hulu's cage bars. Then I made sure my backpack had everything I'd need and tossed in a power bar.

"Time to go," I told the bird while tucking him back inside the cage. "I've got a test today. Wish me luck."

The bird croaked, "Luck, luck, luck!"

"You sound like a duck."

"Quack!"

Even though he hadn't meant to, the bird cheered me up. "See you later, Hulu."

He let out a slow catcall again, and I silently cursed my sister for teaching him that. In the garage, I slid my arms through my backpack's straps, threw my right leg over my pearly-white and matte-black Indian Scout Sixty, and settled onto the seat. Ashlyn nearly lost her mind when I brought the motorcycle home. I got the bike for a steal, though, and couldn't turn it down.

"You'll be killed," Ashlyn insisted.

"I won't be killed." But if my time was up, might as well leave this world having fun.

"Do you at least have a helmet?"

"Don't need one. I'm not planning to fall."

"Not funny." Ashlyn propped her hands on her curvy hips and stared at me the same way Mom used to when she'd find me using the balcony railing at our house in California as a balance beam.

I relented on the helmet. I was studying to be a nurse, after all, and knew I'd likely recover from any other injuries, but the head trauma from a smack against the pavement, even at a slow speed, could be a game ender.

Ashlyn took me directly to the cycle shop and immediately pulled a full-face white helmet with hot-pink swirls off the rack. "This one is perfect for you." She spun it around to show me the hot-pink hibiscus on the back. "And it's pretty."

Normally, I didn't go for "pretty." That was Ash's thing. The helmet fit perfectly, though, and Ashlyn was paying for it.

Along with the helmet, she bought me an entire riding outfit— jacket, pants, gloves, and boots. She spent a fortune that day but insisted there was no price that could be put on her Peep's safety. The white mesh gloves helped maintain my grip on the throttle, so I always wore them and the helmet. I promised to wear the whole outfit if I went for a longer ride. That still hadn't happened. I was too busy. Besides, ninety percent of my trips were three-mile jaunts. Three from the condo to school. Three from school to No Mercy. Three more from the gym to home. I lived my life inside a Kahului triangle.

To emphasize her concern for my safety, the new Jeep sitting a few feet away had appeared in the garage slot next to her Mercedes the day after our shopping trip. A note clamped beneath the windshield wiper read: *For days when you're feeling less reckless.*

Smiling at the memory, I pulled on the helmet and gloves, started up the bike, and let the vibrations rush through me for a few seconds. The Indian made me feel free and relaxed. That was what I'd told Heleena as she checked it out in No Mercy's parking lot.

"I've always wanted a motorcycle," she'd admitted that day three, no, four months ago. "Go with me to look at them?"

"Sure, I'd love to." But I'd kept putting it off, using school and my schedule at No Mercy as the excuse. Now it was too late.

For about the hundredth time today, or so it seemed, my mind had drifted. I'd been sitting there daydreaming for so long I was now going to be late for my test.

CHAPTER FIVE

Professor Hastings often treated time as more of a general guideline than something to be strictly adhered to. Lucky for me, today was one of those days. This meant while I was five minutes late for the test, she arrived ten minutes late and offered no apology. Fifteen years after leaving the mainland and this laidback vibe still didn't fit right with me. The only local customs I'd fully adopted were taking my shoes off before entering the house and the casual style of dress. Shorts and T-shirts year-round were fine by me.

The first question on the exam was easy, as was the second. Then the words dissolved from the page and Heleena's battered face appeared. I set my pencil down and rubbed my eyes. When I looked again, the questions had reappeared, but it was like the words were in the wrong order. I didn't understand any of them so flipped the page. I managed to answer only one question before the words scrambled again, so I turned to the third page. It was an essay question. No way could I put together a coherent essay right now.

I went back to page one. The first unanswered question read: Will the cops really hunt for Heleena's killer?

"What?" My out-loud declaration startled the students around me. The girl at the desk to my right glared, and I whispered, "Sorry."

You've got half an hour left. Set Leena's death aside for thirty minutes.

Just as I finally felt like I was in control, the professor announced, "Time's up. Pencils down."

I blinked at the papers before me and then at the clock over the classroom door. How could the period be over already? I still had three questions to answer on the second page, and I hadn't even started the essay, which was worth twenty-five percent of the grade. A lump, like a hard chunk of lava, formed in my gut. I'd just blown my GPA.

"Another A, Gemi?" Professor Hastings asked with a broad smile as I handed in my test. I was the best student in the class. That wasn't ego talking. It was fact.

"Only if you're feeling generous."

How had I mismanaged my time so severely? I was usually the first one done and reviewing my answers for the third time when time was called.

She flipped through my packet, and her smile fell when she saw the unanswered questions on page two. It turned into a frown at the blank last page. "Is there something we need to talk about?"

I shrugged and glanced out the window at the palm trees scattered through the quad. "You know how I like to get to class early, especially on test days. I was distracted this morning, got here late, and didn't get to meditate."

Some of the other students had whispered about my weird routine the first couple times I did it. When they learned that I'd gotten one hundred percent on my first two tests, they joined me before the third. Five minutes of silent group meditation made a big difference. The average score went way up that week.

The professor held up my packet, third page showing. "You're blaming this on not being able to meditate? What's going on, Gemi? You know this stuff cold."

Using Heleena's death as an excuse felt disrespectful and like a copout. Other people had bad things going on in their lives and managed to stay on track.

"Just some personal stuff." I put my pencil in its slot in my backpack and zipped the bag closed. "I'll do better next time."

Professor Hastings frowned. "You've got a solid A. I think you missed one question on a pop quiz at the beginning of the semester." She tapped her fingers on the stack of test papers in front of her. "If you want to wait, I'll score it right now. If it turns out as bad as it appears it will, we'll figure something out."

It was nice that she wanted to help, except that, for once, my grades felt like the least important thing in my life.

I pointed over my shoulder toward the hall. "I've got another class." It didn't start for an hour but still true.

"You're one of the most serious, dedicated students I've ever come across. Part of that is because that's the kind of person you are. You take on a task, you give it a hundred percent. Part of it is because you're an older student and you understand all that this degree will bring to your life. I know you and I know what you're capable of, so this *personal stuff* must be big. Let me grade this. It won't take more than ten minutes." She thumbed through the half-empty pages. "Five minutes."

"That's okay." I couldn't deal with more bad news today.

Professor Hastings sighed, clearly disappointed with me, and turned her attention to the stack of test papers before her. "All right. Grades will be posted tomorrow afternoon."

I made a show of crossing my fingers and forcing a smile as I backed into the hallway.

The nuts and fruit I'd had earlier wore off about halfway through the test, so I took the remaining fifty minutes to grab a spinach salad with grilled chicken, avocado, and red peppers from the cafeteria. I sat outside to eat it and debated skipping that class. I couldn't concentrate on anything except Heleena today anyway. Who could have done this to her and why? She was the nicest person at the gym and never had a bad thing to say about anyone.

Detective Kalani had asked if Leena and I were close. I considered her a friend, but not as close as I now wish we had been. I knew Heleena the fighter. And Heleena the broken, discarded daughter. She told me some very personal things about her family life, but more in a patient-therapist way, not friend to friend. Why hadn't I ever asked her to stop for girl talk and a smoothie after a workout? With the salon she ran with her girlfriend in Kihei on top of her training schedule, she was almost as busy as I was, but we both needed to eat. We could have found an hour to grab something together. Or a few hours to test drive motorcycles. I'd assumed we had all the time in the world and had missed out on a potentially great friendship.

When I checked the time, more than forty-five minutes had passed, meaning I had to sprint to my health economics class. It was a straight lecture today with no time for questions at the end. A full fifty minutes of listening to the island's most boring man drone on about the cost of healthcare. At least I think that was what the lecture was about. I kept zoning out, trying to come up with any suspects to tell Detective Kalani about.

I flipped to the back page of my notebook and jotted "Steroids????" at the top. Increased aggression, commonly known as "roid rage," was a possible side effect of anabolic steroid use.

Leena's face appeared before me again. Left eye swollen almost completely shut. Nose pushed off to the side. Lips ballooned to three times their normal size.

Whoever had attacked Heleena must have been in an uncontrollable rage to do that much damage. No Mercy members were forbidden from using steroids, but it's not like we tested everyone. Only those competing and only right before fights. Could a jealous gym member, either from No Mercy or another club, amped up on steroids or some other drug have done that to her? Definitely worth checking into.

As I added more things to the page to mention to Kalani next time I talked to her, my legs bounced. There was far too much unspent energy coursing through my body. I was desperate to go for a run or kick something. Anything that would burn off some of this. Good thing I sat in the back of the classroom today. I was so fidgety my constant squirming would have disturbed anyone sitting behind me. The location also allowed me to be the first out of the classroom. As soon as the professor declared class over, I jumped up and left. Hopefully he hadn't given an assignment at the last minute because I didn't hear it. With the way this day was going, he had. And it would be worth half my grade. I'd text one of the other students later.

As soon as I stepped out of the building, I broke into a jog. Like a drug addict desperate for a hit, I needed to feel my muscles working and blood pumping. I took the long way around the campus to my motorcycle.

Faster. Go faster!

On top of the emotional trauma of finding Heleena, I was suffering from physical upset too. My body was letting me know it didn't like having its routine messed with. First, my run was interrupted by Nichole and Ty. I was thrilled that I'd been there for her and wouldn't hesitate to do it again, but my muscles had just gotten warm and loose when we stopped to help. Then, as I was getting close to hitting that runner's high I craved, I found Leena. I needed to be more flexible. I couldn't let glitches in my schedule affect me this way.

Once to my Scout, I pulled on my helmet but didn't bother with the gloves. The only thing I wanted to do right now was get to the gym. The detective should have talked with Salomon by now. Maybe he knew more about Heleena. Also, I needed to clear my head. Nothing would get me back on track better than wailing on a heavy bag. Except for wailing on an actual opponent, of course, but the last fighter who volunteered to spar with me ended up with a split lip. Not that I'd intended to hurt her. If she didn't know to keep her hands up and protect her face, she had no business getting in the ring with me.

Now, volunteers were scarce. Who knew? Split one girl's lip, and bounce around the ring with the gym's current super stud for five minutes without letting him land a blow and suddenly no one wanted to play. Maybe they needed to check their fragile egos and be grateful for the opportunity to work with the island's top-ranked fighter. It would only help them improve.

Damn, girl. You're snarly.

Probably the events of the day merging together. Or it could be a new stage of grief and I'd slid into anger. Fortunately, anger was something I knew how to deal with. The physical side of it, at least.

CHAPTER SIX

The instant I walked through No Mercy's doors, I felt myself relax. It was like someone had draped a security blanket over me or I'd slipped into another world. A safe world where I knew exactly what my abilities were and what I could expect because nothing changed. I liked that. I needed that. Especially today.

No Mercy was housed in a large industrial-looking building and was often mistaken for a warehouse. Inside, the lobby took up the front quarter and was very sleek with orange walls, a silver-gray reception desk, and glossy black flooring. There were also vending machines and four café tables. The locker rooms and Salomon's office occupied the next quarter with the office separating the men's lockers from the women's. That left the back half of the building for workout space.

Right now, a crowd of about two dozen was gathered outside Salomon's office. I squeezed in next to the gym's number two and three fighters in my weight class, Aonani Lincoln and Stacia Hanks. From the stunned expressions on their faces, and everyone's, I assumed they were talking about Heleena.

"I don't know many details," Salomon was telling them. "The police went to Heleena's home in Kihei and talked to her girlfriend. Lana called Heleena's coach, and then Ozzie called me. All I know is that she's dead. I'm not even sure if her parents know yet."

"How did she die?" a fellow featherweight asked.

"Where did they find her?" someone else wanted to know.

"Was it at home? Did Lana do it?"

Salomon held up his beefy hands to silence the questions. The black and red tribal tattoos covering his left biceps rippled along with his muscles.

He fixed a scary stare on the last commenter. It was the same stare that made me perfectly willing to lift ten more times or go five more minutes on the speed bag when I insisted I was too tired to go on.

"I told you, I don't know the details. And that's the last time I want to hear any talk against Lana. We have no reason to think she did anything to Leena. Ozzie told me she's inconsolable, so let's show her the respect she's due, all right? She just lost her girlfriend."

Salomon didn't raise his voice often. He didn't need to because no one dared to cross him. I could only remember two times when his normal low-pitched volume elevated. Once was to stop a nine-year-old from pulling a thirty-pound barbell onto his foot. The other time was to break up a fight between two guys. One of them was doing circuits—rotating quickly between machines—and didn't want the other guy to use *his* rowing machine.

"You want to have private use of the equipment," Salomon had barked, "you make arrangements to come in at four in the morning. And good luck with that, bro. My staff likes to sleep at that time."

Salomon saw me at the back of the crowd and flicked his fingers in a *come* gesture. Aonani glared at me. She *always* glared at me. Whether I was talking with my coach, teaching my kiddos, or doing something mundane like getting a freaking drink of water, Aonani gave me the evil eye. She was the most competitive person I knew and wouldn't be happy until she'd knocked me off the top spot. Maybe she would someday, but thanks to Mele Keahi, an equally persistent fighter from another gym, Aonani and I had never entered the octagon together.

As the others stepped aside for me to pass, Salomon continued, "We'll remain open today, but all classes are canceled in Heleena's honor."

At the far edge of the cluster stood a thin muscular woman

wearing a stern expression. She also looked a little pale, probably from shock. Callie Castro was a gorgeous Hispanic woman with tousled shoulder-length hair and a wicked uppercut. She had a sweet pink teddy bear tattooed on the front of her right shoulder right where her opponents could see it. The bear was part of her ruse. Callie was tough as they came and would have her opponent on the mat before they even knew they'd been hit. That was why she was ranked number one in the featherweight class. Her current serious expression looked much like her game face and was likely a cover-up to mask her emotions.

"And I'm serious about rumors," Salomon stressed. "I hear that you're making up stuff about this or talking bad about Leena or Lana, you're suspended from entering the building for one week. And you'll have to scrub the locker room toilets to regain privileges. If you think you know something, I have the detective's number. You call her. Don't say it here."

A murmur of understanding and agreement spread through the group.

The other person to catch my attention was Johnny Gambino. His name, mumbly voice, and crooked nose made him sound and look like a mobster, but Johnny was one of the gentlest guys I knew. All he wanted to do was fight MMA but didn't have any money, so Salomon agreed to let him clean the building in exchange for his membership. Johnny was also young, painfully awkward, and desperate to date Heleena. It didn't matter to him that she didn't *like* guys. He was in love with her and wanted to go out with her in the worst way. Now, he stood off to the side leaning against a broom as though it was keeping him from falling over. His shoulders shook with silent sobs, and tears trickled down his face.

"Also," Salomon added, "I encourage those of you fighting on Saturday night to dedicate your fight to Heleena. Being a member of this gym means we're ohana. Let's be sure everyone at the fight knows that."

Something set Callie off. Without notice, she spun and stormed out of the building through the large roll-up garage door at the back. We all watched, confused. Was it Salomon's ohana label? Was she overwhelmed by Heleena's death? Or was it something unrelated? Hard to know with Callie. She wasn't one to share her feelings.

Then, to further agitate an already upset and confused group, Johnny took the broom in both hands and cracked it over his knee. The sound echoed like a gunshot throughout the quiet gym, making people jump or cry out in surprise.

Salomon gestured for one of the gym employees to go to Johnny. Then he motioned for me to follow him into his office. There, Salomon dropped onto his black leather desk chair.

I closed the door, my tension level immediately lowering within the privacy of those walls, and took the seat across from the silver desk that matched the one in the reception area. "I've never seen Johnny lose his temper like that."

"It doesn't happen often, but if his emotions get *too big*, as he says, he loses it. He'll be okay." Salomon released a heavy sigh as he sat back. "How did your test go?"

"Could've been better." I pulled my legs up onto the chair and hugged my knees.

He studied me. "What's the matter, Gemi? You're hiding something."

"I'm not supposed to say anything."

Salomon placed a finger on his ear and then on his chin beneath his mouth. His hand signal for "anything that goes in these ears will not come out of this mouth." He used it a lot when instructors became frustrated with entitled students, whether children or adults. We tried to ignore bad behavior, but sometimes we needed to vent.

Right now, I had to tell someone what I had witnessed. Risa knew, I could talk to her about it, but she tended to tell me why I shouldn't be feeling what I was feeling rather than just letting me talk. No, in this instance, I needed my mentor. No one, not even Ashlyn, could guide me through a problem the way Salomon could. Besides, regardless of what Detective Kalani said, he deserved to know the facts.

Quietly, as though the room were bugged and all the members would hear, I whispered, "I found Heleena."

The forty-nine-year-old native Hawaiian sat motionless. Either he was shocked by my words or I spoke too softly and he hadn't heard me. "What do you mean you found her?"

"I went for a run along the bay this morning. I found her body." I closed my eyes like that would prevent me from seeing her face again, but that only made it worse. "Someone beat her up, Salomon. As in, they beat her to death."

He ran a hand over his white goatee and slumped back in his chair. "Who would do that?" A heartbeat later he added, "I'm sorry you went through that, *mahi*. Must've been awful. Are you okay?"

His pet name for me lowered my guard, and a sob formed in my chest. *Moa mahi* meant fighting cock, or more loosely, successful warrior. One of the gym rats had given me the label years ago. Others picked it up, and somewhere along the way, Salomon shortened it to mahi.

"The shock is slowly wearing off. I blew my test, though. Didn't even finish it." Hesitantly, I asked, "Did you notice Callie when you were talking to the crowd?"

It took a second for Salomon to grasp what I was getting at. "You don't think Callie did this."

"I sure don't want to. You've got to admit, though, it's a possibility."

He shook his head. "Why would she resort to that? Callie is secure in the top spot. Leena was improving, but she wasn't ready to unseat Callie."

Focusing on the top featherweight fighters at this gym, I asked, "What about Mona?"

"Mona is off on fishing trips," Salomon replied.

"That's right." Mona ran a charter fishing boat when she wasn't pounding on people in the octagon. "I remember her talking about how the marlin and dorado are biting and that she had group after group booked this week."

Simone "Mona" Randall, the number three featherweight, was physically Callie's opposite. Mona was short at only five-two and had arms and a six-pack that most of the men in the gym envied. Heleena had been somewhere in between Callie and Mona, both physically and in the standings. The three of them were definite rivals but kept things as friendly as was possible. Or so it had appeared. Heleena had come on strong since the last title fight, and Callie admitted once to being distracted by her, worried at how fast she was rising through the ranks. That was locker-room talk Salomon clearly wasn't privy to. During that same conversation, Mona admitted she'd all but given up on ever reaching number one. She still enjoyed MMA, but her focus was on making her fishing business successful.

"Will she be back for the fight on Saturday?" I asked.

"She said she would be. Coach Ozzie isn't happy with her. She should be here focusing if she wants to win." He paused, looked me in the eye, and then cautioned, "Gemi, let the police do the investigating, okay?"

"What makes you think—"

"Keep your mind on this fight."

I nodded. He was right. That would be easier said than done, though.

Salomon rested his head in his hands. "We need to do something for Heleena. Someone mentioned getting together after the fight and toasting her. I thought we could start a collection for Lana too."

"That's a great idea." Poor Lana. My heart ached for her.

"I want to visit her parents." Salomon checked his calendar. "But my schedule is packed with fight stuff."

Good idea. It would be nice to look Mr. Carrere in the face and see if he had any regrets about his homophobic ways. Or, God forbid, if he had anything to do with his daughter's death. And poor little Halle. What must she be going through?

"I don't have class until one o'clock tomorrow," I told him. "I'll get up early for my run, then go be the representative for No Mercy."

"That would be great. They live in Makawao, I think." He opened a desk drawer and dug around in it. "I'll write a card and pass it around for people to sign." Triumphant, he withdrew a card and envelope.

"You got another one in there for Lana?"

He looked some more and shook his head. "I'll pick one up for her. We'll pass that around for signatures, too, and give it to her with the collection. Anything else we need to talk about?"

"That's not enough?"

Salomon chuckled. "It is. You okay to practice?"

"Like I said, the shock is slowly wearing off and anger is setting in. I should probably go punch something."

"Do your warmup. I'll come out in a while."

I gave him a salute and left his office. My mind was a muddled mess with thoughts of all that had happened today. And it was only three o'clock. As I crossed the gym, an image of Heleena's swollen and bruised face flashed in my mind again. Would Lana or Heleena's parents have to officially identify Leena's body or would Kalani take my word for it? What a horrific task. Whoever did this needed to be caught and justice needed to be served.

CHAPTER SEVEN

I slipped into the locker room to change. Off came my khaki shorts and T-shirt. On went soft leggings that fit like a second skin and an electric-blue sports bra that was losing its stretch. I had no idea how it started, but I wore the bra for every practice the week before a fight. Being superstitious, as fighters tended to be, I didn't want to mess with the juju, but I'd need to retire it to my memory box soon.

After pulling my hair into a ponytail, I added my favorite tie-dyed headband to hold back any wispy strands and headed for the gym floor.

"Hey, Gemi," a short, buff guy I knew only by sight greeted as I walked out of the locker room. I also knew, via the grapevine, that he was one of those guys always looking for tips. He didn't want to hire one of the trainers, so instead, he'd follow me or another top fighter around the gym and watch our workouts. Or he'd stop us as we walked past and ask if he was doing a move correctly or using a piece of equipment the right way.

"Hey." I kept walking and didn't make eye contact, leaving him with his mouth hanging open, question unasked this time. I wasn't in the mood today.

Two more people I'd seen before but didn't know by name greeted me. The first was No Mercy's glamour queen. She was always in full makeup, and I had yet to see her do anything other than walk around and talk to people. The second was a guy who came in every day and ate his lunch while using the elliptical machine.

"Do it again and I'm revoking your membership," Salomon threatened the day he dropped lettuce from his sandwich all over.

No more subs, but the guy still showed up with a protein shake. It took all kinds of people to make the world go around, and we had an interesting subsection of them right here.

Like always, I began my warmup on the treadmill. Normally, this meant ten minutes to get my legs and hips loose, but today I did twenty to make up for this morning's shortened run. Cardio was the main component of my workouts. It was important to be strong, too, but if I couldn't outlast my opponent in the ring because I got winded halfway through the second round, it didn't matter how big my muscles were.

Next, I grabbed two twenty-pound kettlebells. With toes on a weight bench, I held tight to the handle of each bell and raised my body into plank pose. Slowly, I lifted one bell, lowered it, then lifted the other. Slow was the key to making each muscle work. My legs were strong from running so strength training primarily involved my abs and obliques. I'd become really good at keeping my hands up to protect my face—due to Ashlyn's irrational fear that I'd be permanently disfigured—but that meant if I did get hit, it was usually on the side or in the abdomen. A strong core turned painful blows into minor distractions. After three sets of fifteen lifts, I moved over to the weight rack to do power squats then grabbed the handholds overhead for a few sets of hanging crunches. Finally, I was warm and ready to hit stuff.

For an actual fight, we had to wrap our hands with gauze strips held in place with surgical tape. For workouts, I used reusable cotton wraps, methodically weaving the strip between my fingers, over my knuckles, and around my wrists. Fight regulations required commission-approved fingerless MMA gloves over the gauze and tape. I preferred to keep everything well-protected so wore full boxing gloves during practice.

I could feel eyes on me from various places as I pulled on the gloves. One set of them, surely, was Aonani's. Let her and the others watch. I'd likely give them a good show today. I was devastated about Heleena and furious over blowing that test. And then Salomon canceled classes for today. That was understandable, but it meant I didn't have my little warriors to look forward to. Instead, I'd focus all this anger and frustration on the scumbag that had done this to Leena.

When I shoved my mouth guard in and bit down, it was like plugging in a lamp and flipping the switch. No longer was I Gemi, baby-faced younger sister of gorgeous Ashlyn Kittredge. I was Gemi the Bull, my fighting persona, future MMA bantamweight world champ.

With each blow to the heavy bag, that persona took over more and more. I kicked all worries out of my head and made them wait in the corner. At that moment, I didn't care if that damned test grade came back an F. I let loose with one uppercut after another. Jabs, punches, hooks, and crosses alternated with front kicks, side kicks, and round kicks. Then I turned my back to the bag which in my mind had become the attacker, one who hid in the heliotropes to attack innocent people. Or jumped out of the shadows in dark parking lots to assault defenseless little girls. I nailed him with an elbow strike squarely to the Adam's apple, another to his nose, and followed that quickly with a backfist to the temple. The final blow was a solid donkey kick to the balls. The smack to the bag and my accompanying *kihap* echoed through the gym.

You got him! the little girl from the parking lot cheered in my head.

I paused for a beat. What was she doing here?

Dismissing her, I started the routine again, letting my left side take the lead this time. Sweat soaked my headband and ran in a stream down my spine. By the time I'd finished that second round and stopped to catch my breath, I found a half-moon of gym rats behind me watching.

"Mercy," someone called.

"You mean *no* mercy," someone else corrected.

"Uncle," a third rat cried out, "I give."

I smiled and lisped through my mouth guard, "Bunch of wimps is what you are. I was just getting warm." Focused on Aonani, I asked, "Anyone want to spar?"

"I'm warm. I'll spar with you anytime."

I turned to see a blond guy with wide shoulders and a narrow waist—"I'm a perfect triangle."—leaning against the wall and leering at me. Ross Donnelly, aka Super Stud. At least that was who he was in his mind. I flashed to the last time he and I had sparred. Not only did he not land a blow, he'd been arrogant about it, claiming he'd gone easy on me. God, how I wanted to lay him out cold. And I could do it. One carefully placed right cross to his left temple—my signature close-the-deal move—and pretty boy would be face down on the mat.

Ross was one of the biggest jackasses I'd ever met. He tended to show up uninvited, like now, and almost always asked me out. There were times he practically insisted I go out with him. Caught between being a member of this gym and being No Mercy's assistant manager, I wanted to handle things professionally and without making a scene. I always told him no and walked away, hoping he'd get the hint. But responding that way ate at me. It went against everything I told the women who came to me for guidance. I encouraged them to go ahead and make a scene if they found themselves in a situation where they weren't comfortable. This was their life we were talking about. Literally in some cases.

I found Donnelly to be supremely annoying, like a fly that wouldn't quit buzzing around my head, but I didn't feel threatened by him. He had never once touched me. If he ever laid a finger on me, I would fight back and have him on the ground in seconds. Like I had with Ty this morning. Except I wouldn't be so cautious about not damaging Ross's shoulder.

Or so I said. Why did I back down when he was in front of me? Why couldn't I follow my own advice when it came to him? Maybe because I knew the other side of domestic violence. The side where people, mostly men, were wrongly accused and branded sexual predators for the rest of their lives. I understood why women hesitated. They'd worry that maybe they were wrong. As in, maybe they'd given the impression that they were interested when they really weren't. Or perhaps they'd misinterpreted the guy's words and he hadn't intended to be a jerk. Valid concerns if true. Not of the remotest importance if she'd said no. Even if she'd already said yes.

Was this why I didn't confront Ross? Was I worried that I'd misinterpreted his intent?

Then I remembered the day that Heleena made a formal complaint about him. She and I had been goofing around and laughing about something. Other women joined in on whatever we were talking about and out of nowhere, there was Ross.

"Go out with me," he said in what he'd presumably meant to be a sultry tone. "Just once."

Then he winked like they were buddies sharing an inside joke. He glanced at me and the other women standing by, all of us ready to jump in and back Leena up if she needed it. When he saw the looks on our faces, he backpedaled, trying to make it seem like he hadn't been serious. Except we'd all assumed he had been and that his underlying implication was, go out with me just once and I'll turn you from gay to straight.

Factoring in the words, his tone of voice, and the wink, that was what he meant. Wasn't it?

It was certainly the way Heleena took it. She barely considered him an acquaintance let alone a buddy that she would share that kind of a joke with. She stepped in close, looked him up and down, and replied, "I guarantee, your extra little appendage wouldn't have *any* effect on me let alone the kind you seem to think it would. Your greasy ways may work on lonely desperate women who would do anything to have a man in their lives. But me? You make me want to puke."

Then she stormed into Salomon's office and demanded he do something about Ross. Clearly, Heleena Carrere didn't need anyone to rescue her. Except for last night.

I got chewed out from Salomon that day for not stepping in on Leena's behalf. He said it was part of my job to make sure every member felt safe here in every sense of the word. Even Ross Donnelly, who had the audacity to state that Leena could have simply said no. Even though he didn't seem to understand the definition.

"I'll do better with that," I promised Salomon, "but don't try and pin this all on me. You get so wrapped up in the business side of things you forget to step out of your office and pay attention to what's going on with your members. This is your gym. Ultimately, member safety is on you."

The look he gave me made me feel like a little girl who'd disappointed her dad. That was the problem with my coach not only being my boss but a father figure for me too. Fortunately, our closeness also meant we got past the spat quickly.

Salomon had a talk with Ross. He behaved for three or four months, although his workouts were the more testosterone-fueled grunting kinds during that time. Then he slowly returned to his lecherous ways.

Had he approached Leena again? She'd done a fine job of humiliating him in front of the other members that day. Had he carried around that anger for all these months? Did he do this? Did he follow her last night and punish her for embarrassing him? Honestly, I'd pick her over him in a fight any day. But embarrassment led to anger. Anger fueled adrenaline. And too much adrenaline could be a dangerous thing.

Now, as he waited for my response, I turned away from him and back to the heavy bag.

"Seriously," he pushed and held up his gloved hands. "You want to spar?"

Ross wasn't a little guy, but he wasn't the biggest either. Closer to a buff Sheldon from *The Big Bang Theory* than Dwayne "The Rock" Johnson. Honestly, my concern was that I might hurt him.

"Afraid to take on a guy?" he taunted.

I shook my head. "Don't do that, Donnelly."

"You won't like her when she's angry," someone called out the cliché, overused *Incredible Hulk* reference.

Aonani crossed her arms, leaned against the wall, and smirked at me.

"Come on." Ross motioned to the ring.

I wasn't in the mood to deal with Ross today.

No, that wasn't true. I was in exactly the right mood. The bag served as a nice warmup, but I still wanted to hit someone. No one in the gym better to take my frustrations out on than Super Stud.

"You're on," I agreed, and Ross put both hands in the air as though he'd already won. I got a drink of water and climbed into the ring, slipping through the ropes. Game face in place.

"You're sure about this?" I asked, giving him one last out. My fists quivered to reach out and connect with his perfect nose.

He deflated a smidge when he looked in my eye. Embarrassingly, his voice broke when he answered, "I'm sure. One round."

A roar of laughter came from the other rats. When one of the other fighters in Ross's weight class shouted, "Five bucks on Gemi," they started collecting bets.

We danced around each other for the first fifteen seconds. The crowd booed and hissed, wanting action, not a dance. So Ross swung hard and landed a punch on my left shoulder. It didn't hurt, but it reminded me that I'd be doing this for real in three days. I couldn't risk any bruises or strains that might interfere with that fight. I'd been training too hard for that win. And best of all, he'd asked for it.

I sidestepped away from him and inhaled deeply. I needed to visualize an opponent that truly motivated me. Ross only annoyed me. Heleena's killer didn't have a face yet and even though the possibility was there, I doubted that Ross was the guilty party. Out of nowhere, the parking lot attacker appeared again.

Get him, the little girl whispered in a quivering voice.

As I let out a slow breath, I swung and solidly landed my signature right cross to Ross's temple. Super Stud refused to wear headgear no matter how many times we told him he should. Finally, Salomon made him sign a waiver stating that he wouldn't hold any other fighter or No Mercy responsible for a serious injury. My blow stopped him for a second and made him sway like he was going to go down. Without hesitating, I hooked his legs with one of mine and dropped him hard to the mat. An instant later, my legs were around him, one behind his head, the other over his chest. I grabbed his left arm, the one closest to me, and pushed his body to the right with my hips while pulling his arm straight back toward me. Finally, using my leg as a fulcrum, I pushed his arm toward the mat, threatening to dislocate his shoulder. An instant later, he tapped out.

That's good. The little girl sounded relieved but . . . *But he touched you. He got you on the shoulder.*

She was right. A true defeat of an attacker meant no contact.

A cheer of victory rose from the crowd. Aonani glowered and stomped away.

Satisfying as it was to best him, I wasn't celebrating. Ross had landed a blow. If I wasn't in top form Saturday night, one blow could be enough. My winning streak of twelve consecutive matches would be broken. I wanted a baker's dozen of consecutives and fifteen wins overall. Some of the gym rats had started calling it the baker's fifteen.

I jumped to my feet and held out an arm to help Ross up. He sat there, signaling that he needed a minute. The body's natural response to preparing for pain was to inhale, hold the breath, and seize up. That was probably what he'd done when I had his arm locked that way. He might have been close to passing out. It was supposed to be good clean fun, but sometimes, like now because the little girl spoke to me, I had a hard time controlling myself.

When Ross finally held up an arm, I locked elbows with him. The first tug knocked me off balance, so I linked both arms around his and leaned back to pull him to his feet.

"Sorry about the armbar," I lied as I pulled off my gloves, "but you gave me the go-ahead."

"Are you done working out? Can I buy you dinner?"

Un-freaking-believable.

Before I could reply, a voice behind us said, "She's got plans with me."

I spun and found Risa standing there. She had mentioned stopping by to check on me.

"When will you be ready?" she asked.

"I need another hour and a half. I've got to train with Salomon and then take a shower.

Risa checked the time on her phone. "That works. I still need to go to the grocery store. I'll be back."

I nodded and turned to find Ross still there. The look of disappointment mixed with anger on his face chilled me. Was that anger directed at me or Risa? Had I been right before? Had Heleena seen that same look of anger last night?

"See you later," he grumbled and walked away.

Heading toward the treadmills for a cooldown, I mentally took the hand of the little girl and led her away from the attacker.

CHAPTER EIGHT

Risa and I stared up at the massive chalkboard menu above the counter at The Juice Bar. They originally opened with a menu of only smoothies and juice drinks. They'd slowly added muffins, salads, burgers, wraps, and a variety of light entrées, but they were still best known for their beverages. All of it was delicious, not to mention healthy, and I always had a hard time choosing.

"What would you like?" Risa asked. "My treat. You could use a little pampering."

I was about to argue, but the look of compassion and eagerness on my friend's face silenced me. She was right, I *could* use a little pampering today.

"I'll have a large Green Glory." My favorite smoothie was the perfect blend of coconut milk, spinach, avocado, mango, chia seeds, and protein powder. The protein- and healthy-fat-packed drink would hold me for the rest of the night.

Risa ordered the smoothie and a mango iced tea and tuna wrap for herself.

I told Kym, who was working the counter, "A tuna wrap sounds good. I'll have one of those, too."

As we settled into a small table by the front windows, Risa went into enforcer mode. "Is Ross Donnelly still hitting on you?"

I rolled my eyes. "He doesn't understand the word *no*."

"Do we need to report him? I can call Malia . . . Detective Kalani. She'd be happy to issue a restraining order."

I might call her to add him as a possible suspect in Leena's death, but not because I couldn't deal with his flirting or whatever he thought he was doing. "It's not to that point."

"Are you actually waiting for it to get there? Boot his ass out of the gym altogether. No one deserves that kind of harassment."

"You're preaching to the choir, sister. We can't just boot him, though. Heleena's the only one to ever make a formal complaint about him and that was months ago. He's mostly a pest, but I did mention his constant asking me out to Salomon during our session tonight. He's going to have a chat with him."

"Since when are you afraid of direct confrontation? Drag him out back and show him your mighty muscles. I saw you beating him up earlier." She grinned. "I mean, sparring with him. I've never seen you so focused."

"I had motivation." The little girl could be relentless. "Look, it's not that I'm afraid to confront him. I think the guy is more clueless than anything. I mean, he can be so awkward it's almost comical sometimes."

She leveled her evil eye on me as Kym placed an extra-large smoothie on the table in front of me. "Good luck Saturday night, Gemi."

"Thanks. This smoothie might last me until then." Maybe I shouldn't have the tuna wrap. No, I could use more protein. "You know what? Just give me the guts of that wrap. I should skip the carbs."

"Side salad with tuna," Kym quipped. "Got it."

"Catch me up on your life," I told Risa. "What's been going on at work?"

After the first sip of the smoothie, I realized my workout and the emotions of the day had left me famished. Good that I had stuck with the salad. I forced myself to release the straw or I'd drink the whole thing before our food arrived.

"Ordinary ER stuff for the most part." Risa looked side to side and then leaned across the table. "There's been an increase in yakuza activity on Maui."

I leaned forward and, matching her confidential tone, asked, "What's yakuza?"

"You haven't heard of them? They make the news every few months."

"Between training, teaching, and studying, I don't usually have time for the news. If I ever have downtime, I like to read action-adventure novels."

"Okay." The way she shifted in her seat said she was excited to teach me something. "It depends on who you ask, but most people compare the yakuza to the Italian mafia. They're an organized crime syndicate involved with gambling, drug dealing, arms trafficking, blackmail, and prostitution. To name just a few of the pies they have their fingers in. They come across as being humanitarians at times by showing up at disasters with food, water, clothing, and other essentials."

"And why do I need to be worried about them?" I waved at a girl from my self-defense class who had just entered the café.

"Hi, Miss Kittredge."

She placed her hands with her palms together and bowed slightly from the waist. She was the only one of my students to do that in public. Most called out, "Hey, Gemi," from fifteen yards away. This was much more respectful.

"Hi, CJ."

"I'm sad," CJ said with a deep frown. "No class today. Heleena got hurt. No class Saturday either because of the competition."

Heleena got worse than hurt. I'd let CJ's parents deal with that, though. "I'm sad too." I thought of Heleena and then the little girl who'd been attacked in the parking lot. I knew how important it was for my warriors to learn self-defense, but this drove it home. I tapped the tip of CJ's nose. "We're going to have a class tomorrow at five o'clock instead if you can make it."

Salomon had made this decision during my workout. The next regularly scheduled class wouldn't be until Monday night. He didn't want the kids to go an entire week without one.

This brought an enormous smile to the tiny girl's face. She looked hopefully up at her dad who nodded. "Okay! I'll be there." She bowed again and skipped off.

"That kid," I told Risa, "is an up-and-comer. She's fierce. Absolutely nothing scares her."

Kym brought our food. "Anything else?"

"We're good, thanks," Risa replied with a smile. As soon as Kym walked away, she returned to her topic. "These guys, the yakuza, are nothing to fool around with. I don't know exactly what's going on, but there's been a wave of violence on the island that the cops are crediting to the islands' biggest group, Tanaka-kai." She leaned close again. "Rumor is, they found a beheaded man on the beach south of Kahana."

Beheaded? A shiver ran through me. She wasn't joking around about them. "How do you know all this? Detective Kalani?"

Risa shook her head as she chewed and swallowed a bite of her tuna wrap. "I heard some officers talking about it outside a room in the emergency department. I was stocking the cart in a room next door to one they were guarding. I don't know what happened to the guy in their room, but there was a lot of blood."

Risa had an eavesdropping addiction. Usually it was annoying. Sometimes, though, it could be helpful. Like the time she was outside the professors' lounge and "overheard" a group of them planning surprise quizzes for the day after a four-day weekend. She even knew the topics. We had cram sessions every night and were the only ones in our classes to ace the quizzes.

I was loading my fork with tuna and mixed greens, thinking about poor beaten Leena and the beheaded man, when a disturbing thought slammed into my head.

"What are you thinking?" Risa asked.

"Nothing. It's crazy."

"Tell me. Sometimes crazy is spot on."

"What if—" I sighed. "This is really out there. I'm tired, and my brain just combined the two deaths. What if Heleena was somehow involved with these yakuza people? What if that's why she was killed? I mean, they sound like a pretty violent group, and whoever killed Heleena was definitely violent."

"What if?" Risa sat back in her chair looking like she was analyzing this option. "I guess it's possible, but the yakuza have a preference for blades and bullets over fists to get their messages across."

I couldn't imagine Heleena being involved with a crime organization anyway. Of course that assumption came from thinking I knew her well based on the discussions we'd had. What did I know about her otherwise? Did she prefer fruit or vegetables? No clue. What was her favorite color? What did she like to do when she got home at the end of the day? Did she have a cat? A hamster? I didn't know any of these things.

What about the other gym rats? We knew each other's fighting styles. We knew who to target and how to fight that person in order to climb the ranks. But what about personal things?

Then again, the rats might know plenty about each other. It was possible they got together all the time and were super close. As Salomon's second in command, I had to maintain a little distance to avoid being accused of favoritism. At least that was what I told myself. Was that the truth or a convenient excuse? Except for interacting with other fighters and students at the gym, I didn't socialize. If not for Salomon and Risa, I'd literally have no one other than Ashlyn in my life. Of course, as Risa loved to point out, we made time for what was important.

I took a sip of my smoothie, barely tasting it. "You said the yakuza are involved with local businesses?"

"Yeah. Why?"

"I'm sitting here thinking about how I don't really know any of the gym rats all that well. People are complex. What I see on the gym floor doesn't mean that's who they are at home. I can't believe Heleena would ever be involved with something illegal, but maybe she was. I know she and her girlfriend have dealt with one struggle after another recently."

"You mean haters?" Risa sat forward in her chair, ready as always to go after anyone who harassed someone for their lifestyle.

"I hadn't thought of Leena's death being a hate crime, but that's a possibility too. She had been practicing with her coach until closing last night. Her habit was to go for a slow run after practice to cool down and clear her head before she went home. Sometimes another rat would join her, but she usually went alone."

"If she ran alone last night," Risa concluded, "it's entirely possible a hater followed her."

A chill ran through me. "She did have some tiny-minded people in her world. But what I meant by struggles was that they've had financial troubles." I tapped my fingers on the table while chewing a mouthful of salad. "Maybe Heleena's parents can offer some insight. I'll try to steer the conversation that way when I go to their house tomorrow."

"Why are you going to her parents' house?" Risa asked, wrap poised at her mouth for a bite.

"I told Salomon I'd bring them a card and offer our condolences."

"Where do they live?"

"Makawao."

"You're going clear over to Makawao to deliver a card?"

"It's not like it's on the other side of the island. It's twenty minutes. It'll be a nice motorcycle ride."

Risa sat silently for a few seconds, eyeing me. I knew that look. She wanted to analyze my motives. Dig around in my brain to find some buried truth.

Before she could start down that path, I asked, "How do I look into these yakuza people?"

Risa winced. "Be careful with that, Gemi. The chances that they're responsible for Heleena's death are very slim. You don't want to fool around with them. They're tricksters, coming across as caring for the public while terrorizing people in private."

"What do you mean by that?"

"Like I said, they show up with trucks of food and supplies when natural disasters strike. They work their way into the public's good graces and offer help if it's needed. But for those that don't need any help, they offer protection. And by offer, I mean force it on them. For those who need financial help, they give loans. You miss a payment, they employ scare tactics. You miss another payment, things get physical."

"Let me guess, you don't want to miss a third payment?"

She gave a slow nod.

"Heleena and Lana have a little hair salon in Kihei. That's the other thing I meant by struggles. Leena said that some months they have a hard time covering rent, let alone all their bills. Once, she even mentioned shutting it down and renting a chair at another salon." I paused and then added, "Sounds like the exact type of people the yakuza would be interested in *helping*."

Risa rubbed her neck as if it ached. "If Heleena and Lana did get involved with these folks, it could mean trouble for you if they think you're nosing around in things that are none of your concern. Tread carefully."

I munched a few more bites of salad, trying to decide if this was a path worth following, and a different option struck me.

"What if it was Lana? Maybe she got involved with this gang. No better way to get a message across to her than to go after the person she cared about most."

Risa didn't respond, which told me the thought had some weight behind it.

We changed the subject then, talking about if I was ready for the fight on Saturday and weird non-yakuza things Risa had encountered at work. The whole time, in the back of my mind, I couldn't stop thinking about Heleena and wondering what she'd gotten involved with.

CHAPTER NINE

I left my helmet sitting on the Indian's seat and entered the condo. I could immediately tell that Ashlyn was home. The obvious clue was her brilliant-blue Mercedes convertible tucked into its spot in the garage. Also the bird roamed free, swooping down from atop the bookshelf to land in front of me when I walked in. Finally, the refrigerator was wide open. As were the silverware drawer and dish cupboard door. How could she forget to close doors and drawers? Open, remove the desired item, and with hand still on the knob, shut it again. Not difficult.

"Aloha, Gemi," Hulu's squawky voice called out.

"Aloha, Hulu." I closed everything and grabbed a glass of water. As I headed for the stairs to the second floor, a *meow* sounded from the corner. That was new. Through a laugh, I scolded, "You're not a cat, Hulu."

The bird giggled, a perfect imitation of Ashlyn, then meowed again.

As expected, Ash was in bed with her tablet propped on a pillow in her lap, a bowl of yogurt with mango in her hand, and the television on.

"You forgot to close the refrigerator again." The mostly full bowl of fruit and yogurt led me to believe it hadn't been open for long.

"Did I?" She grinned big around the spoon and then pulled it out of her mouth. "Sorry. The phone rang. Speaking of which, there was a message on the machine from Professor Hastings when I got home. Why is she calling the condo instead of your cell?"

"She did." The professor had called while I was at No Mercy. "She left a message there too."

Ashlyn turned off her tablet and lowered the television volume on the episode of *The Good Witch* currently playing. "She said to check your email."

Knowing she would literally follow me around the condo, into the bathroom if necessary, until I checked, I pulled my phone from my shorts pocket and flopped onto the bed with her. After tapping a few times, I found the email in question, received a little after two o'clock.

I'm concerned that there's something big going on with you. Not only did you miss those last three questions, you got half of the questions you did answer wrong. Call me ASAP and we'll figure this out.

Nothing new there. Except for getting so many of the answered questions wrong. I glanced over at Ashlyn who was sitting with her arms crossed and a look on her face that was her version of a disappointed mom.

"Well?"

"I blew my test today."

"What?" She switched the volume to mute and snatched my phone out of my hand. Her mouth dropped open as she read. "How?"

"That thing that happened this morning—" I paused as my voice shook and tears threatened. "It's really bad, Ash."

While I told her everything, starting with spotting Heleena's body on the beach and going clear through to the discussion with Risa at The Juice Bar tonight, Ashlyn played with the infinity necklace at her throat. I absently reached up and touched the matching one at mine. When we realized Mom wasn't coming back, we bought matching silver necklaces. We designed them together, choosing an infinity symbol to represent our bond as sisters, a tiny leaf-shaped charm with our first initial engraved into it, and another small round crystal charm with our birthstone. As soon as we'd put them on, we took them off again and switched. Hanging from the infinity symbol around my neck was a tiny leaf with an *A* for Ashlyn and the clear crystal that was her April birthstone. The leaf on Ashlyn's had a *G* and the crystal was March's aquamarine.

"Oh my God, Peep." Ash had paled beneath her tan. "That's horrible. Are you okay? You must be absolutely devastated."

She draped an arm over my shoulders and pulled me in for a hug.

"I'm okay." But my voice caught as I let my guard all the way down with my sister.

"No, you're not."

She turned to shove her tablet into the nightstand drawer. When she did, I noticed a small pink hibiscus tattooed on her right hip. It was beautiful.

"When did you get that?" It wasn't inflamed or angry red, which happened with new ink, so must have been there for a while.

Ashlyn looked at my finger poking the tattoo. "Months ago. You never saw it?"

"Would I ask if I had?"

"I guess not. Stay right there." She strode down the hall to my bedroom and reappeared a minute later with a tank top and pajama shorts.

"Put on your jammies. I'll be right back."

While I took off my T-shirt and shorts and swapped them for a baby-pink sleep tank and cotton boxers with rainbows and unicorns all over, a gift from my sister, I heard Hulu let out an objecting squawk. That meant she was putting him into his cage for the night. Then came the sound of a spoon tapping on a dish.

"I hope she remembers to close everything," I murmured and noticed her packed suitcase sitting in the corner. Right, she was leaving in the morning. I'd almost forgotten.

"Goodnight, Hulu," Ashlyn said at the bottom of the stairs.

"Nighty-night. Sleep tight," the bird replied.

I smiled at the nightly ritual. When Ashlyn was home, that was how she ended every day. Wishing her bird a good night. I was a big fan of routine.

She entered the room with another bowl of yogurt and fruit and handed it to me. Honestly, I was still stuffed from the smoothie and salad, but I couldn't turn down such a sweet gesture.

By this time, Cassie the good witch had brought her inn's visiting struggling couple together. So Ashlyn clicked over to the Hallmark mystery channel where the next *Murder, She Baked* episode was just starting. Considering the events of my day, a murder mystery felt appropriate. Ash tucked pillows around me and then rubbed massage oil into my feet and calves. My legs and feet almost always ached.

Two hours later, when I rolled over to go to my bedroom, she stopped me.

"No, you don't. We're having a slumber party tonight."

A perfect ending to an otherwise rotten day. What would I ever do without my sister?

* * *

I woke at six thirty the next morning, confused to find an arm draped over my torso. A couple blinks later and I remembered I'd slept in Ashlyn's bed. I tried to go back to sleep, but when I closed my eyes, images of Heleena's battered face slammed in behind my eyelids. That image had haunted my dreams overnight too. I bolted awake once, sure I'd heard a noise in the condo. The killer coming after me because . . . why? Because I found her body? No. If the killer had wanted to keep Heleena's death quiet, he wouldn't have left her on a public beach. I'd gone back to sleep only to be wakened again. That time I could have sworn I'd heard Leena crying out for help.

As I tried to go back to sleep now, my mind went to the suspect list I'd come up with. The worst option being . . . No, the worst option would be that one of Leena's family members had killed her. I shuddered at that thought. The second worst option being someone from the gym. Callie Castro's name sat at the top of that list. I'd rather learn a serial killer was preying on women in the Kahului area than find out Callie or anyone from my ohana had done that to her. More likely, we were looking for one of the many drugged-up homeless persons wandering around Maui. It made much more sense that the killer was someone who had gotten hold of some bad drugs and went on a stupor-induced attack than it being one of the gym rats.

What about that guy who'd been at the beach near Heleena? What was his . . . Homeless Harry. Could he be the killer? Wasn't it a generally accepted rule that the guilty party returned to, or stayed at, the scene of the crime? I'd told Detective Kalani about him. Hopefully, she'd tracked him down. Did the homeless stick to their own areas of the island, or did they wander? Harry ran when I tried to talk with him yesterday. Maybe I'd go back, track him down, and try again.

I flipped onto my right side, away from Ashlyn's morning breath, and tried to dismiss thoughts of murderers and fall asleep again. Right about the time my body started to feel heavy, my schedule for today slammed into my brain. I should still be asleep at six thirty. But last night's slumber party meant I hadn't done any studying. Fortunately, I didn't have a test or anything due today, but since I was awake and obviously not going back to sleep, I might as well get up and be productive.

Sliding out from beneath my sister's arm, envious of how deeply she was still sleeping, I rolled out of bed. At least this was a peaceful time to get in a run. I gathered my pile of clothes from the floor and brought them to the overflowing hamper in my bedroom closet. Laundry. I'd meant to throw in a load last night.

After trading my pajamas for jogging shorts and a sports bra from the hamper, I paused in the kitchen for water. As I drank, I uncovered Hulu's cage.

"Good morning, Hulu," I whispered.

"Rise and shine," Hulu whispered back. As much as a parrot could whisper. "It's a beautiful day in the neighborhood."

I loved that my sister taught him primarily happy phrases. The world needed more happiness.

I finished the water, strapped on my shoes, and headed left for Iao Valley State Park. This route provided the peace and solitude of towering mountains and rich foliage. So much nicer than the busy streets of Kahului. Then again, being able to run along the ocean made navigating the town worth it. Of all the problems life presented, which bit of beauty to subject myself to was a nice one to have.

When I got to the Iao Valley parking lot, not quite five miles from the condo, I smiled at finding only a handful of early-bird tourists waiting for the gates to open. That meant the path to the lookout would be clear.

I paused my music, pulled out an earplug, and jogged in place next to the older couple in matching aloha shirts who were first in line. "If you don't mind, I'd like to cut ahead of you."

"Are you going to run to the top?" the woman asked.

I nodded and unclipped the water bottle from my waist pack. "That's my plan."

"By all means." The man held out a hand, indicating I could go first. "You'll likely be up and back down before we're halfway."

I thanked them, sipped some water, and once given the okay, took off up the paved path that became a series of zigzagging stairways. It was a hundred-and-some steps to the top, the reward being a spectacular view of the valley. I paused there to take it all in. There was no disputing the physical beauty of this island. The lush green of Iao Valley. The reddish-orange towering peak of Haleakala in the distance. Straight ahead, the ocean faded from a turquoise ring of water closest to the island to a royal blue a few yards out and then a deep dark blue. Not to mention plant life in every shade of the rainbow. We truly lived in paradise. Why then, after fifteen years, did I still feel like a tourist on an extended visit? Maybe because we came here to escape our old life, not start a new one.

I heard voices from below me and looked to see that the couple from the start of the line were almost to the top.

"You made it," the man congratulated me.

"Did you think she wouldn't," his wife jokingly scolded. "Keep taking care of yourself like this, sweetie. You'll be happy you did when you reach our age."

We chatted about the view for a minute and then I started back down. The steps were slick in spots from all the moisture, so I took the descent at half the pace of the ascent. While this full route provided a great cardio workout with the addition of steps, it was only eleven miles. I took the long way around the neighborhood on the way back to extend it a bit more.

I waved at Mrs. Ly, watering the flower beds along the front of her condo. Her mother was outside with her this morning. Ancient, very wrinkly, and adorable Mrs. Voong stood on the front porch, deadheading the pots. As she plucked a dead blossom from a plant, she stuck it in her pocket instead of tossing it in the weed bucket at her feet. Mrs. Voong had sticky fingers. If anyone on the street discovered something missing from their property—yard ornaments, abandoned kids' toys, a pair of shoes left outside the door—they knew to check with Mrs. Voong first.

Back home, I found Ashlyn's suitcase and makeup kit waiting by the front door for departure.

"There you are." She was in the kitchen making coffee and toast. "I would've gone for a run with you."

She looked gorgeous in a figure-hugging white sheath dress with pink hibiscus flowers and green leaves trailing down her sides. I couldn't imagine ever wearing something like that, especially the beige high heels that completed the look. But even in the land of shorts, T-shirts, and *rubbah slippahs,* aka flipflops, my polar-opposite sister looked completely at ease.

"You wouldn't have liked this one." I refilled my water bottle and took a long drink. "Up to the Iao lookout."

"You're right." Ashlyn stirred plenty of creamer into her coffee. "I probably would've tripped on the steps and messed up my nails." She flashed the new manicure in my face. "Do you approve of the color?"

I inspected the rosy-pink shade I hadn't noticed last night and grinned. "I'll call it *Ashlyn's Embarrassment*, and yes, I approve. When are you leaving?"

"Jeannie's picking me up in forty-five minutes."

"Good, plenty of time for a shower."

"Yes, please shower." Ashlyn put a hand to her nose, then squealed and ducked out of the way when I came at her with arms open wide for a sweaty hug.

While scrubbing suds through my hair, I reviewed the day's schedule again. Workout done. Breakfast next. Was I supposed to visit Heleena's parents this morning or another day? Salomon was going to check with them. Lunch and then classes from one to four thirty. Grab some dinner, teach the kiddos how to get away from an attacker, then train again with Salomon. Training was never off the schedule, but as fight day grew closer, my sessions with him got progressively lighter.

"You know what to do in the octagon," Salomon told me the first time I had pushed for more. "The last thing you want is an injury two days before a fight. Run, hydrate, stretch. The night before, review footage of your opponent's fights and visualize your attack on her."

Salomon was big into mindset and had converted me to the power of meditation. It didn't matter how well the body was prepared, if the mind wasn't equally ready, a fight could easily take a turn toward disaster.

"Busy day," I told myself as I rinsed out the shampoo. "Guess it's a good thing I was up early."

I pulled on a pair of loose khaki shorts and a one-size-too-big T-shirt with surfboards and *Life is Better on the Beach* on the front. After toweling most of the water out of my hair, I shook my head, arranged the waves into a somewhat organized style, smeared a little moisturizing sunscreen on my face, and declared myself ready for the day.

I had just slid my egg white omelet with chicken strips, sweet potatoes, and red peppers onto my plate when the doorbell rang.

"Can you get that?" Ash called from the half bath.

I looked from my hot breakfast to the front door and sighed. Knowing this would likely involve more than simply opening the door, I switched on the oven's "Keep Warm" feature and then slid the plate inside.

"Good morning, Gemi," Jeannie Yamaguchi greeted in her usual cheery way from the front porch.

Jeannie was stunning with flawless porcelain skin and sleek black hair. Like Ashlyn, she was always impeccably dressed. Today she wore a dress similar to Ash's, except hers was sleeveless and the flowers trailed diagonally from her right shoulder to her waist and then diagonally across her legs to the hem.

When Ashlyn emerged from the bathroom, I noted that while her dress was white and Jeannie's black, the pink hibiscus flowers were identical.

"Did you guys plan your outfits?" I asked.

Ashlyn flushed the color of her nails, and Jeannie's perfect bow mouth formed an O.

"We shop at the same stores," Ashlyn replied with a slight stutter. "We loved both dresses, but black looks so much better on Jeannie."

I hadn't expected an explanation. It was a joke. Since they hadn't taken it that way, though, the dresses now looked more like uniforms to me. And with all the possible flowers to choose from, why hot-pink hibiscuses on both?

Jeannie took Ashlyn's makeup case. "We should get going. I'll have her back in time for your fight, Gemi. I hope to come too."

"That would be great." My words faded as Jeannie turned to leave. Her dress had a high crew neck in front but plunged low in back and revealed a tattoo between her shoulder blades identical to the one on Ashlyn's hip. They must have shopped for tattoos at the same store too.

On their dresses, their tattoos, and on the motorcycle helmet

Ashlyn bought for me. Maybe this was like buying a new car and then seeing that same model everywhere you went. Or was there something else going on?

"What's wrong?" Ash asked, preparing to hug me goodbye.

"Jeannie's tattoo." I suddenly felt like a sprinkler in a rainforest: completely unimportant.

"You're not upset about that, are you?" She frowned. "Don't be. It was a spur-of-the-moment thing. If I remember correctly, there was a Mai Tai that sparked the idea. Two more and we were numb and on the tables at the parlor."

She was right. It was a stupid thing to be bothered about. I shared things with Risa that I didn't share with my sister, after all. Didn't I?

Ashlyn went to Hulu's cage and scratched the top of the bird's head with a long blush-pink nail. "Short trip this time, buddy. See you in two days."

With eyes closed, he leaned into the scratch. "Bye-bye, Ashy."

Returning to me, she put one hand on my shoulder and adjusted some of my curls with the other. "How are you doing regarding Heleena this morning?"

I shrugged. "I'm as okay as I can be."

She pursed her lips and hummed, not believing me. "Hydrate, stay loose, get enough sleep. I'd say eat well, but I don't know anyone who eats like you do. I'll call and text and see you on Saturday."

We gave air kisses, to not mess up her lipstick, and then Ashlyn left, dragging her overstuffed suitcase behind her.

I stood in the doorway, staring at the place on Ashlyn's hip that held the tattoo. I waved as she got into the passenger's seat of Jeannie's Lexus sedan, as sleek and black as her hair, and wondered, not for the first time, what exactly Ashlyn did when she went on these *business* trips.

CHAPTER TEN

I breathed in the heady fragrance of the spring-blooming flowers planted near the lanai while I ate my now slightly rubbery and warm but no longer hot omelet. Even from four miles away, I could tell that the ocean was peaceful today. I exhaled, grateful for a bit of serenity no matter how brief. Then my phone buzzed with a text from Salomon.

Heleena's parents will be home until 11 this morning. The earlier you can stop over the better.

So much for peace. I gobbled the rest of my breakfast and, fifteen minutes later, was on my way to Makawao, the card from the No Mercy gang tucked into one of the Indian's saddlebags. I took Highway 37 there. It was a straight road, kind of boring, but I opened up the bike and cruised along, relishing the feeling of the wind against my bare skin. I'd take Baldwin Avenue back. That route was a little longer but had plenty of curves I could lean into.

I arrived at my destination before I knew it, the twenty-minute trip having passed far too quickly. I'd checked online for a flower shop in Makawao and stopped there to pick up a small arrangement of pink-and-yellow king protea and deep-pink ginger flowers. At least that was what the woman working there told me they were. All I knew was that the arrangement was simple but pretty. Hopefully, it was appropriate for mourning. Guess I should have asked about that.

The GPS on my cell phone, which I'd clamped between my handlebars, guided me to a sky-blue single-story house—not too small, not too big—with a covered front porch and tidy, simple landscaping. Halle was sitting on the steps, holding a black-and-white kitten. She looked so much like her big sister with her long wavy dark hair, darkly tanned skin, and sparkling medium-brown eyes. Except her eyes had lost their sparkle today.

Seeing her this way tore at my heart. Halle loved coming to classes at No Mercy and was always one of my more enthusiastic students. While she didn't have quite the MMA aptitude Heleena had, I expected her skills to take off at any time.

"Hi, Ms. Kittredge."

My voice caught before I even tried to speak. What was I supposed to say to her? I hadn't thought about that until this moment. What would I want to hear if it had been my sister? I'd want strength and support, not a reminder of how horrible this was and how sad I must be. That meant I had to stay in control of my emotions. I sat next to the girl, close but not touching.

"How are you doing, Halle?"

"I've been better," she admitted and shrugged her small shoulder.

"I'm so sorry about Heleena." Halle's eyes filled with tears. That wasn't what I wanted. Ten words and I'd already said the wrong thing. I poked a finger into the kitten's stretched-out paw, tiny needle-sharp claws exposed. "Is this Feral?"

Halle had been so excited the day her mother let her adopt the kitten. Mrs. Carrere wasn't so happy with the name her animal-loving younger daughter chose, however. Maui had a huge feral cat problem. Thousands and thousands of them had taken over, especially along the coast, and posed a danger to marine life. Heleena helped her choose the name, and Halle swore she'd never tell her parents where it had come from. One of their many sister secrets.

"I'll think of you every time I say his name," I heard Halle tell Heleena that day only a couple of weeks ago.

"Isn't he cute?" Halle held the squirming kitten up for inspection.

"He's adorable." Tiny Feral purred like my motorcycle when I scratched his ears. "Is your mom home?"

Halle nodded. "Daddy is too." Her eyes shifted to the flowers in my hand. "They told me you were coming and that I should wait outside. You can go in. They're in the kitchen."

I wasn't comfortable just walking into someone's house, but Halle assured me it was okay. I untied my sneakers, left them on the porch, and then opened the door to find gleaming koa wood floors and soaring ceilings. From the front entry, I saw a large open space that took up the center of the house.

"Mrs. Carrere?"

"Aloha, Gemi," a woman's voice sang out. "We're here. Straight ahead and to the right."

Ten feet inside the house was a freestanding wall that delineated the kitchen from the entry. The Carreres were on the other side. I placed my palms together, the bouquet sandwiched between them, and bowed. A greeting of respect picked up from years of studying taekwondo. I held out the flowers and card to Heleena's mother, a woman who always managed to appear both laidback and pulled-together at the same time. Mrs. Carrere usually wore simple sundresses, and her collarbone-length bobbed hair always looked perfect, even on the most humid days.

"How lovely." She went to a cupboard and retrieved a vase that suited the protea and ginger flowers perfectly. She read the card and handed it to her husband. "Thank you, Gemi. And please give Salomon and the others our thanks as well."

Mr. Carrere glanced at the card before tossing it into a basket on the counter filled with others. "Yes, very thoughtful for someone to come all this way." He had the same pulled-together-casual appearance in pressed khaki shorts and an aloha shirt in subdued rather than vibrant colors. He was a stocky man with wide shoulders, a thick neck, and salt-and-pepper, military-style hair. Leena and Halle had his eyes. "We understand you found Heleena's body."

Something was off with these two. First, the too-bright "aloha" when I entered, and now the proper demeanor of welcoming people into their home. They struck me as being unemotional about their daughter's death. I hadn't expected to find them sobbing and understood that they, or at least he, hadn't approved of Heleena's lifestyle, but I had anticipated some amount of sorrow. She was their daughter, after all. Maybe they were just in shock.

"Yes, sir. I was running along Kanaha Beach when I found her."

"That must've been quite upsetting," Mr. Carrere noted, still with little emotion. "I'm sorry for your distress."

For *my* distress?

Mrs. Carrere brought Halle to No Mercy twice per week for lessons. She usually ran errands while Halle was in class, but on the few occasions she did come into the building, I found her to be a pleasant but not exactly warm woman. That was the vibe she conveyed now. I had never met Mr. Carrere before. He'd never come to any of Halle's classes or demonstrations and never to Leena's matches, so I didn't know what to expect. Where his wife was poised and proper, he verged on icy.

Their phone rang, and Mr. Carrere excused himself to answer an extension in another room.

"It's been ringing constantly," Mrs. Carrere commented. "So many people calling to offer condolences."

Figuring I might not get the opportunity again, I asked, "Forgive me if this is too forward, but do you have any idea who could have done this to Heleena?"

She shook her head. "As I told Detective Kalani, I don't know much about Heleena's personal life."

While that didn't surprise me, I couldn't reconcile the comment with the woman who was so obviously concerned about Halle's wellbeing. At least once a month, Mrs. Carrere made a point of asking how Halle was doing. The girl would stand at her side, her cheeks pink with embarrassment over all the questions her mom would fire at me.

One time, Halle had been so embarrassed by the interrogation, she blurted, "Heleena's doing well too. She's the number two fighter."

Tears shined in Mrs. Carrere's eyes as she glanced across the gym at Leena. She excused herself and went out to her car where I saw her crying. I held a guilty-looking Halle back and told her to give her mom a few minutes before going out there.

Now, that same woman sat pensively, staring at the bouquet on her kitchen island. Quietly, she offered, "A young man came by a few weeks ago looking for Heleena."

"He came here?"

She gestured at the barstool next to her. "I have no idea why. Heleena hasn't lived at home for five years."

I sat. "She moved out when she was eighteen, right?"

She nodded while glancing in the direction her husband had gone. "That was when Heleena told us she was lesbian. My husband didn't react well."

"You kicked her out?" I asked, playing dumb.

This time, the woman arched a disapproving eyebrow at my directness. "A fact I'm sure you're already aware of, Gemi." She lowered her voice and confessed, "My husband doesn't tolerate that kind of thing. He told Heleena she had two choices. Break up with her girlfriend or move out."

She verbally stumbled over the word girlfriend. Did she feel the same way her husband did or was she simply obeying his command in order to keep the peace in the household? The woman had never struck me as being anything but self-assured, but people could be very different behind their closed front doors.

"Heleena had a horrible time at first," Mrs. Carrere continued. "Maui is godawful expensive, and she and Lana had no money. Lana did something with tourism. Or was it restaurant work?" She paused, thinking, then dismissed the question with a shake of her head. "Anyway, they lived in a tent on the beach for a while. Fortunately, the weather is consistent here, so the only danger there was getting soaked in an afternoon shower." She paused. "Or picking up a meth habit. Or being assaulted." She laughed, although it was more of a sob. "Anyone who tried anything on Heleena would be in for a rude awakening, wouldn't they?"

Had Detective Kalani told them how Heleena had died? Would she hang on to that information for some reason?

I offered a gentle smile. "She was definitely able to protect herself. When was the last time you saw her?"

"You mean when did we last have a conversation? It's probably been a year." She stared into the distance and thought. When she came up with the answer, her shoulders slumped slightly. "Closer to two years. I would see her now and then when I dropped Halle off at the gym." She held a hand in the air as though greeting the ghost of her daughter in the corner. "We always waved."

"But you didn't speak?" I hadn't meant that to come across as being so judgmental. Luckily, Mrs. Carrere was still lost in thought and didn't seem to hear my comment.

"No"—she looked relieved as she lowered her hand and rested it on my arm—"it hasn't been two years. I gave her money one day a few months ago. I stashed away a few dollars here and there and kept it in my car's center console. Once I had a tidy sum that could actually make a difference for her, I met her outside the gym. We talked for a while that day. She told me about the salon and how she'd been climbing the MMA ranks. She promised to use the money for a sofa." Mrs. Carrere smiled, but it faded quickly. She removed her hand from my arm. "It seems like such an empty gesture now. But what else could I do?"

In other words, she wasn't allowed to do anything meaningful for her daughter. I'd heard this time and again from the women at the shelter. They weren't allowed to . . . fill in the blank. But I'd also noticed that even the most compliant women had a way of making things happen.

My instincts about abused and controlled women and children were usually strong. To not have seen this in Mrs. Carrere until now was proof of how skilled the woman had become at hiding her truth. She was mourning the loss of her daughter and not just because she was now deceased. Mr. Carrere appeared to rule this household and had likely forbidden his wife from having any kind of relationship with their daughter. What did he threaten to do if she broke his rule? Kick her out too? Take Halle from her? Both?

I returned to the statement that had sent us down that emotional path. "You said a young man came looking for Heleena?"

"Oh, yes. He seemed surprised that she didn't live here. As we just discussed, Heleena hasn't lived here for years. I thought he was kidding around."

A bad feeling slithered up my back. "Do you remember his name?"

She chuckled and shook her head as though amused. "Oh, I remember. Johnny Gambino. For a minute, I thought he was a mobster."

My breath caught. Johnny had come here looking for Heleena?

"Johnny is one of our gym members," I confirmed. "He had quite a crush on Heleena."

"Barking up the wrong tree, wasn't he?" She was trying to make light of it, and I wondered again about Mrs. Carrere's mental state. Joking this way when her daughter had just died, but grief took many shapes. Then her laughter turned into a sob again. And this time, that sob became a hairline crack in her honed exterior.

"Did you mention Johnny to Detective Kalani?"

She sniffed and blinked. "No, I forgot about him until just now. I'll give her a call."

I would too. "Is there anything else you can think of that might help us find who did this?"

Help us? Like I was part of this investigation.

She shook her head but very quietly suggested, "You should talk to Lana. If anyone can tell you about Heleena's life, it's her."

"Do you happen to know her address?"

"I don't. That's why I didn't give it to Mr. Gambino when he asked." She paused. "I know that Leena lived in Kihei." At this, the tears hovering at the brim of her eyes spilled, opening that crack a bit more. "How disgusting is that? I don't even know my own daughter's address."

I reached across and placed a hand on hers. "That's okay. I'll get it from Salomon."

The phone rang again, giving us another minute together. Mrs. Carrere walked me to the front door.

"If you find out anything," she asked, "will you let me know?"

"Of course. Hopefully, Detective Kalani will get answers quickly. I'll go see Lana and let you know of anything I find out from her. Today is Thursday, no classes Saturday, so I'll see you and Halle next week."

"Halle will be in class tonight," Mrs. Carrere stated, shocking me one more time. "Her father says she is not to miss any classes and that—" She cut herself off, flushing a deep red.

"That what?" I spun when Mr. Carrere cleared his throat behind me.

"I told Halle she has the potential to be better than her sister. All she has to do is apply herself." He pushed his wide shoulders back, appearing even bigger than he already was. And, I had to admit, scarier. "All those lessons. All that time and money. Heleena let herself get distracted by . . . that girl and the growing public attention around her rising in the ranks."

For someone so disgusted by his daughter's lifestyle, Mr. Carrere seemed to know quite a bit about her. "You didn't like the attention she was getting?"

He huffed. "It's fine if the recipient deserves it."

My body tensed, ready to fight. "You didn't think Heleena deserved the attention she got?"

Or did he think she got what she deserved Tuesday night?

As though reading my mind, his eyes narrowed. To someone less physically capable, I saw how intimidating he could be.

He paused, regaining control, before saying, "She clearly wasn't the big MMA star she wanted people to believe she was. If she had been, she could have fought off her assailant."

So they did know how Leena died. I stiffened more at his comment, my fists involuntarily clenching at my sides. Even the world's best fighter lost a bout at some point. And if faced with two attackers, as I feared Leena had been, they likely didn't stand a chance. Reality was far from what television portrayed.

"Thank you for stopping by, Ms. Kittredge." The phone in his hand rang, and he sighed as though weary of hearing condolences about his dead daughter. "Halle will see you in class tonight."

Once he'd left the room, Mrs. Carrere pulled me into her arms, her breath coming in ragged little gasps, and her body shook. She was fighting to bottle up her emotions again. If she didn't let them out soon, that crack would split wide open and she'd explode. Then there might be another murder on the island.

So softly I had to strain to hear her, she said, "*Mahalo.* Thank you so much for coming over."

I nodded and left the house. I wanted to say goodbye to Halle, but she was no longer on the porch. She'd probably run off with Feral to play somewhere else. It seemed I'd see her tonight anyway.

As I squatted to tie my sneakers, my thoughts turned to Johnny Gambino. Who had given him this address? What had he hoped to accomplish by coming here? Everyone knew how desperate he was to go out with Leena. Had his desperation turned to obsession? I thought of him breaking the broom handle in half over his knee yesterday. Like I did with Ross, Heleena had said no to Johnny every time he'd asked her out. Had he heard no too many times and took out his *big emotions* on Heleena like he had on that broom?

CHAPTER ELEVEN

As badly as I wanted to talk to Detective Kalani about Johnny and get down to Kihei to talk with Lana, school came first. Fortunately, that wasn't a struggle today. I enjoyed the mental health class with Professor Hastings a lot, but I liked Care of Women even more. It meshed well with my passion for teaching self-defense to women and kids.

"Quiz on Tuesday," Professor Sato announced, with one minute left in class, "test on Thursday. This will be the last test before your final exam next month. Any questions?"

Yeah, how did this class always fly by? For that matter, how did this year fly by?

Professor Sato stopped me on my way out of the room.

"One of my student tutors is graduating this year," he explained. "I wondered if you would be interested in filling the spot. There is a nominal hourly pay rate attached, but more importantly, it will look fantastic on your resume."

He wasn't the first professor to ask me to be a tutor, but this was the most appealing offer so far. To discuss women's and children's healthcare with new students sounded like a passion project if ever I'd heard of one.

"I'm honored by the offer. Thank you. How soon do you need an answer?"

Professor Sato's smile drooped at the question. "Positions on my tutoring team don't open up very often, Gemi. I only offer them to the best and most mature students. Honestly, I expected you'd jump at it."

Without thinking, I placed my palms together. It was a calming gesture for me and a sign of respect to him. "I would love to take it. But between school, training, and teaching classes at the gym, my schedule is already packed. I wouldn't want to take on something like this if I can't give the students the attention they deserve."

He held my gaze and then sighed. "Take a scalpel to your schedule and let me know. I'll hold the spot for you for one week."

Take a scalpel to my schedule? The only way I could carve out time to tutor would be to drop something else or sleep less.

"I appreciate that, professor. Thank you again. I'll see what I can do."

I headed toward my next class and thought of the follow-up email Professor Hastings had sent while I'd been talking with Mrs. Carrere. Since tomorrow was rotation day, I didn't *have* to deal with my blown exam until Monday, but I knew what a privilege it was for professors to take this kind of interest in a student. There were twenty-five minutes before my three o'clock public health class, so I pulled a protein bar and a bottle of water out of my backpack and changed course for Professor Hastings's office. Once there, I steeled myself before rounding the corner. She was at her desk grading papers, a red pen behind one ear and another in her hand. I knocked softly on the doorjamb.

"Oh, Gemi. Good. Have a seat." The professor indicated a nearby chair. "You didn't reply to either of my emails, so I wasn't sure if I'd see you or not." She took a folder from her satchel on the credenza behind her, thumbed through it, and removed a test packet. "You failed the test. What's going on?"

Detective Kalani told me not to discuss Leena's death with anyone. My grade was on the line, however, so I had to tell the professor something. I'd skip over the details. She didn't need to know that.

"I imagine," I began, "you heard about the woman found dead on the beach yesterday."

"I did." She frowned. "So tragic."

I let out a heavy sigh and blurted, "Not only am I the one who found her, she was a member of my gym. A fellow fighter. Ranked second in the featherweight class."

A student appeared in the office doorway. Professor Hastings held up a hand, waving him off as she got up to close the door and then gestured for me to continue.

"That was upsetting for multiple reasons. On top of my normal schedule, I've got a title fight on Saturday, and my sister is on a trip again." To my horror, a couple of tears ran down my face, and my voice shook. "It's just been a lot, I guess."

"What a traumatic experience that must have been," Professor Hastings stated, her voice full of empathy.

"It was."

"You said you knew this woman from your gym. Were you close? Was she a friend?"

She couldn't know how loaded those questions were. "She was a friend, yes, but we weren't anywhere near as close as we could have been." I swiped at my cheeks and laughed, embarrassed. "Thought I was coming in to discuss a bad test."

Professor Hastings smiled. "I'd like to think I'm here for more than delivering lectures." She absently tapped her fingers on the test packet. "This just happened yesterday. How are you doing?"

"I'm all right." I had to keep it together until after the fight on Saturday. Once that was over and Heleena's killer was caught, then I could fall apart.

"Are you sleeping and eating? That's often the first sign of distress."

"I had a few bad dreams last night," I replied, deciding to be honest with her since she was taking time for me. "Woke up a little earlier than normal, but that might have been because I slept in my sister's bed." I smiled at the memory of Ashlyn's arm draped over me and continued as though checking off items on a to-do list. "I ate a decent breakfast this morning and had a big dinner last night." I pulled the protein bar wrapper out of my shorts pocket and dropped it in her trash can. "Had a snack on the way over here." My neoprene water bottle sticking out of my backpack pocket caught my eye, so I took a long swig. "I never seem to drink enough."

My words answered her questions but didn't seem to ease her mind. "You're aware that effects from trauma like this can linger in the background and sneak up on you. If you feel you need to talk more, I'm available. Or I can put you in touch with someone else if you're not comfortable talking to me."

"Thank you, professor. I'm all right, all things considered. Once they figure out who did this, I'll be even better. You know?"

"I do." Her look of concern turned to one of empathy. Without warning, she tore my test papers in two. "You know this information. We don't need a test to prove that. Maybe we'll get together again in a week or so and revisit a few of the questions. For now, I won't include this test on your grade."

I probably should have felt a greater sense of relief over my salvaged GPA. But the only thoughts racing through my mind were that I needed to get to my next class and how I should contact Lana and set up a time to visit her.

Professor Hastings hesitated before saying, "There's something else I wanted to talk to you about. The timing is a little awkward, considering what you're going through, but it's kind of time sensitive."

"What is it?"

"I know how full your schedule is," she began, "but there's an internship position open at a clinic in Wailuku. It would be over the summer so wouldn't conflict with your classes and other commitments. There will be an option to extend it for a semester at the end of the summer if you feel it's right for you. It's paid and I'm sure they'd work with your training schedule."

A tutoring position with Professor Sato and an internship. Wasn't I the popular one today?

"I'll think about it." I stood to leave and realized I should say a little more. "It sounds like a great opportunity. Do you have any information so I can read more about it?"

Professor Hastings frowned. "You've been through a lot. I should have waited to mention it. They want to make their decision soon, though, and I wanted to offer it to you first because you're the best fit. I'll email you the details. Look it over and let me know next week."

I gave her a simple nod in response. Why wasn't I jumping at these opportunities? Both this and Professor Sato's offer would be great on my resume. The internship took place over the summer, so fitting it in wasn't a factor, and the tutoring spot would let me spend time with students who shared a common interest. For the sake of my resume, I should do both.

"Thank you, Professor Hastings. I'll look for your email."

Her expression mimicked Professor Sato's. I wasn't displaying the eagerness she'd expected to see. I was honored by the offer and wouldn't hesitate if nursing was still my passion. Still, I shouldn't burn any bridges. Especially none that led somewhere I might need to go.

She looked a little closer at me. "You're sure you're okay?"

I stood and reached for the doorknob. "I've just got a lot of irons in a lot of fires, if you know what I mean."

She nodded. "I understand that. We all overextend ourselves at times. Be gentle with yourself right now. Show yourself a little grace. That's not a weakness, Gemi. You've experienced something very upsetting."

"I'll try. I will tomorrow night for sure. My coach insists on downtime the night before a fight."

She gave a crisp nod, satisfied with that answer.

I raced to my next class, took a seat in the back of the room, and zoned out. If offered a million dollars, I couldn't have said what the lecture topic was today. The second I sat down, my mind started making the rounds from Heleena and her killer to contacting Lana, to what I'd teach my warriors tonight, to training with Salomon before I could go home and fall into bed. I should eat dinner at some point too.

The next thing I knew, my classmates were putting their laptops and textbooks away.

"I checked out," I admitted to the girl next to me. "Is there homework?"

"Don't blame you," replied the girl with a long auburn braid down her back. She held a hand in front of her mouth like a shield and whispered, "Class was a real snoozer today. Read the next chapter."

Partway to the parking lot, my phone buzzed with an email from No Mercy. When I opened it, I found a photo attachment too. It was of Heleena the day a year ago when she'd beaten Mona Randall, her arms raised high in the air in victory. Heleena had been ranked number four before the fight, and the win moved her to the number three spot, bumping Mona down to number four.

Mona took it well enough. Callie Castro, however, did not. Leena climbing the ranks, seemingly out of nowhere, rattled Callie's confidence and set off her temper. She turned her anger onto her opponent that night by pounding and kicking the hell out of the poor girl. At least it hadn't lasted long. Callie won her fight two minutes into the first round and held the top spot. Minutes later, temperament once again sweet as her pink teddy bear tattoo, she joined Mona in congratulating Heleena.

I smiled at the picture and the message on the email.

Saturday after the fights. Memorial gathering for Heleena Carrere.

"I'll be there."

As I completed the walk to the parking lot, I wondered again about Callie. Had her temper finally gotten the best of her? Had she been the one to batter Leena so severely?

Salomon always altered the gym's closing hours for the two weeks before a fight. The scheduled fighters had the gym to themselves for the last hour and a half, no one else was allowed. Everyone scheduled for this weekend's fight was at the gym

Tuesday night, except for Mona if memory served. Heleena's routine was similar to mine. She would have worked out first, then spent time with her coach, fine-tuning her plan of attack for Saturday's fight. After that, she would have gone for a cooldown run. Maybe Callie offered to go with her. She could have waited until they got to that secluded spot where I found Heleena's body and attacked.

It was possible, I guess, but was Callie that shallow? Would she really beat a friend to death to maintain her ranking? Or was it that she had so little control over her temper? Or was something else going on between the two that I didn't know about?

I had just shoved my backpack into the Indian's saddlebag and was thinking I needed to talk to Detective Kalani when my phone buzzed. Text from Ashlyn.

How are you doing? Regarding Heleena, I mean.

I'm okay. I went to talk with her parents this morning.

How did that go?

Long, very involved story. I'll tell you about it when you get home.

Had a chat with Professor Hastings. She's giving me a pass on the test.

Also offered me an internship. I didn't want to open that topic right now, though.

Super cool.

How's Honolulu?

Big. Crowded.

I smiled at her standard response to any big city. *Enjoy your workshop thing. Gotta run. Talk to you later.*

Love you, Peep.

I sent her a dozen heart emojis and then checked the time. One hour before I needed to report for duty at No Mercy. Just enough time to run home, grab a snack and my already packed gym bag, and get over to the gym to stretch before class. A typical day. I thought of Professor Sato's directive for finding time for tutoring and chuckled. There was no room to even insert a scalpel into my schedule let alone carve time out of it.

CHAPTER TWELVE

The moment I walked into the condo I heard a distinctive metallic clanking sound. That could only mean Hulu was out of water. Sure enough, I found him tapping his beak on the outside of his empty stainless-steel water dish.

"Goofy bird. What's the matter?"

"Water," Hulu demanded.

"You had plenty of water this morning. Did you try to take a bath in your dish again?"

Hulu lowered his head, ashamed. The bedding at the bottom of his cage was soaked. Now I'd have to change it tonight. We really needed to get a second parrot. Hulu was lonely and bored by himself all day and demanded attention the moment one of us walked in. That was why we moved his cage near the window. He could at least see people and animals outside when we were gone.

I sighed and went to the kitchen to get him more water. While there, I whirled two handfuls of greens, frozen mango, coconut water, and a scoop of protein powder in the blender. I drank my smoothie and filled his dish then misted him with a spray bottle.

"Do you want a bath tonight?"

He bobbed his whole body up and down. "Bath please."

As I downed the last of my drink, I gave him a couple more squirts. "That's all for now. I've got to go teach self-defense."

Hulu raised a foot in the air. "Hi-yah!"

I grinned. It had taken a week for him to get that right.

* * *

"There she is," Kenny said from behind the reception desk as I walked into No Mercy. Kenny was a part-Islander part-Asian man with the widest shoulders and biggest biceps I'd ever seen. And I'd seen some big dudes over the years. He could bench press three hundred pounds without trying hard, but his arms were so big he couldn't lower them all the way. He typed on the computer keyboard with his elbows out to the sides and his hands twisted at an awkward angle. That had to mess with his wrists. Unfortunately, Kenny didn't give equal attention to the lower half of his body and had scrawny legs by comparison.

"What's up?" I asked.

"This is Aria Vega and her dad, Manuel," Kenny said of the tall blond girl and the man standing next to her. "She'd like to try your self-defense class today. Dad is interested in classes too."

"How old are you, Aria?"

"Fourteen," the girl responded with eyes locked on me. She never once looked at Kenny. In fact, she was turned slightly away from him.

"You're a little old for tonight's class. It's for younger kids just starting out. My women's class would be a better fit. I don't teach men, but we've got options for you, too, Mr. Vega."

Salomon fought me on my refusal to teach men at first, but I was adamant.

"Kids and women or I don't teach here," I'd said without apology. "There are other gyms in town that will welcome me."

Salomon said he'd seen my potential within my first week at No Mercy. He wanted to coach me—or rather, didn't want anyone else coaching me—so agreed to my demand.

"Aria's never taken a class like this before," Mr. Vega said.

I understood the look on the man's face. Something had happened to his daughter. As in, she had a bad encounter at some point. Given the way she was avoiding Kenny, I guessed a boy at school or maybe a male neighbor had assaulted her.

"I figured," Kenny began, "since there are no classes on Saturday this week, and she'd have to wait until Tuesday night for the next women's class, it would be okay for her to try it with the younger kids tonight."

I glanced past Aria at Kenny. He raised an eyebrow and gave me a pointed look, silently letting me know my instincts about Aria were right.

"That's a good idea." I smiled warmly at the girl. "We'll start you tonight, and if you like it, you can join the women on Tuesday."

"How old are the women?" Mr. Vega wanted to know.

"Various ages and skill levels. I move girls over to that class when they turn thirteen, but plenty of the women are new students. The oldest lady is in her late sixties. She's amazing. After they've been at it a while, some of them move over to the MMA classes. Not necessarily to fight but to learn different skills."

"MMA. That's what you do, right?" Aria asked, her eyes sparkling.

Kenny fielded that answer. "Gemi is the top-ranked fighter on the island. If you want to learn self-defense or MMA, Gemi is the instructor you want."

Halle Carrere walked in the front door then. I was both pleased to see her, because I knew how much she loved class, and concerned because the girl should be home tonight mourning the loss of her sister. I stopped her after she'd signed in on the member computer at the far end of the front desk.

"Halle, this is Aria. She's new. Would you show her where class is going to meet?" I turned to Aria, noting her capri leggings and loose T-shirt outfit. "You can wear that for class or you can change first. Either way, Halle can give you a tour of the locker room too."

Aria looked up at her dad, and he gave a go-ahead nod.

"You're welcome to watch class, Mr. Vega. You'll see the visitors' section above the gym floor when you're in there."

"Great." He looked both relieved and nervous. "Do you have

time to have a talk about Aria?"

I nodded and promised, "After class."

Once Dad had left the lobby, I turned back to Kenny who was creating something tiny out of pastel yarn and skinny knitting needles.

"What's the project this week?"

"Booties," he explained, focusing like this was the most important thing he'd ever done.

Kenny was one complex guy. When not bench pressing the equivalent of three of me, he was tending to his collection of bonsai trees or knitting booties, beanies, or blankets for newborn babies. His knitted creations were beautiful and got distributed throughout the islands at hospitals, clinics, and shelters.

"I don't know how those big hands of yours can work those tiny needles."

"Determination. Anything is possible if you want it badly enough."

"A motto to live by. You working out later? I could use a sparring partner."

"Planned on it." Kenny squinted at the bootie that looked like it would fit snuggly on his thumb, counting the stitches. "I'm game. Long as you go easy on me. I heard what you did to Donnelly last night."

"Not my fault if he doesn't protect his head." I flashed him a quick shaka or hang loose sign. "See you later."

I took five minutes to change into leggings and a sports bra with a loose tank top over it. In the far corner of the otherwise empty gym—only Salomon, instructors, and students were allowed on the gym floor during classes—fifteen eager future MMA stars were waiting for me. Well, fourteen eager kiddos and one nervous Aria. The girl's eyes darted from the other kids hovering in the area to her dad in the balcony. Mr. Vega sat on the edge of his seat, hands gripping the railing. He gave her an encouraging nod and smile. Attending this class might be a bigger deal for her than I realized.

"Take things at your own speed," I told her before starting class. "I'll push the other kids, but they've been at this for a long time. Do what you can and don't worry about keeping up or trying to do things perfectly. If you decide to keep coming, you'll catch on in no time."

Aria nodded, her long ponytail swaying, but didn't say a thing. There was something about her that felt familiar, but I couldn't say what.

Six more warriors straggled in over the next five minutes. At the top of the hour, I clapped my hands loudly, making skittish Aria jump.

"Class, line up!" I hollered, and the kids scrambled into four straight lines, starting with the most senior student to the newest, Aria. I nodded at the boy at the head of the line. "Darren, will you lead warmups today? I'm going to work with our new student for a bit. Everyone, give Aria a warm aloha."

When the kids turned to look at their newest classmate, Aria's cheeks flamed red as a Maui sunset.

"Aloha, Aria," the kids said.

"Mahalo," she answered quietly.

I stood at her side during warmups, showing her the proper way to do every stretch and explaining which muscle was being targeted.

"You're really flexible," I commented. "Have you done sports before?"

"Yes, ma'am. Ballet and water polo."

"You must already have great endurance, then. Now we'll work on your strength and reflexes. You're going to be one tough little cookie in no time."

I expected to see her grin. Instead, Aria's jaw set, and a determined, steely look crossed her eyes. "That's what I'm hoping, ma'am."

Once they were warm, I had the kids partner up. With what had happened to Heleena foremost in my mind, I decided to have them practice how to get away if someone grabbed them.

"Watch first," I told Aria, "then you can work with Darren. He's my second in command and knows more than anyone in this group." She stiffened and a panicked look crossed her face. Having my number one student work with a new one was automatic for me. I hadn't thought of her reaction to Kenny. "Do you think you'll be okay working with him?"

She hesitated before agreeing.

The class broke into pairs and took turns being the attacker and the defender. As the attacker approached, the defender shouted, "Stop! Back off!" at the top of their lungs. It never took more than two "attacks" for the kids to get fully into character. They loved having the freedom to yell without being told to quiet down. Next, the attacker would grab the defender by the shoulders. Without hesitation, the defender would shove their hands up through the attackers' arms, swipe their own arms wide to break the hold, and then spin and run a few steps away.

"If this were a real attack," I explained, standing behind Aria, "you would run fast and far. Preferably to a group of other people. Adults if possible."

Aria nodded but said nothing as she observed with an intensity that practically radiated off her.

"Watch for another minute and then try this move with Darren. He'll take it slow until you're comfortable with the motions and are ready to go faster."

I circulated among the kids then, giving pointers and tweaking positions. The more experienced students moved on to escaping from more persistent attacks or those that came from behind.

"Remember," I called, "sometimes a strong, sure voice is all it will take to stop someone. Other times, you're going to have to fight harder."

"Is this what Heleena did?" one of the boys asked.

The question caught me off guard, and I immediately looked to Halle. I knew word would spread among the adult members, but I hadn't thought about the kids hearing it. Which, of course, they would. Halle's face pinched as though she was fighting off tears, but then she blew out a shaky breath and nodded to me that it was okay to talk about it.

"I'm sure Heleena fought very hard," I began.

"This stuff doesn't really work, then, does it?" the boy challenged.

I froze and noted the part-defiant part-scared set to his face. Scanning the group, I saw the same expression on some of my other warriors. Salomon would want me to wait until the police had answers about Heleena's attack, but my kiddos needed answers now.

"Class, gather round."

I motioned for Halle to stand next to me as the others formed a half-circle in front of us and dropped to one knee. All twenty-one faces stared at me, waiting for me to tell them the secret to not ending up like Heleena.

"First," I began, putting a protective arm around Halle, "any comments regarding this incident will be respectful or I'll ask you to leave class. Understood?"

A chorus of "yes, ma'am" sounded, and heads bobbed in the affirmative.

"Good. We've talked about this before. You all know that the best way to stay safe is to always be with another person." A memory flickered at the back of my brain. I immediately shoved it away. No time for that right now. "The skills I'm teaching you will help, but you always have to be on your guard. That doesn't mean you should be scared. Chances are, you'll never need these skills. That would be the best possible outcome." The memory flickered again. "Stay aware of your surroundings. Never go into dark places by yourself. If you do end up alone, trust your instincts. Again, I'm not trying to scare you, but if you're someplace where there's another person and your gut tells you that person might not be safe, turn around and go the other way. Better to be late getting where you need to go and arriving there safely than to risk someone harming you. And remember to use your voice. That's your first line of defense."

The same boy raised his hand. "Is that what Heleena did? When she saw the person who hurt her, did she go the other way?"

"The truth is," I began, "I don't know exactly what happened Tuesday night." *But I'm going to find out.* "As soon as I do, I'll tell you."

I paused then, waiting to see if any questions arose. When none did, I clapped my hands once. "All right, back to work. If you want to talk with me, we can do that after class. Any of the other instructors are available for you too." I faced Halle. "Are you okay to continue with class?"

"I'm okay. Leena would want me to be brave."

I had to bite my lip to fight off my rising emotions. I wanted to tell her that being sad over the loss of a loved one wasn't the same as not being brave. It wasn't my place, though. Hopefully, her mother would find the courage she needed soon and explain this to her.

"Okay, go ahead." I turned to Aria next. She was staring at Halle as if confused.

"Who's Leena?"

Another test. Maybe I should get her dad down here for this one. No, this girl still had that determined look on her face.

Start with the simplest answer possible. She'll ask if she wants to know more.

"Heleena was Halle's sister. She died two days ago."

"Someone attacked her?"

I nodded, hoping she wouldn't ask for details.

"She was a fighter here?"

I swallowed before saying, "She was one of our best."

Aria thought on this for a second and finally said, "Halle's brave to be here right now."

"She really is. Are you ready to give this a try again?"

The girl squared her shoulders. "Yes, ma'am."

Darren took it slow with her, explaining what he was going to do and how she should react. Within a couple of minutes, Aria was ready for more. They moved on from verbal defense to him putting his hands on her shoulders. Again, Darren explained in detail what Aria needed to do, and they slowly went through the movements.

"Ready to take it at full speed?" he asked five minutes later.

Aria blew out a breath. "Ready."

I glanced up at Mr. Vega. He had released his grip on the railing and looked a little more relaxed. His eyes met mine, and I gave him a reassuring smile. Aria was doing fine.

And then, Darren "attacked" without giving her a warning first.

"No!" Aria screamed, backing away, her arms crossed in front of her face.

Thinking Aria was using her own script, I let Darren continue. She continued stepping away until her back was against the wall. When Darren placed his hands on her shoulders, she screamed again and burst into uncontrollable sobs.

"Daddy! Help me!"

I froze, the memory of the night more than sixteen years earlier as vivid as if it were happening now.

I'd been thirteen and had gone to the movies with a group of friends. We were in line to buy tickets when I realized I'd forgotten my phone in the car. I got the keys from the driver—I couldn't remember her name anymore, but she was the older sister of one of the girls—and asked the group to wait outside the theater for me.

All I had to do was run to the parking lot behind the theater and grab my phone. A task that should have taken thirty seconds because the car was parked in the second row. I pressed the fob button to unlock the door and as I reached for the car's door handle, a man came out of the shadows. He pushed me up against the car, held a knife to my neck, and grabbed my breast. Then he stuck his hand up my skirt and ripped off my panties. He would have done God only knows what to me if my friends hadn't shown up.

"I'm so sorry, Gemi," the driver kept saying. "I should have come with you."

"We all should," someone else in the group said.

"We weren't thinking," another added.

They called Mom, but she was busy with something and couldn't come. They tried Ashlyn next. She and her date arrived in minutes and took me home. Ash bandaged the wound behind my ear from the knife, and the next morning my mom, realizing the driver hadn't been goofing around when she called, made a counseling appointment for me. A few weeks later, at the strong recommendation of the therapist, she signed me up for self-defense classes. Two years after that, we left California and moved to Maui. Mom claimed it was because the guy had never been caught and I didn't feel safe. At that point, I was confident with my abilities, but Mom insisted.

"It'll be safer there," she promised. "Besides, I've got a great job lined up. The people are begging me to come, so we have to go."

I wasn't stupid. I knew the move was all for her and had nothing to do with me and my well-being. Mom wanted the glamour and romance of the islands.

It's okay, the little girl soothed. *It was a long time ago.*

I blinked, returning to the present. Thankfully, what had felt like an hour of reliving the event was only a flash of seconds. I rushed to the pair, told Darren to stand down, and squatted to look Aria in the eye. With that blond hair and terrified expression, she reminded me so much of the little girl, the me from seventeen years ago. When Aria finally calmed down, I spoke gently to her.

"I don't know what happened to you," I said softly, "but I think it might be similar to what happened to me."

Her tear-filled eyes went wide. They said, *you too?*

I nodded. "You're doing great. I hope this didn't scare you off. If you want, we can talk after class and share our experiences. With your dad at your side, of course."

After a few seconds, Aria agreed, got to her feet, and flipped her ponytail behind her shoulder. She glanced at Halle and then faced Darren. "I'm ready. I don't want to be scared anymore."

And that was exactly why I taught.

CHAPTER THIRTEEN

After class, Aria, her dad, and I sat in Salomon's office, the only private place in the gym. I pulled the desk chair around so we could sit in a triangle, and we talked about what had happened to Aria. She was still a little emotional from the incident with Darren so let her dad get things started.

"It was after one of her water polo matches," Mr. Vega explained. "I couldn't be at the match because of work but checked in on it via the livestream. When it was over, I called and told her I was on the way, but then traffic held me up, and it took even longer to get to her than I'd planned."

"I waited for him outside." Aria's voice was just above a whisper.

"Alone? Your coach didn't wait with you?" My blood boiled.

"Coach was with me at first," Aria recalled, "but she forgot something in the locker room and said she'd be right back. She was only gone for like two minutes,"

"That's all the time it takes," I replied sympathetically.

"You said something happened to you," Aria prompted.

"It did. I was about your age, a little younger. I went to the movies with friends and ran out to the parking lot to get my phone from the car. A man was waiting in the shadows and assaulted me."

As I told them what happened, without getting graphic, the color drained from Aria's face. "That *is* like what happened to me. I was leaning against the building on the parking lot side. That's where Dad said he'd meet me."

"I should have told her to go out front where there were more people," Mr. Vega murmured, guilt clear in his voice.

"Daddy, I told you it's not your fault."

No, it was her coach's fault. She never should have left her alone. She should have taken Aria inside with her or waited until Mr. Vega arrived.

Aria continued, "Two older boys from my school came out of the building. They waved and I waved back. I didn't *know* them but knew who they were."

Her words came easily although a little shakily. She'd clearly talked about the incident many times. That was good. She'd taken control of the story instead of letting it control her.

"They came up to me and congratulated me on the win. I was kind of nervous with them being so close to me. I said thanks but nothing else. One of them stepped closer and kissed me on the cheek. I told him not to do that. So the other one said, 'How about this way?' and he kissed me on the mouth. Then he grabbed me . . . between my legs."

"Two boys?" My heart pounded. "That had to be really scary."

"It was." Her voice had gotten small again.

"Her coach came back then and caught them in the act." Mr. Vega looked both furious and relieved. He placed a gentle hand on top of his daughter's head. "My girl was so brave. She told her principal that night what had happened. In the end, both boys were expelled."

"That takes tremendous courage," I agreed. "I'm guessing this happened recently?"

"Last summer," Aria said. "Almost a year ago."

"She's been going to counseling," Mr. Vega added, "but still gets scared. Like you saw today."

"It's okay to be a little scared. Sometimes, a bit of fear will help you stay alert and avoid other dangerous situations."

"That's what my counselor said." She looked me right in the eye. "Are you still scared?"

I thought of the little girl appearing in my head yesterday. "Not as much anymore, but sometimes, yes, I am." I took Aria's hand. "I'm sorry Darren scared you. I trust him, though, and hope you know he wouldn't have hurt you. And I hope you know you can trust me."

Aria nodded as her eyes filled with tears.

"He scared you, but you made it through and did an amazing job working with him afterward. If you think you want to continue, I'd like you to join the women's classes. You'll feel safer there. No boys."

"I want to," Aria insisted and looked at her dad. "Can I?"

"That's why we came here. Yeah, I think you should give it a try. I will, too, and we can practice together."

"I'd like that." Aria glanced out the office window at the members who'd flooded the place once the classes were done. "Can I go look around the gym?"

"As long as Ms. Kittredge says it's okay."

I nodded. "Keep your distance from the people working out and don't use any of the equipment."

While Aria went to explore, I turned to Mr. Vega. "I'm so sorry this happened to her."

"Thanks. I'm sorry it happened to you. I think you'll be the perfect teacher for her."

I placed my hands palms together and bowed. "I wanted to commend you for letting me handle the incident during class."

A laugh burst out of him. "I was about to leap off the balcony."

"Understandable. Letting her work through this at her own pace in a place she feels safe is really important."

Mr. Vega grew quiet, then asked, "This young woman who was killed, she attended this gym?"

"She did. I'm going to work with the owner and arrange a special session for the kids to talk about this once the police have answers for us. The adults, too, but separately. Everyone has questions, and right now there's not much we can say."

Once Aria returned, I invited them to the fight Saturday night. "Otherwise, I'll see you on Tuesday?"

"Can we go?" Aria asked her dad.

"We'll check our schedule and see what's going on. She'll be here Tuesday for sure."

With all my warriors gone, it was time for me to be the student. I told Kenny I was starting my workout and would be ready to spar soon. He decided to join me for all of it. First, we hit the treadmill. After ten minutes, I was just getting warm, but Kenny was huffing and puffing. Then we did some lifting. Kenny clearly had me beat there. I wanted to do a little balance training, which involved standing on one foot on a half balance ball while tossing a five-pound medicine ball to each other. Top-heavy Kenny was horrible at that even with both feet on the balance ball so stood on the floor instead.

"Are you done embarrassing me?" he asked ten minutes later. "Is it time to spar?"

"Didn't you just ask if I was *done* embarrassing you?" I winked.

"Let's go."

We pulled on headgear, plugged in mouth guards, entered the ring, and Salomon came out of his office to bark orders. He was my coach, but he directed Kenny just as harshly this time. There was a reason he called his gym No Mercy.

"You want to be the best," he'd told me from the start, "you give it your best every time. No exceptions. No mercy."

Kenny and I tapped gloves. I immediately started dancing foot to foot, where Kenny lumbered around the ring. I bobbed and weaved, threw jabs, and landed a round kick, then backed away before he could react. The thing was, despite my speed, I couldn't do damage to a man his size. Kenny was wicked strong. One well-placed blow and I'd be flat on my back looking at stars.

"Combos!" Salomon hollered. "Show me combos . . . Mix it up, Gemi . . . Change your angle. Don't stand in front of him that way. He's going to knock you on your ass."

I trusted that Kenny wouldn't actually hit me hard. He was a bodybuilder, not a fighter, but enjoyed sparring. He liked the challenge of blocking punches and kicks and had gotten good at protecting his torso. So that was my goal. To make contact with that rock hard abdomen.

"Keep your chin down, Kittredge!" Salomon yelled. "How many times do I have to tell you that? Chin down ... Go for the takedown."

"Takedown?" Aonani scoffed. She glanced around at the crowd gathered by the ring. "No way she can take him down."

That was all the motivation I needed. I started my attack. Two punches followed by a knee to the thigh. That was Kenny's weak point. He could protect himself from a body blow, but his arms, unable to lower all the way, couldn't block shots to his legs very well. He took a step away from me, so I did it again, distracting him with a jab and a cross, then bringing a knee to his thigh. He took another step back. In seconds, I had him in the corner. I leaned in, taunting him, and he went for it. When he took a purposely wimpy swing with his right, I ducked down, then dove for his legs. I wrapped both of my arms around his ankles and pulled. Just that fast, Kenny was on the mat. I went for an armbar, and the crowd went wild.

Kenny raised his head to look at me. "Is that supposed to hurt?"

"On a normal-sized human," I replied, "yes. I can't straighten your arm."

"Neither can I."

"Do you have pain?"

"A little."

"You need to ease off on the lifting," I advised in my clinical voice. "Take a few days away to let your muscles and tendons rest. This is a good chance to give your legs a little attention."

"What's wrong with my legs?" He held one up in the air, and I made a sound like a clucking chicken. "You saying I have skinny legs?"

"Have you ever looked at them? Or are you too busy admiring your arms?"

He lay back and stared up at the ceiling. "Are we done? I think I've suffered enough humiliation for one day."

I shrugged. "I can go longer."

"Let him up," Salomon told me. "You're mine now."

I offered a hand to Kenny to help him up, and he laughed at me. True, I'd be as successful trying to pull a bus. Once he was upright, we bumped fists, and then he went to use a leg press machine.

In the corner where I held class, Salomon praised me for the takedown. "A round kick to the temple might have worked too."

"Yes, and it also might have broken my foot. Kenny has a hard head. Besides, I didn't want to knock the guy out."

"And here I thought you were ruthless. Go easy on your workout tomorrow, nothing too strenuous or anything that might result in an injury." Salomon got paranoid this close to a fight. "We'll review footage of Mele's last match tomorrow night, and then I want you home, resting and meditating."

Mele would be tough, but I wasn't too worried. The number two bantamweight was fueled more by desire than skill. Not to say she wasn't good, she was, but I was better, and as long as I kept my head in the game, I'd be fine.

"Yes, coach," I replied with respect. Shortly after becoming my coach, Salomon said he wanted to know the Gemi he didn't get to see in the gym. So one night we went to dinner and then for a walk on the beach. We talked about our home lives. He told me about his wife and daughter. I told him about my attack. He seethed, insisting he'd kill the man if he ever got his hands on him. That was the night my coach and mentor also became a father figure for me.

Salomon was saying something more about Mele, but my attention had strayed to Callie Castro on the far side of the gym. She was tossing a medicine ball back and forth with her coach, Ozzie, and laughing hard at something. Ozzie's stern scowl clearly stated he was irritated by her lack of attention.

"Something more important than discussing your fight?" Salomon asked.

"Hmm?" I faced him. "Oh, no. Sorry, coach. I was just noticing that Callie seems to have recovered well from the shock of Heleena's death."

"After the initial blow from news like that, people move on with their lives. Family and close friends need much longer. Since we're on the topic, tell me what happened with Heleena's parents this morning. But let's go to my office. This isn't a discussion anyone else needs to hear."

I felt eyes on me as we walked across the gym and turned to find Ross Donnelly staring at me while doing waves with a battle rope. I was almost impressed with the speed he was generating with the heavy rope until he lost his grip on one and sent it flying into Kenny. Kenny shoved him up against the wall and held him there with one hand while drinking from his water bottle with the other.

I bit back a laugh. "He's going to hurt someone."

"Kenny?" Salomon asked. "He wouldn't hurt a flea on a fly. The man knits for babies."

"I meant Ross."

Salomon looked closer and didn't bother disguising his grin. "Oh, yeah. Donnelly's a danger. Thankfully mostly to himself."

In the office with the door closed, I told him about my visit with the Carreres. "Mr. Carrere is pretty much what you'd expect from a man who kicked his own daughter out of the house. Arrogant, concerned with appearances, demanding of both his wife and Halle. I'm a little worried about Mrs. Carrere."

Salomon held up a hand. "You can't save the world, mahi."

"But I think she's being controlled."

He gave me an empathetic smile. "I understand why that's important to you, but you need to stay out of the Carreres' business."

He was right. I knew that. A victim needed to ask for help. They couldn't be forced. Right now, all I could do was find a way to let

Mrs. Carrere know I was able to assist when she was ready.

"What else happened during your visit?" He was curious about Heleena's relationship with them too. He just wouldn't admit it.

"Not a lot. I wasn't there that long. Mrs. Carrere told me that Johnny came to their house."

"Gambino?" Salomon turned an angry, sunburn red. "Why?"

"All she said was that he was looking for Heleena."

"How did he even know where they live?"

"I'm not sure. He has access to the office when he cleans. Maybe he got into the computer. Although you and I are the only ones who know the password."

Salomon twirled a pen through his fingers, an additional sign that he was aggravated. "I'll talk to him. If that's what he did, it's grounds for expulsion from No Mercy. I might have to start locking the door and cleaning the office myself." He gazed across the desk at me. "Or you can do it."

"What?" I held a hand to my ear. "Sorry, there's so much noise in the gym today. I didn't hear what you said."

"I said—"

"What?" I leaned closer.

He swatted a hand at me and made a face.

"Speaking of Heleena's address," I said, serious again, "I need the one for her apartment in Kihei."

He fixed a suspicious stare on me. "Why?"

"I asked Mrs. Carrere if she knew who might have done this to Heleena. She told me she knew little to nothing about her daughter's personal life and suggested I talk to Lana."

The suspicious look intensified. "Or did she suggest that Detective Kalani should talk to her? I don't want you getting involved with this, Gemi."

Too late for that. I was already in it. "The detective knows about Lana. If she hasn't been there already, she's not doing her job. What's the harm in me asking a few questions?"

Salomon knew how I felt about cops and why. He also knew I

114 I SHAWN MCGUIRE

could find the address myself so grumbled while clicking a few times and then scribbled the address on a piece of paper.

"I know you. There's no sense in me trying to forbid you because when you get focused on something, you don't let go. Can't you focus on the fight right now and play detective later?"

I should. I wasn't so sure I could, though. "What if this guy is targeting fighters? How long should he be allowed to wander around Kahului picking us off?"

Should I mention the yakuza twist? That was the real reason I wanted to talk with Lana. To find out if she and Heleena had been so desperate they turned to a crime syndicate for help.

He scowled and handed me the paper. "Go check on Lana. Give her our condolences and make sure she knows we'd like to see her on Saturday. If she doesn't want to watch the fights, ask her to come to the memorial for Leena."

I left the office, Lana's address in hand, and was almost to the locker room when someone grabbed my arm. I spun to find Ross Donnelly.

"Are you done for the day?" Ross asked. "Can I buy you a coffee?"

"How many times have I told you—"

"It's coffee, Gemi. Or a smoothie. Or a bowl of sprouts or whatever you're into."

Two female members exited the locker room and paused behind him, waiting to see if I needed help. Their gesture of solidarity touched my heart.

I thought of my warriors and the lesson on feeling safe and staying out of danger we'd just had. What kind of example was I if I couldn't shut down this loser?

"Kill them with kindness," our aunt always joked. "Less chance of going to prison that way because there's no weapon."

I often wondered, what would Auntie Amelia think about me punching people in the face for fun? Would she consider my fists weapons?

I took a wide stance, pushed my shoulders back, and clenched my hands. "Do you harass all women this way, Ross, or just me?"

"Harass?" He laughed like I didn't know what I was talking about. "I like you, Gemi, and just want to get to know you better."

"And I've repeatedly said no. Salomon has told you to leave me alone as well."

The women stepped closer, and I held out a hand for them to stay where they were. I could do this. I needed to do this.

"Since you don't seem to understand the definition of 'no means no,' let me be really clear. Stop asking me out. I'm not interested in going out for coffee, for dinner, or to a movie. I'm not interested in having you walk me across the parking lot to my bike. Not today, not tomorrow, not ever. Not with you, not with anyone. I don't know how to make this any clearer. Do you understand what I'm saying, or should I get Kenny to explain it to you?"

Ross paled and then pouted. "You don't need to get like that about it."

"I do because you refuse to listen to me." I took a step closer, and he cowered. "If you ask me out again, I will have your membership revoked. You will be banned from this gym, and I'll contact the other gyms on the island to let them know you shouldn't be accepted there either. If you continue to cause problems after that, I'll call the police and press harassment charges. Do you understand that?"

Ross took a step back. "I understand. I'm sorry."

The women behind him pumped their fists in victory.

I gave them a grateful smile and continued into the locker room.

Good job, the little girl praised. *You used your words.*

CHAPTER FOURTEEN

It was after seven o'clock when I left the gym. My stomach was complaining loudly for dinner, but I needed to make a phone call first. While straddling my bike, I popped the protective case off my phone, and exposed Detective Kalani's card. She told me to call if I felt I had information about Heleena's killer.

"Kalani," the voice on the other end of the line greeted. If it could be called a greeting. It was more the bark of an irritated guard dog.

"Detective, this is Gemi Kittredge. I'm the one who found—"

"I know who you are, Ms. Kittredge." The bark had softened a little. "What can I do for you?"

"You said I should call if I had anything to offer regarding Heleena's death."

"What did you think of?"

"It's more something I learned. I went out to Heleena's parents' house in Makawao this morning to deliver flowers from the gym."

"You went all the way to Makawao for that? Why didn't the gym have flowers delivered? You're not messing around in this investigation, are you, Ms. Kittredge?"

"Salomon wanted a personal touch in this instance and wasn't able to go himself. Besides, it was a beautiful day for a motorcycle ride."

As most days here were.

"You ride?" Detective Kalani's voice took on that interested tone that said she did too.

"Indian Scout Sixty. White and black with brushed chrome pipes."

"Saddlebags?"

"Of course."

"Nice bike."

"Thanks. You?"

"Harley Softail. All black."

"Also nice. And very badass."

Silence fell over the line. I heard background noise so knew the call hadn't dropped. Finally, like she'd been waiting for me to say more, Kalani prompted, "So you delivered flowers?"

"Right. I talked briefly with Mrs. Carrere while I was there. She mentioned that Johnny Gambino showed up at their house a couple of weeks ago looking for Heleena. We both found that strange, because Heleena hasn't lived with her parents for five years. Everyone knows that."

"Who's Gambino? Why is he important?"

Kalani's barely interested attitude surprised me. "He's a member at No Mercy and was obsessed with Heleena. I don't know if he could legally be considered a stalker, but he asked her out two or three times a week. She always said no, but he wouldn't back off."

Just like Ross. Which reminded me I wanted to mention my concern about him as well.

"Did Ms. Carrere feel unsafe? Did she ever make a formal complaint about this guy?" Kalani sounded slightly more interested now.

"Not to the police, but Heleena did talk to the gym owner about him. Salomon told Johnny to leave her alone. He did for a while but going out with Leena was more important to him than following Salomon's orders even if it got him kicked out of the gym. Going out to the Carreres' place tells me he was taking things to a different level."

She hesitated before acknowledging my concern. "That's possible."

I had her attention so pushed on. "To get the Carreres' address, he must have dug through the gym's files, but I can't figure out how he did that. The system is password protected, and only Salomon and I know it."

"So you're saying that somehow Mr. Gambino got into the gym's secure computer and took the Carreres' address instead of Heleena's. Then he drove clear over to Makawao to ask her parents for the address he really wanted."

"I don't know the exact chain of events, Detective, but I do know that Johnny went to Makawao looking for Heleena. He doesn't let things go. If he decided he wanted to go to Leena's home, he would have fixated on that and not stopped until he got there. If that meant driving to her parents' house, he'd do it. If they weren't home when he got there, he would have waited for them to get back. If it turned out he had the wrong address, he'd search until he got the right one."

After a short pause, she said, "I still don't understand why you feel Mr. Gambino's visit is significant. Maybe he went to deliver flowers too." Sarcasm oozed from the comment.

She wasn't taking this seriously. I let her sucker me into believing she was. If Kalani wrote off Heleena's death, I'd talk with Johnny myself. And anyone else who might have done this to my friend. I wasn't about to let this go.

"Detective Kalani, don't you think it's significant that a probable stalker showed up at a victim's residence, even a former one, not long before she died?"

Kalani sighed softly, as though resigning to spend more time on this. "Is Mr. Gambino a violent person?"

"He likes to box and sometimes goes a little crazy on the heavy bag. He's strong, but I've never seen him attack another person." I told her about him breaking the broom over his knee.

"Outbursts like that can be concerning," Kalani agreed and remained quiet for a few seconds. "It's possible that was the first he'd heard of Ms. Carrere's death and was simply releasing emotional tension."

"That *is* possible," I conceded. "Johnny has a hard time controlling his emotions. When they get *too big*, as he says, he bursts and does things like breaking the broom or beating up a bag. Heleena never saying yes would definitely have made the pressure build up." I got off the motorcycle and paced beneath a parking lot light. "I don't know if Johnny did this, Detective, but I think it's worth pursuing. Like I said, he was obsessed and crazy in love with Leena."

"And he loved her to death? Is that what you're saying?"

A violent shiver shot through me. "I sincerely hope not."

"I think this is a hell of a lot of speculation, but I'll talk with him. Was there anything else you wanted to tell me about?"

Yes, actually. I wanted to tell her about Ross, but she would surely say that was speculation too. Especially because there had only been the one incident.

"Mrs. Carrere told me that you spoke with her," I stated. "Did you also talk to Mr. Carrere?"

"Briefly. He was about to leave for an appointment when I got there."

"Are you aware of how homophobic he is?"

Kalani sighed again. "You think Mr. Carrere might have killed his daughter?"

"I don't know, but aren't family members prime suspects?"

"You're going to have to explain this one to me, too, Ms. Kittredge. You said Heleena hadn't lived at home for five years. Mrs. Carrere's statement corroborates that. She told me she had occasional contact with Heleena, but her husband never did. She said Mr. Carrere wouldn't allow any of them to even mention Heleena's name. It appears he'd written off his eldest daughter. Why would he suddenly go from ignoring her existence to driving clear over to Kahului to murder her on the beach?"

I knew this was a stretch, but to me, all leads were worth following. If the cops had followed a few more leads ten years ago, I might know where my mother had gone. For all I knew, she could be living down the street, watching me jog by every morning.

"That's the thing," I objected, "he wasn't ignoring Heleena.

They didn't talk about her, but Mr. Carrere kept track of her. He knew she was rising in the ranks and didn't like the attention she'd been getting." I paused, anger rising over his final statement to me. "He said if she was really the MMA talent she appeared to be, she would have been able to fight off her attacker."

The detective hissed out a breath at this.

I pressed on. "There had been a lot of buzz about Leena's ability to knock Callie Castro out of the top spot. Based on what I observed while at their house and from talking with Heleena, Mr. Carrere is obsessed with public appearance. His lesbian daughter was drawing attention to herself, which in his mind put a bad light on him. He couldn't tolerate that."

"That's a lot of dime-store psychology, Ms. Kittredge. You think he snapped? Is that your diagnosis?"

The detective had a way of asking otherwise innocent questions that made me feel stupid. "It's possible, isn't it?"

"Anything's *possible*." She paused, then murmured, "I'm willing to believe this could have been a hate crime, but I don't think Mr. Carrere was involved. I'll make a note of his behavior in the casefile, however."

I was about to thank her for her time and end the call when she said, "Talk to me about Callie Castro. I spoke with her once, but I'm wondering if there's any reason to look more closely at her."

"Sounds like you think you should."

"Ms. Castro is the number-one-ranked fighter in her weight class, correct?"

"Right. Featherweight."

"It's weak, but protecting her rank could be motive."

I kicked at a pebble next to my bike's tire. "I hate to think that another fighter, especially one of ours, had done that to Heleena."

"And most abused women never thought their partners would strike them."

Her words hit me like a sucker punch. I got it. I was being incredibly naïve. "Honestly, I wonder about Callie too. But why would she suddenly take out Heleena? She was number three overall. Why not the number two fighter?" I paused to let those questions settle. "And no matter how competitive we all are and eager to win, we're not talking big money here. Certainly nothing to kill a person for."

"You also get bragging rights, correct?"

"I suppose."

"You suppose?" She sounded surprised by this response. "Why do you fight?"

A flash of the night I was attacked in the parking lot shot through my mind. Like it did every single time someone asked how I got into fighting.

"I started in martial arts because I wanted to know I could defend myself should the need arise. MMA offered a new challenge, new skills. Getting into the octagon with an opponent is real. It keeps those skills fresh and reminds me what I'm capable of."

"What about being in that top spot? What does that do for you?"

I couldn't remember anyone ever asking me that. "I won't lie, I like it. Sitting atop the leader board feels pretty damn good."

"You have bragging rights."

"You could put it that way. It doesn't go to my head like it does with some. That's not what I'm in this for. The only person I want to prove anything to is myself." Specifically the little girl. And maybe that jerk from the parking lot.

"For some folks, winning translates to power, and power is an incredibly strong motivator. We live on a tiny island in the middle of a huge ocean. The world can feel really small when you're isolated the way we are."

"Power," I echoed, understanding the correlation to a murder but not to murdering Leena.

"People have killed for less. If, for example, this is all Callie has in her life—no family, no career she's passionate about—to lose her title could be devastating. Or perhaps someone has been taunting her, telling her she's fading and losing her edge. Proving someone wrong, someone who constantly doubts your ability, for example, can also play into situations like this and create a strong incentive to win at any cost."

As it had when she made the comment about a victim never expecting that their partner would hit them, the detective's voice held an edge of emotion as she talked about Callie's possible motives. What was Malia Kalani's story? What made her so tough?

"Does this sound anything like Ms. Castro's life?" she asked.

Images filled my head of Callie, Mona, and Heleena hugging after fights and congratulating each other no matter their personal outcome. Of course, Callie hadn't lost in three years. It was easy to be happy for a competitor when you weren't in danger of losing your spot on the podium.

"Ms. Kittredge?" Detective Kalani had raised her voice slightly. "Are you still there?"

"Sorry, yes. I'm here. I have no idea what Callie's personal life is like. I don't want to believe Callie could have done this, not for a small purse and bragging rights. She does have a temper, though."

"What do you mean by that?"

"I've never paid close enough attention to notice a pattern, but on rare occasions something will set her off. She'll explode, swearing and taking out her frustration on a piece of gym equipment. It only lasts a few seconds. Before Salomon or her coach, Ozzie, can cross the gym to calm her down, she's back in control."

"How often have you witnessed this type of behavior?"

"I don't know. Five or six times? She had an outburst yesterday. We were discussing what had happened to Heleena, and Callie stormed out of the gym without a word to anyone."

"What set her off? Did you notice?"

I thought back to the discussion. "Salomon was talking about how we were an ohana, but I couldn't say if that had anything to do with it."

Kalani didn't give any clue as to whether she was going to pursue that line. "Anything else you think might be helpful or anyone else you feel we should talk to?"

Ross entered my head again, and I shoved him aside. I closed my eyes and did a mental scan of the gym when it was busy. There were the fighters, both those defending their titles this weekend and those new to the sport. There were bodybuilders like Kenny. There were the beauty queens and the selfie addicts. The guys who came to hang out with their bros. The kids and the women who came to learn self-defense. And the "members" who showed up once or twice a month to make themselves feel good about their health.

"Unless someone had a personal beef with Heleena and they hid it really well, I can't think of anyone else who could have wanted to harm her."

"All right. If you do, let me know. Okay?"

There was Lana Madison. Should I mention that I was going to visit her tomorrow? No, that would only raise questions and I didn't want to make false accusations. "Okay."

"Thank you for the call, Gemi. I hope you understand that we can't follow every lead. On top of what you've just told me, I've gotten dozens of phone calls from people sure they know what happened to Ms. Carrere. Some have merit, and I'll look closer at them. Ms. Castro deserves some more attention. And because something does seem a bit off about Mr. Gambino, I'll have a chat with him too."

"Thanks for that. If there's anything I can do—"

"You can stay out of this," she warned. "I understand you want answers, but if you start digging around in an investigation, you could cause more harm than good. This is not your territory. You are free to call me with any thoughts—" She cut off her statement. "Let me amend that. You can call me within reason. Let me do my job. I'm pretty good at it. And please remember, this isn't the only crime I'm investigating."

That was the second time in the last hour I had been told to stay out of Leena's death. I didn't like to make promises I wasn't sure I could keep so simply said, "Good luck, Detective."

CHAPTER FIFTEEN

Before leaving the gym's parking lot, I called Risa. "I know it's late, but I haven't had dinner yet. Want to come over?"

"You're a mind reader," Risa replied. "I was just thinking about eating. Should I bring something?"

"Nope, I've got it covered."

"I assume that means we'll be eating chicken breast, broccoli, and rice?"

I grinned and could practically see Risa's eyes rolling. "Mahi-mahi is super fresh right now. Thought I'd grill some fillets."

"That sounds way better. Can I bring something to drink?" That meant a bottle of rosé.

"Bring what you want. I'll be drinking lemon water."

I knew plenty of fighters who abused their bodies horribly to meet weight restrictions. Days before a fight, they'd basically dehydrate themselves and drop a ton of weight to be sure they fit within the range for their class. Then immediately after weigh-in, they'd start pounding down the protein to build their muscles back up. It was so dangerous. As much as I loved the sport, I wouldn't risk my health for it. I preferred to keep my body clean. Fruits and vegetables, chicken or turkey, fish, nuts, Greek yogurt with honey for dessert, and plenty of water. Studying to become a nurse made it easier for me to take care of myself. I knew what could happen if I didn't.

"I'm just tossing in some laundry," Risa said. "I'll be right over."

Laundry. I knew I was forgetting something. I was down to

only holey T-shirts and my last pair of underwear. Ashlyn sent her laundry to the cleaners. Of course, most of her clothes were high end, not the shorts, T-shirts, and athletic gear that I wore. I didn't need a service. I just needed to stick to my schedule.

Half an hour later, the washing machine was swishing, and the parrot was wandering around the condo when the doorbell rang.

"I'll get it," Hulu called out.

I laughed out loud when I got to the door to find Hulu standing there looking up at the knob.

"Okay, genius. How are you going to open it?"

Hulu responded by waddling back into the living room.

"Are you going to let me in?" Risa called from the porch.

I opened the door. "How many times have I said you can just come in? You know we never lock it. Except at night."

"That's not safe," Risa scolded as she entered.

"We live in Maui. We're pretty safe."

"I'm sure that's what Heleena and the man beheaded by the yakuza thought too. Speaking of Heleena, how did it go at the Carreres' this morning?"

She followed me to the kitchen and sat on a barstool. I relayed the shortened version of the visit while preparing a marinade for the mahi-mahi. By the time I'd finished, the fish fillets were soaking in teriyaki sauce, pineapple juice, and crushed garlic cloves.

"As the oldest of eight," Risa began, "I took care of my seven brothers and sisters."

I knew what was coming. She'd told me the short version of her life story a million times. The longer version half a million.

"After my dad drank away his paycheck one too many times, Mom kicked him out. She worked three jobs—"

"Four," I interrupted.

Risa paused and counted on her fingers. "Right. She worked four jobs, and every penny went for rent, utilities, and food."

"Did she have to walk six miles through three feet of snow uphill both directions?"

"It never snows in the Philippines." Then she realized I was teasing her and muttered something offensive in her native language. At least it sounded offensive. "If we wanted extras, we had to beg for money on the corner."

"You let your little brothers and sisters beg on the corner? And you accuse me of not being safe. A good caretaker would do the begging for them."

She scowled at me. "My point is, I still had it better than someone like Heleena. I never had any haters on my back. And I've got a family where we all know we can count on each other for anything."

Risa and I had initially bonded over challenging childhoods. Ashlyn and I didn't have to beg for food, but it came close some days. We never knew if there would be enough to pay the rent. If our mother decided the money would better serve one of her whims, she spent it. All of it. Ashlyn and I used the money from Ash's minimum-wage, part-time paycheck to eat during those times. Mom, however, lived like a queen, insisting her way was right, that it would all pay off in the end, just wait and see. I'd wished so many times that she'd just walk out the door and never return because the stress over what she'd do next was too much for us to handle. We didn't need material things. All my sister and I needed was our ugly tiny house, a meal a day, and each other. Salomon made sure we got at least two meals per day and that the power was always on. Ashlyn refused to take more from him.

And then one day, my wish came true. We entered our cramped, questionably healthy house after school to find a note:

I've decided to take that job in Honolulu. They're absolutely begging me to come help open this nightclub. It's going to be a huge success. We'll make millions. Probably billions. Take care of each other. Love to you both.

That was it. No indication of when we'd hear from her again or how to get in touch with her. We tried to call, but she never answered her phone, and her voicemail was always full. After a couple of weeks, Ashlyn went to the police. They spent maybe an hour with her putting together a missing person's report and sending it to other stations around the islands. And that was all they did. No matter how many times she followed up, they never did more than refresh the report and note that Mom was still missing. They never actively investigated, never contacted anyone on the list we gave them of people who might know where she went.

Ashlyn had been twenty at that point, a legal adult, but I was only seventeen. Just about to graduate high school. To keep social services from taking me away, we didn't tell a soul Mom had left for ten months. If the school needed something from my parent, Ashlyn forged Mom's signature or pretended to be her on the phone.

Ash took all the waitressing shifts she could get. My small paycheck from working the front desk at No Mercy paid for our food, but every other penny went for rent. Our landlady figured out that Mom was gone and since the lease was in Mom's name, she threatened to kick us out.

"How about a month-to-month basis?" Ashlyn begged. "Please, we have nowhere else to go."

"Fine, but you miss one payment and you're out," the landlady warned, jerking a thumb over her shoulder.

Between the two of us, we always made the payments. After a few months of the checks arriving on time, the landlady rewrote the lease in Ashlyn's name. Then Ash got this new job doing whatever it was she did, and we hadn't worried about money since.

Pushing all those memories aside, I returned to dinner and started the rice. Then I pulled mango, papaya, red pepper, pineapple, red onion, and a variety of fresh herbs out of the refrigerator for fruit salsa and set them on the counter between us.

"If you ever want to change careers," Risa began and stopped. "Guess you need to have a career before you can change it."

I made a face at her.

"If you ever change your mind about becoming a nurse, you could go to cooking school." She snatched a chunk of mango from the cutting board. "This looks amazing."

"I've got motivation. Can't bounce around the ring for twenty-five minutes if I feed my body crap."

"Your bouts never go that long."

"Championship bouts do. Otherwise, they're fifteen minutes."

"No, I mean you either do that punch to the temple thing or have them on the mat in that arm thing in the first round."

Risa's descriptions always amused me. "That 'punch to the temple' is a right cross. The 'arm thing' is an armbar and hurts like hell."

"Which is why it's your go-to move whenever possible. You have a wicked side, you know?"

She followed me out onto the lanai and flopped down on the loveseat while I waited for the grill to heat up.

"You look relaxed," I observed.

"I love days off. Don't get me wrong, I wouldn't change jobs for anything, but puttering around the apartment and running errands is fun for me."

"It probably reminds you of taking care of your siblings."

"Never thought of it that way. You're right. I went shopping and bought enough food to last me at least two weeks, did all my laundry, and cleaned my apartment. I even scrubbed my toilet. How's that for being an adult?"

I raised a hand and slapped an air high-five at her. "Great job. Speaking of laundry, the washer is out in the garage. Since you're feeling so domestic today, you want to hang my things to dry?"

"I'll pass. I don't need to see your undies, sister. Besides, with my household chores done, all I want to do is chill for a while. You should try it sometime." Before I could issue a snappy response, she added, "Oh! That reminds me, I got invited to go out on a yacht tomorrow, and you're coming with me."

"Who owns a yacht?"

"He doesn't own it. He knows someone who knows someone . . . who knows someone. Something like that."

"Who is *he*?"

"One of the doctors. It's his thirtieth birthday, and he's about to finish his residency. He wants to celebrate on a boat. You have to go with me. I know these people, but it's weird socializing with people you work with."

Great. Celebrate someone turning thirty who was about to enter the phase of his career he'd been working for years to get to. I was thirty and still hadn't finished college. The grin I forced almost hurt. "And you are not exactly a social butterfly."

Risa gasped and placed a hand over her heart. "You wound me."

"Right."

As we ate, we chatted more about work, the gym, and the upcoming fight. I mentioned Ashlyn and Jeannie's matching outfits and tattoos and the offers from my professors.

"The outfits and tattoos are a little odd," Risa agreed. "They should stay away from Mai Tais. You should for sure take that internship this summer. The tutoring thing would be good, too, but not as impressive."

After dinner she helped me with Hulu's cage. The bird perched on top, inspecting the process while we pulled out the old bedding, wiped down the bottom, and put in fresh stuff.

"Now," I said, "it's bath time."

Hulu bounced up and down excitedly. "Bubbles, Kenichi."

I pointed a finger at him. "No bubbles for you." He liked to perch on the edge of the tub when Ashlyn took baths and pop the bubbles with a talon.

"What does Kenichi mean?" Risa asked.

"Who knows. Some of the things he says he learned from his first owner. Or Ash teaches him something new, and he butchers it for a while."

Before we knew it, it was eleven o'clock.

"I'm going to head home," Risa said as she teased Hulu with a food pellet.

"Hulu sad." He lowered his head and made a sound like he was crying.

"I'm sorry. Here." Risa held the pellet out. Hulu grabbed it and then laughed.

"You're such a sucker," I said.

"Sucker," Hulu repeated.

"No respect. I'm out of here." Risa slid her feet into her sandals outside the door. "So tomorrow on the yacht, right?"

I thought about my schedule. No room for a scalpel, but she was right. I needed to relax now and then. "Lahaina harbor or Kahului? My day is pretty packed."

Lahaina Harbor was a forty-five-minute drive. Over an hour if there was a lot of traffic.

"Kahului. That way they can stop more often to pick up and drop off people who need to work or can't stay all day."

Tomorrow was Friday. The most important thing was weigh-in at eight o'clock tomorrow morning followed by my rotation at the women's shelter. As emotional as the fallout could be, I really enjoyed my visits with the women and kids there. The afternoon should be fairly open, so I had no reason to say no.

"All right. I'm at the shelter until two. I can do the yacht after that."

She pointed at me. "I'm going to hold you to this. No skipping out on R&R."

I did the nightly shutdown routine—made sure the garage door was shut, hung my laundry, locked the front and lanai doors, and covered Hulu's cage.

"Goodnight, Hulu."

"Sleep tight."

I'd just snuggled into bed with pillows propped around me and my novel opened to the marked page when a text came in from Ashlyn.

Are you still awake?

I am.

A few seconds later, my phone rang.

"How was your day, Peep?"

That led to yet another retelling of what I'd learned from the Carreres and the rest of my day.

"Wow," Ashlyn mumbled through a mouthful of something. "Used every minute today, didn't you?"

"It's my superpower. What are you eating?"

"Chocolate covered macadamia nuts. You've got weigh-in in the morning?"

"Yep, at eight. The shelter is next and then a yacht ride."

"Wait. A yacht?"

I explained Risa's invitation. "Oh, and I wanted to go down to Kihei—"

Damn. I hadn't meant to say that out loud. I just remembered I hadn't confirmed a time with Lana yet, and it slipped out.

Ashlyn pounced on it. "Why are you going to Kihei?"

Reluctantly, I explained.

"How about," she turned on her big sister in charge voice, "you call that detective instead and she can go talk to Lana?"

I just realized that Ashlyn's in-charge voice sounded a lot like Risa's.

"Because with Detective Kalani," I replied, irritated now, "Lana would have to explain who all the people in her life were first. With me, she can just talk, and I'll understand. At least when we're talking about No Mercy folks. I also have this little niggly feeling that Leena and Lana got involved with some nasty people, and I want to ask her about that."

"Nasty people?"

"Yeah, have you heard of the yakuza?" I explained my theory that they needed money.

Ashlyn didn't reply.

"Ash?"

"Have you lost your mind? Because you sound like a crazy person. First you say another fighter did this to her, then you think it could be a hater, and now a crime syndicate is involved? What is going on with you?" Before I could speak, she added, "You and Heleena were acquaintances. Fellow gym members. It's not like you were close friends. And yes, I know the gym rats are your ohana. You need to stay out of this."

"Everyone keeps saying that."

"So why aren't you listening?

I slipped out of bed and over to the window. A breeze blew in, bringing the smell of flowers and recently cut grass with it.

"Gemi?"

"What if it was one of them?" I asked softly.

She hesitated before asking, "Them who?"

"One of the rats. After talking to Detective Kalani tonight, it seems more and more like it might be."

"That would be awful, but there's nothing *you* can do about it. Gemi, please. You put yourself in physical danger every day. If it's not letting people throw punches at your face, it's that dang motorcycle. Let the police handle this one."

Always so worried about my face. I couldn't help but smile. "My opponents wear gloves, so it doesn't hurt that much if they connect. I've never even come close to having an accident on the bike. And you know how helpful the cops can be."

"By the grace of God, you've stayed upright on that bike. And don't discount Detective Kalani yet."

"Yeah-yeah."

"*And* you've got a scar on your left eyebrow to remind you it does hurt to get hit. That kid popped you in the eye, and you cried like a baby. Blood running down your cute face . . ."

I could picture Ashlyn grimacing with disgust. The scar on my eyebrow wasn't my only one. The other, not quite an inch long, was behind my left ear. A physical reminder of my attacker and his knife. It was ugly because Ashlyn treated it at home. We probably should have gone to the hospital for a stitch or two.

"I cried because the kid hit me, not because it hurt."

"You played it up like it did."

"I was nine, and Auntie Amelia said booboos deserved ice cream. She bought you a cone that day too."

Ashlyn laughed. A lighthearted, happy sound. "Emotional trauma over seeing my baby sister bleeding. Who do you think taught you how to work the system? Don't say Mom."

I heard a door open and close in the background. "Is someone with you?"

"Oh . . . that's just Jeannie."

"You're sharing a room?"

Ashlyn never shared a room. After it became obvious Mom wasn't coming back, Ashlyn took over her bedroom at the tiny house and vowed to never share with anyone ever again. Except for a future husband.

"Sharing? God, no," Ashlyn answered. "We've got adjoining rooms. You know, with a door between them? I need to kick her out before she steals my towels. Again."

When she said nothing more after that, I knew what she was waiting for. I climbed back into bed and pulled the covers up.

"Ready," I told her.

"Nighty-night, sweet Peep."

"G'night, Ashy. Talk to you tomorrow."

CHAPTER SIXTEEN

I woke to fluttering nerves. As in excitement, not fear or worry. I always felt this way the day before a fight. I'd never had an issue at weigh-in. My weight might fluctuate a little, but I naturally hovered near the middle of the 125-to-135 range for bantamweight fighters. There was a touch of irritation swirling around in me, too, which came from the rules I'd have to follow today. All imposed by Salomon, they completely messed with my normal daily routine. Starting with my morning run.

"Five miles is all you need to stay loose," he'd said last night as he had before every fight. As though I'd forgotten. "Treadmill is best. Stay inside where you won't get hit by a car."

Salomon was abnormally paranoid about injuries. Among other things.

"So it's all right for me to get hit at any other time?" I couldn't help poking at him.

"That's not what I mean, and you know it."

"Treadmills cause more injuries, coach," I'd responded, as I did every time. "Easier to pull a groin muscle or hamstring on a treadmill."

Then he glowered in that scary Polynesian way of his before relenting. "Fine. But stay in quiet neighborhoods. I don't understand why you insist on running on busy narrow roads." He crossed his arms over his expansive chest and added, "Watch for debris on your path. One wrong step and you twist your ankle. Just that fast"—he snapped his fingers—"and this fight is done before it starts. And in the name of Ku, stay off that motorcycle."

Ku was the god of war and Salomon's favorite of all the Hawaiian deities. I found it amusing that a man who trained people to fight honored a war god. To be honest, Salomon's freak-out stage before every fight calmed me. If he didn't worry about everything, I would, and I'd be a jumble of nerves.

Maybe that's why he did it.

He'd spouted his superstitions at me so many times over the years, I'd adopted some of them. That meant I put on my running gear and stuck to only five miles through the quiet streets of my neighborhood. Today, that turned out to be a good plan because I wasn't paying attention. Mrs. Ly called out to me twice before I heard her and waved.

Heleena was distracting me. In fact, I could almost feel her ghost running next to me.

I usually dismissed supernatural things, but the islands were chock full of myths and lore. Like the Night Marchers, ghosts of ancient warriors who roamed specific areas to the beat of drums during certain phases of the moon. Pele's Curse stated that bad luck would come to anyone who took sand, rocks, or pumice off the island. It was said that pretty much anyone who grew up here had encountered a ghost, even if they didn't realize it. I figured a few of the legends must have some truth behind them due to odds and the sheer number of stories.

As for who was running with me today, it was more likely the little girl at my heels than Heleena. Since finding Leena's body on the beach and especially after meeting Aria yesterday, I could feel her hovering around, trying to protect me. Which was ironic and sort of sweet since no one had been there to protect her that night so many years ago. Not right away, at least. Friends showed up when it mattered most.

"I'm trying to find out what happened to you, Leena," I said out loud in case she was listening. Could spirits hear thoughts? "Detective Kalani is investigating, and I promise this won't go unsolved. If she doesn't find out the truth, I will."

Why you? the little girl asked. *Why do you need to do it?*

Ashlyn had asked almost the same thing last night.

Almost immediately after we moved here, I found a taekwondo studio. Mom had complained about the tuition but agreed to let me stick with it until I earned my black belt. That took a year and a half. I wanted to do something different after that. While touring No Mercy, I watched some of the members sparring MMA style and immediately knew that's what I wanted to learn next. Like with Johnny Gambino, Salomon let me clean the gym to pay for membership. After a few months, he moved me to the front desk. That was right around the time our mother left. Not long after that, I was earning a paycheck as an instructor. When I turned twenty-one, he asked me to be his assistant manager. Salomon's trust in me changed my life. Over those thirteen years, he became more of a parent to me than my mother had ever been, and his ohana of gym rats became my ohana as well.

"Why me?" I repeated the little girl's question. "One of my ohana was killed. For whatever reason, I'm the one who found Heleena's body. That means I have to make sure that circle gets closed."

But it's not your responsibility, she insisted. *You should stay out of it.*

Ashlyn said that last night too.

My irritation level spiked, so I pushed my run to seven miles. Salomon didn't need to know.

By the time I got home, I was dripping with sweat and starving. Fish and fruit never stayed with me long. I should've had more substantial protein last night. A shower would take care of the first problem, but I couldn't have anything to eat or drink until after weigh-in. As the tepid shower slowly cooled me, I tilted my face into the stream and let my mouth fill. Like a dry sponge, my tongue swelled and rehydrated. After a couple of seconds, I spit out the rest. On the off chance I came in overweight, which could disqualify me,

Salomon would make me do burpees for an hour until I sweated it off. I hated burpees.

Once dressed, and knowing this day would be packed solid with no time to return to the condo, I prepared three bags. One was a duffle bag with clothes and gear for the minor "workout" Salomon and I would do later tonight. The second was a canvas tote with my swimsuit, cover-up, towel, rubber slippers, and sunscreen for the yacht ride this afternoon. I was looking forward to that more than I'd expected. Third was a Kahului College string bag with a notebook, folder, and pen to take notes during my rotation later this morning.

All that wouldn't fit in the motorcycle saddlebags, so I'd have to take the Jeep today. That would keep Salomon happy too.

I filled Hulu's food and water dishes.

"Thank you." He grabbed a pellet from the dish.

"You're welcome. I'll be gone all day, so you're in charge."

He straightened on his perch as though standing at attention. I should teach him to salute.

"Ashlyn will be home sometime tomorrow, so you won't be stuck with just me much longer."

"Ashlyn," Hulu practically purred then gave a long, low catcall whistle.

"Dirty bird," I scolded with a grin. "See you later."

"Have a good day." I swear he released a sad sigh as he turned to stare out the window while nibbling on his pellet.

* * *

"You're a pound underweight," Salomon scolded while staring at the number on the scale in his office. "Have you been eating and hydrating?"

"I have. I've been a little distracted, though."

One pound under was allowable but also easily fixable. Since Salomon liked things neat and tidy, he handed me a bottle of water. "Drink this. "You've got too much going on. Like always."

Grateful, I took a long swig. My stomach immediately clenched at the sudden addition of cold liquid.

"What do you suggest I cut? I have to go to school if I ever want a decent job. No offense." As much as I loved being his assistant manager, it wasn't a career. "Teaching my classes here is important to my soul. Working out is crucial to my physical and mental health. The only thing optional in my schedule is fighting."

That sort of fell out of my mouth. Did I mean it? Could I seriously walk away from fighting?

Salomon scowled, as unhappy with my statement as I was shocked by it. "You're almost done with school for the summer, right?"

I nodded. I'd get a three-month break, but my final eight weeks of classes would start up again before I knew it.

"Good, don't fill that time with anything," Salomon ordered. "Relax a little. Read a book. Plant a flower."

"Plant a flower?" I grinned at him, amused.

"You know what I mean. Do something different. Take some time to breathe." He waved at the owner from one of the other gyms. "I need to go talk with her."

I drained the water bottle and then went to wait for the weigh-in official with the other fighters. We rotated locations to keep things fair. The last two times we had to go to one of the other competing gyms. This time No Mercy got to host.

The official arrived right on schedule. Salomon hauled the scale out to the middle of the gym where the official verified it was properly calibrated. Then he called for the fighters to line up by weight class, men first, lightest to heaviest. There were eight classes for the men: flyweight, bantamweight, featherweight, lightweight, welterweight, middleweight, light heavyweight, and heavyweight. For this fight, the top four overall fighters in each class were eligible. This meant I had to wait a long time for my turn.

"Stop fidgeting," Salomon hissed. "You're going to burn off the pound you just gained. Why don't you sit?"

"You worry way too much," I chided in return as I bounced foot to foot.

"Do you really want to forfeit over a pound?"

I didn't bother reminding him that underweight was fine.

"He made me do burpees," Stacia complained. "I came in at 134."

"You could be over once the scale gets calibrated," Salomon insisted.

"Then I better drink another bottle." I stared him in the eye as I chugged. He was being ridiculous.

Aonani and Mele stood off to the side, glaring at us. Aonani looked pale and a little unsteady on her feet.

"She hasn't had anything to eat or drink since Tuesday night," Stacia whispered and pointed out a dozen other fighters who looked equally shaky.

"I hate that part of this sport," I whispered back.

"Me too," she agreed. "And Aonani is fighting me. She knows I don't weight-cut."

I understood the strategy. Fighters fought in the class they weighed in at. This meant they wanted to weigh in at a lower weight class and then quickly rehydrate and eat enough to get back to normal weight. This, theoretically, gave them an advantage over their opponent. It was what everyone learned on the playground. The bigger kid can wallop the smaller kid. Some fighters dropped twenty or more pounds before weigh-in. It was incredibly dangerous. And the thing was, if everyone did it, where was the advantage?

In Aonani's case, she should fight in the heavier featherweight class. Stacia and a few others had told me Aonani wanted to fight me. I was the top ranked woman fighter on the island, and she wanted that spot. I sure hoped she didn't kill herself before we got the chance to face each other.

Stacia and I glanced around, commenting on various fighters and how we thought they'd do. The mood was different today.

Where there was normally a lot of swagger and smack talk being tossed about, a more somber feel hovered over the gym this time because of Heleena.

"I give her a lot of credit for being here," Stacia commented.

"Who?" I asked.

She nodded at a very subdued Callie sitting a few feet away with other fighters. Quite the difference from the laughing, joking-around Callie I saw working out with Ozzie last night.

"Where's Mona?" Stacia asked.

"She called Ozzie early this morning," Salomon answered. "There's a problem with her boat. Guess they're waiting for a tow to haul them into the marina. She has until six o'clock tonight to weigh in or she'll forfeit her fight."

"The featherweight girls can't catch a break," Stacia stated.

"Ozzie talked with Callie and Mona about backing out," Salomon said, "but the ladies insisted on going forward in Heleena's honor."

"Good decision." I bounced on the balls of my feet. After drinking all that water, now I needed to use the restroom. "Leena wouldn't want them to forfeit because of this."

"He's ready to start." Salomon nodded at the official. "I should be up front."

Everything went smoothly until they got toward the end of the line.

"What do you mean I'm overweight?" demanded Lono, a rising star in the heavyweight class from a competing gym. "That's impossible."

"I can only go by the number on the scale," the official said. "You can stand there all day and tell me it's wrong, but it's not going to change anything. Go to the bathroom. Run around the building a few times. Do whatever you need to do. You can get back in line once."

Grumbling and shaking his head, insisting the scale had to be wrong, Lono went to the end of the line, grinned big, and removed his shoes and his jeans.

"Good God, Lono," one of the other men said. "Bro, put your pants back on."

"At least he's wearing clean undies," someone else called out.

Stacia shook her head and laughed. "The rats are going to be talking about this one for a long time."

When Lono got on the scale again, he weighed in at 259 pounds, well within the limits of 205 to 265 for the heavyweights. The big man grinned and threw his arms in the air as though he'd already won his fight.

"No one wears jeans and shoes to weigh in," I noted. "I'm surprised the official let him on the scale that way."

With appreciative eyes locked on Lono, Stacia said, "He did it to draw attention to himself."

"Looks like it worked," I teased and bumped her shoulder with mine.

"Women," the official called out, "you're next."

There were only four groups for the women—strawweight, flyweight, bantamweight, and featherweight. Someday I would find out how each of the rankings got their names. Why, for example, were the flyweights heavier than the straws? And surely a feather would be the lightest.

"What's a bantam anyway?" I mumbled to no one in particular.

"It's an aggressive male chicken," Mele replied from behind me in line.

I blinked. "Really?"

"Hand to God."

Well, a chicken for sure weighed more than a feather.

My turn finally came. I stood on the scale and watched my official weight come in at one twenty-five and a half. I'd consumed the equivalent of a pound and a half of water. My coach gave me a little pat on the back, and I ran for the women's restroom.

"Do you need me for anything right now?" I asked Salomon from the doorway of his office. The rest of the women had finished weighing in. Members from the other gyms had left, leaving only No Mercy rats gathered and talking excitedly. "If not, I need to eat before I pass out."

"We're done for now. Come back tonight so we can go over last-minute strategies. Going to The Juice Bar?"

"Yep. I've been thinking about an extra-large Green Glory and an egg white omelet with avocado and red peppers all morning."

"Don't eat too much at once," he cautioned. "You'll make yourself sick."

I swatted a hand at him. "I'll have that worn off by lunchtime."

"What's on the calendar today?"

I leaned against the doorjamb and told him about visiting the women's shelter. "I'm also hoping to go see Lana. I should call or text her rather than just running down there. Would you look up her number?"

"You're not riding that motorcycle, are you?"

Don't ride the motorcycle, Gemi, you'll kill yourself. Don't eat too much. Hydrate more. You need to relax now and then. Why did people think I needed a keeper? Especially Salomon, Ashlyn, Risa, and occasionally a professor. Rather than defend myself, I either ignored the statements or replied with a tight smile.

"You'll be happy to know I'm using the Jeep today. I won't have time to run home between appointments and can't fit everything in the saddlebags."

"That does make me happy, but you need to ease back."

And cue the smile.

He clicked his mouse a few times and then pointed at Lana's number on the screen. "That's her cellphone. I don't think they have a landline."

I entered the number into my phone and sent a quick text: *Lana, this is Gemi from No Mercy. Would it be all right for me to stop by this afternoon?*

Her response came a minute later. *Sure, I had an appointment cancel, so I'm free from 2 to 3. Can you come then?*

I was supposed to meet Risa at two thirty. No way I'd be back by then. I'd have to push that out.

That works. See you at 2:00.

She verified that I should meet her at the apartment, not the salon. Then I sent another quick text to Risa. *Something came up. I'll be to the marina by 3:20.*

"All set?" Salomon asked and I nodded. "Be sure to invite her to the fight. And don't forget our strategy session tonight."

"I'll be here but don't freak out if it's not until later. I'm going out on a yacht with Risa this afternoon. Actually going to relax for a while."

"That's great. Don't forget sunscreen. You know how much it will sting to get punched in a sunburn? You should probably wear long sleeves and pants. Put on a hat and sunglasses too. Maybe a pair of gloves."

I was fairly sure he was joking about the clothes. "Yes, to the sunscreen. But that's a big no to the rest. I packed my bikini and plan to soak in as much vitamin D as possible."

"Bikini?" asked a voice from behind me.

My shoulders dropped. I didn't even need to look to know Ross Donnelly was standing behind me. No wonder I'd had an itchy feeling for the last half hour. Where had he been hiding? Usually, he was front-and-center where I was sure to see him.

"If you need someone to help you with that sunscreen," Ross continued, "you know, rubbing it on your back or wherever, I'm available."

I looked him in the eye and shook my head slowly. "I warned you." Taking two steps back into the office, I stated, "Salomon, I'm making a formal complaint. Ross Donnelly is sexually harassing me."

Salomon clenched his hands and barked, "Donnelly, in here now."

As I walked past him, I noted that Ross had turned a sickly shade of green.

"I'm heading to The Juice Bar," I called out to the fighters still in the gym. "Anyone interested?"

Ten hands shot into the air, so I asked Kenny at the front desk to call over to the restaurant and let them know we were coming.

"Will do," Kenny replied. "They said they planned ahead this time and have extra inventory on hand."

That had to be why Kym asked when weigh-in was. The last time a group of us showed up unannounced, they had to work off an abbreviated menu for the rest of the day. Fifteen MMA fighters consumed a lot of protein.

Kenny stuck out his lower lip while reaching for the phone. What was the pout for?

"Would you like to come with us?" I asked, guessing he felt left out.

His face lit up. "I'll see if Gambino or someone can watch the front desk for a while."

Pausing at the mention of Johnny's name, I wondered if Detective Kalani had talked with him yet. "Just don't tell him where you're going or he'll follow. You and the others come when you're ready. I need to scoot over there. I've got rotation at ten thirty."

CHAPTER SEVENTEEN

After ordering my smoothie and omelet, I chose a seat at the table in the back corner Kym had reserved for us. Sitting alone in the relative silence of the café for those few minutes was almost as rejuvenating as the food would be. I closed my eyes, rested my hands in my lap, and took in the surroundings. My stomach rumbled at the smell of frying bacon. The clinking of dishes in the kitchen was oddly comforting as I thought of someone making food for me. I heard traffic driving by outside and the murmuring voices of the staff. The aroma of toast mingling with the bacon made me feel conflicted. I loved bread but couldn't have any. Especially not right before a fight because it would make me sluggish.

When the café's door opened, I peeked an eye open, expecting to see the gym rats coming in. Instead, I saw a striking Asian woman in loose white linen pants, a snug black tank top, and rubber slippers. She was on the skinny side of slender and had a curtain of slightly mussed, straight black hair that hung to her waist. I couldn't see her face because her back was to me, but the thing about her that really caught my attention was her tattoos. They covered both of her arms from shoulder to wrist and her upper back. There were intricate floral designs among swirling waves, Koi fish, dragons, and other things I couldn't make out from across the room.

As though sensing me, she glanced over her shoulder and locked eyes with me. I flushed hot with embarrassment at being caught staring and placed my palms together in apology. She gave a crisp nod, accepting the gesture, then turned back to finish placing her order. I hadn't meant to be rude, but if a person put that many tattoos on display, people were going to look.

"Isn't she gorgeous?" Kym whispered while placing my smoothie, the omelet, and a tall glass of water on the table in front of me. I was so entranced by the tattooed woman I hadn't even seen Kym coming my way. "She doesn't come in often, but when she does, people usually give her the same reaction you are."

"My sister has one small tattoo on her hip of a Hibiscus flower. It's about this big." I held my thumb and index finger about two inches apart. "She said she needed a few Mai Tais to numb her enough to have it done. Can you imagine the pain this woman went through? I mean, if she's got that many on both arms and her back, it's a safe bet she's got more somewhere else."

"True. I've never seen her in anything but pants, so can't say what her legs look like, but they're probably covered too." Kym leaned close and kept her voice low. "Rumor is, she's yakuza."

Again with that group. Was I the only one who'd never heard of them? "Why? Because of the tattoos?"

Kym gave a slow nod and absently ran a hand over the trio of black Polynesian-style turtles swimming across her upper left arm.

I'd been joking. "What do the tattoos mean?"

"I guess they started out as identifiers. You know, to show which faction a person belonged to. I'm not sure how they got to the point of covering their whole body."

"Their *whole* body?" I repeated, winced, and squirmed.

We stared for another few seconds while the woman waited for her order, a smoothie of some kind, and then Kym let out a contented sigh. "The others are coming, I assume?"

"I thought they were right behind me. Either way, I've got something"—I glanced at my watch—"in forty-five minutes, so I need to eat and run."

"Are you ready for your fight?"

"I'm ready. Will you make it?"

"To see you achieve your baker's fifteen?" Kym asked with

enthusiasm. "I'll do whatever I can to be there. It's in Paia, right?"

"As always. See you there."

I'd just put the first forkful of eggs in my mouth when I got the feeling I was being watched. I turned to see the tattooed woman staring at me. Not just a glance but full-on staring, like she was studying and memorizing me. With smoothie in hand, she leaned against the counter and didn't look away.

Since I wasn't the one to start it this time, I stared back. Her face was as beautiful and delicate as her tattoos were strong and bold. The low scoop neck of her tight black tank top revealed a mass of tropical flowers inked right up to her collarbones. I smiled weakly, but she didn't react. I was about to compliment about her tattoos when she strode directly over and bent at the waist to get a better look at . . . something.

What was she looking at? Before I could ask, she spun away, getting swallowed by the throng of No Mercy fighters who'd just walked in. Relief flooded me. I wasn't too proud to admit the woman unnerved me.

Ross arrived with the others and made a beeline in my direction the moment he spotted me.

"Please, don't say anything." He sat down and blew out a shaky breath. "I want to apologize. I'm really sorry about the comment I made earlier. I meant it as a joke, not to be offensive, but it's a little hard to—"

"You offered to rub sunscreen on my 'wherever.' Do you honestly not see how that was offensive?"

His head dropped forward. "I didn't mean that. I swear."

He appeared genuinely ashamed. Still, it was vulgar. "For the record, saying something like that and then trying to brush it off as 'that's not what I meant' only makes you look like a bigger jerk. Own up to it."

He inhaled and looked me square in the face. "I apologize. I like you, Gemi. A lot. And no matter what I say, it comes out wrong. I try to be flirty and sound like a pervert. I try to be macho, or whatever, and come off as a sexist ass. I try to be alluring and look like a clueless jerk." He put his hands over his face and talked through his fingers. "I try to get your attention and only succeed at humiliating myself and looking like the class dunce."

Really? Alluring and flirty? It seemed he was trying to be sincere, so I made an equally sincere effort to not laugh at what he thought would work with women.

"What about that comment you made to Heleena that time? The one about turning her."

He looked completely confused. "Turning her?"

"You said, 'Go out with me. Just once.'"

"*That's* what you thought I meant?" His face flared lava red behind his hands. "I hadn't even thought about her being gay. She was the closest woman to you, and I thought asking her out would make you jealous."

Didn't expect that answer. "Um, why?"

A groan came from behind his hands this time. "I don't know."

When he let his guard down this way, Ross was more clueless boy-next-door than creep that needed to have some sense beaten into him. He was a couple of years younger than me but, like me, looked even younger. He fought in the lightweight class, which meant he was muscular but lean.

"Class dunce is a pretty good description." I took a long drink of my smoothie, letting him stew in his embarrassment. "Look, I meant what I said. I'm not interested in dating anyone. *Anyone*, not just you."

He spread his fingers wide, exposing his deep-brown eyes. "Are you interested in a friend?" He lowered his hands before I could respond. "Nothing remotely romantic. We could just hang out." He paused, giving me a minute to respond. When I didn't, he slumped back. "I know, I'm coming off as a desperate loser."

I loaded my fork with eggs. "That's a good way to put it."

"I'm sorry. I'm truly sorry. I never meant to be offensive." He looked away and back a few times. "Trying to talk to you is the most frustrating thing ever. I want to get to know you, but honestly, you scare the hell out of me." He held his hands out as though framing my face to determine the best angle for a picture. "You have this beautiful, soft image, but then you get in the octagon and beat people to within an inch of their lives."

This time, I couldn't hold back my laugh. "That's my rope-a-dope."

Ross tilted his head, confused.

"You've never heard of rope-a-dope?" He shook his head in the negative. I shook mine in astonishment. "And you call yourself a fighter. It was Muhammad Ali's classic move. He'd let himself get 'trapped' in the corner against the ropes and keep his hands up, protecting his face. His opponent would throw one blow after another. Then once the guy had exhausted himself, Ali moved in for the kill."

My mind faded to watching old telecasts of Ali's fights with my uncle in California when I was little.

"Bill idolized Ali," Uncle Lonnie had told me, chuckling. "After two beers, he'd prance around doing his rendition of Ali's 'I am the greatest' speech."

I would've loved to see that. My dad died when I was five years old.

"Gemi?"

I inhaled and blinked until Uncle Lonnie and Dad faded away and Ross came back into view.

"You okay?"

My eyes stung, so I blinked a few more times. Ross stared with concern. "Yeah, I'm fine."

I was vividly aware that I wasn't following the advice I would have given other women in a situation like this. I'd tell them if they didn't feel safe, get away.

That was the question, though. Did I feel unsafe with Ross? I didn't want to date him, no doubt about that, but what if I'd been wrong about his intentions? Since the attack so many years ago, shutting men down had become my go-to instinct. I defaulted to not trusting them, to believing that they were all out to hurt me. But my gut was telling me Ross was a dork, not a pervert, and I should give him a chance. There had to be a reason I hadn't already shut him down.

Could I trust him?

What are you doing? the little girl asked. *You can't trust boys.*

"Tell you what, Ross."

He sat straight, like a dog waiting for me to throw a ball.

"I meant what I said about not wanting to date anyone." When his shoulders dropped, I added, "There's a reason for that, but I'm not going to explain it to you, so don't ask. I could use more friends, though, so I'm going to trust my gut and say okay to that part. We can give it a try, but you play by my rules."

"Which means what?"

I was just trying to set boundaries and hadn't thought that far. "If you can go for one week without offending me or anyone else, we'll discuss getting a coffee or something. As friends, not a date."

A faraway look filled his eyes, like he was working through a plan for how he'd manage this.

"After that week," I continued, "flirting or whatever it is you think you were doing is still not allowed. And getting together won't happen often. I've got a really full schedule."

"Will you forgive me if I slip now and then? Being an idiot has kind of become a habit."

I considered the question while loading the last bite of eggs onto my fork. At least he admitted it. I held up two fingers. "You get two slips. Any more than that and you're not trying hard enough. Of course, if I've made the wrong decision here, I can always beat you to within an inch of your life."

By the way the color drained from his face, he wasn't sure if I was joking or not. Good.

He cleared his throat and held a hand across the table to me. "Deal."

As we shook, I wondered what I had just agreed to. From the shocked looks the other rats were shooting at me from across the room, they wondered the same thing. Kenny was staring at us with his arms crossed like a bouncer denying entrance to the hottest club in town. He arched an eyebrow, silently asking if everything was okay. I smiled and nodded. Time would tell if compassion for Ross was justified or if I'd need to eat crow.

Ross abruptly changed topics. "You've been digging around in Heleena's death. Haven't you?"

How much should I tell him? The truth would get out eventually, so if he slipped it wouldn't be the end of the world. "Salomon is the only person at the gym who knows this. If word gets out, I'll know you spilled it."

He remained silent, waiting for more.

"I found Heleena's body."

I explained what had happened Wednesday morning on the beach, my conversation with the Carreres on Thursday, and my various discussions with Detective Kalani. All while being conscious of not revealing any details that could harm the investigation if they got out. Or so I hoped.

"I didn't realize you and Heleena were so close," he said when I'd finished.

"It's not so much that we were close. It's more like I feel called to do the right thing. If that makes sense."

He frowned. "Not sure investigating a death would fall under doing the right thing. That's the detective's job." He waited for me to react. When I didn't, he pressed on. "Have you come to any conclusions?"

"About who the killer is?" I didn't want to reveal anything specific to him. He hadn't earned that much of my trust yet. "I've got a few ideas."

The back of my neck prickled, and the hairs stood on end. I turned to find the woman with the tattoos sitting at the table behind me, her expression neutral. A mostly full smoothie sat on the table in

152 | SHAWN MCGUIRE

front of her, her hands clasped loosely around the cup. She appeared to be listening to our conversation.

Ross leaned closer and whispered, "She's been staring at you the whole time we've been talking."

Was this woman one of the yakuza? Did they know I found Heleena's body? Was I in trouble for some reason? Maybe they sent her as an enforcer, or whatever, to silence me. Or maybe she had killed Heleena. She had a physique similar to mine and looked capable of delivering a series of nasty blows. Was she here to find out what I knew and didn't know?

You're being stupid, the little girl chided.

I hoped she was right. But then why was this woman so interested in me?

With eyes still locked on mine, she slowly rose from her chair, leaving her drink behind. Everyone watched as she glided out the front door. My tension level should have dropped, but I could still feel her there. Like her ghost had taken her place at the table.

"That was weird," Ross noted dismissively. "So what were you going to say about possible suspects?"

Forcing myself to forget the woman, I asked, "How well do you know Johnny Gambino?"

"Wow." Ross sat back, stunned. "You think he did it?"

"I'm not sure." I paused while one of the café employees took my empty plate. "You know how obsessed he was with Heleena."

Ross smiled, blushing a little. "I'm aware."

I blinked and took a sip of my water. "He showed up at Heleena's parents' house a few weeks ago looking for her. Apparently he had the wrong address so asked them for hers."

"Did they give it to him?"

"They didn't know it."

"They . . . really?"

I gave him a thirty-second recap of Heleena's relationship with her parents.

He looked stunned. "I had no idea. He must have gotten it from the gym somehow."

"That's what I think too. I'm a little concerned about his temper as well." I described the broom breaking incident, which Ross remembered. "Have you ever seen him go off like that before?"

Ross stared into the corner, thinking. "I want to say yes but can't come up with specifics. I'll think on it and pay closer attention to him. Maybe I'll ask some of the other guys."

"You promised—"

He held up a hand. "I won't say anything about Heleena or you. Believe it or not, I can talk like a normal human being around guys."

I bit back a grin. "I do believe that. Girls are scary."

"You have no idea."

I glanced at the clock over the door. "Dammit! Is that seriously the time?" I looked at my watch to verify. Yes, 10:25. "I've got five minutes to get to the shelter. Gotta go."

CHAPTER EIGHTEEN

Fortunately, the shelter wasn't far, just a few miles from The Juice Bar, but I'd never make it on time. And on top of being late and distracted about Heleena, now I wondered if I'd done the right thing by confiding in Ross. Would he keep my secret? Would it be that big of a deal if he let it slip? Before the fight tomorrow, yes, it would be a big deal. Rats from every corner of the gym would pounce on me, wanting to know details and taking my mind off the fight.

"You better keep your mouth shut, Donnelly," I murmured to myself. If he was stupid enough to talk, our friendship would be over before it started. And my ability to trust anyone other than Ashlyn, Risa, and Salomon would be back to zero.

I turned south down a narrow vegetation-lined street where the houses had a good amount of space between them. This was a great location for the shelter as it offered more privacy. I pulled into the driveway of a nondescript single-story white house. My supervisor's royal-blue Tacoma was the only vehicle parked there. For safety reasons, the women who stayed here parked at a different location. That way a husband, boyfriend, or whoever their aggressor was wouldn't see their car and come looking for them.

Terri Riggs, psychiatric nurse practitioner and my supervisor, met me out front. She had shiny shoulder-length deep-blond hair and was twenty years my senior but looked like she could be my older sister.

Through my open window, I called, "I'm so sorry I'm late."

She gave me a disappointed frown as I walked up to her.

"You're here. That's the important thing."

"Thank you for understanding."

"You've never been late before. I'm sure you've got a good reason."

The underlying warning was that she could easily fill the spot with another student. Message received.

"You can stay a little longer to make up for the lost time."

I winced. "Actually, I need to be in Kihei by two o'clock. Can I do an extra hour next week?"

She considered this, lips pursed, fingers tapping on crossed arms. "Since this is the first issue I've had with you, I'll okay it. But I will expect that extra hour next Friday."

"Yes, ma'am. I promise."

"All right." She inhaled, her tense expression softening. "Are you ready?"

"I am."

She held out her hand for mine and joined me in a two-minute meditation, encouraging me, as always, to clear my mind before entering the house. Once I crossed the threshold, nothing mattered except the women and children staying here.

"We've got a full house today," Terri informed when our two minutes was up, "but we've already got help arranged for most of them."

"That's great news. Who would you like me to visit first?"

Terri was both an RN and a psychiatric nurse, so we also evaluated and treated minor physical problems. If injuries or issues were more severe, we would contact a doctor at a local clinic to take over. Terri was mostly concerned with mental health issues, however, so we spent a lot of our time talking with the women so she could assess their needs upon leaving the shelter. This wasn't intended to be a new home for them, but rather a safe place where they could catch their breath while we helped determine and arrange their next move. An otherwise physically fine woman with mental issues wasn't ready to tackle life. Doubly so if she had a child.

"A young woman in her early twenties came in this morning," Terri explained, frustration over my late arrival forgotten. For now. "She's been here before. Her name is Dani. I have no clue how she got here, but she showed up about an hour ago. She said she didn't want to talk to anyone and went right out to the lanai. Go sit with her. See if you can get her to open up. If you can, I'll join you and we'll talk more about her situation. If not today, I'll try again tomorrow. Since she's been here before, she knows the rules. She can't stay long, so she'll need to help us if she wants us to help her."

Sometimes, I hated that I only had four hours on Fridays here. I saw either the start of cases or the end but rarely got to know the women. Maybe that was for the best since I wouldn't be involved with their lives once they left here.

I went to the lanai and spotted Dani right away. Easy since she was the only one out there. She was sitting in a tight ball on a patio chair, her knees pulled to her chest, and staring into the lush foliage that made up the untamed backyard. She looked up at me, paused, and her eyes went wide.

"Hi, Dani. I'm—" I knew her. It took me a second to place her as a woman who had taken one of my self-defense classes. "I remember you."

She nodded, her waist-length light-brown hair partially covering her face. "I did one of your free Saturday morning classes."

"That's it." Her voice was so soft, I sat close to be sure I heard her properly. "About a year ago."

Dani smiled, pleased that I remembered her. Then she winced, and her hand slid beneath her hair to a purplish-blue bruise covering her left cheekbone. Her left eye was also swollen. For a split second, a battered Heleena was sitting before me. Maybe the yakuza had nothing to do with this. Maybe this had been a hate crime. Or worse. Had Lana done it?

I blinked to refocus. Dani now. Lana and Leena later.

When she realized what I was looking at, Dani blushed. "I'm a klutz."

No accusations, no judgments, but I knew what that meant.

Dani wasn't a klutz. She was a victim of domestic violence, which was why she came to my class that day. I clearly remembered discussing the signs of an abuser at the end of that class. Something I did every time a woman asked for a free self-defense lesson. The other students knew to expect it and were very supportive. That day, like now, Dani wouldn't look at me. But she had been listening closely with one ear tilted my direction. Also like now.

"I haven't seen you at No Mercy since that day. Have you been taking classes at another gym?" When she didn't respond, I added, "As long as you're getting quality instruction, I don't care where you learn. The important thing is to develop those skills."

Dani fidgeted. Uncomfortable with this topic?

I pushed on but gently. "My classes are also great exercise. I'd love to have you come back."

She shook her head, her hair covering her eye and that bruise again. "Oh, no, I don't have—"

"No charge for the first month."

This was the agreement I had made with Salomon. If I suspected a woman of being abused, or knew it like in this case, she could come in for all the classes she wanted for one month. Salomon had objected at first and told me he'd allow two free classes instead of one like we gave all potential students. I spent a half hour pleading my case, explaining how my class helped to develop not only physical strength and confidence but mental strength as well.

I'd ended with, "We could save lives, Salomon."

Finally, he agreed. "Just don't go overboard, okay? I know you. Half your class will be free. I'm trying to run a business, not a charity."

Dani didn't respond to my free month offer, but she also didn't turn away. I hadn't lost her yet.

We sat quietly, watching birds hopping around in the bushes. After a few minutes, she asked, "Do you still fight? I remember you talking about . . . MMA? Is that right?"

"That's it. I still fight. In fact, I'm defending my title this weekend."

"Maybe I'll come and cheer you on. My boyfriend left this morning for a job at a construction site on Oahu for ten days. So my schedule is clear."

Smack her around before leaving to keep her in line while he's gone? Mark up her face so no one will take an interest in her? Was that his strategy? Well, *I* was interested. So were all the other women here.

"I'd be honored." I gave her the location and time.

She nodded, grew quiet again, and then asked with a whisper I had to strain to hear, "Do you ever get hit? During your fights, I mean."

My heart stuttered. "Sometimes. I do my best to not let that happen, though."

"Doesn't it hurt?"

I needed a second to swallow the sudden surge of rage rushing through me. She wasn't asking about me. The bruise on her face was the one he left that would either keep her inside or force her to label herself a klutz. It was the one everyone could see. How many more were hidden beneath her clothing?

"It can hurt, sure, but we wear gloves with a good amount of padding. That helps." I forced my voice to stay light and added, "No one wants to get hit with a bare fist."

This time, Dani met my eyes. She let me see the pain and fear there. When she reached for my hand, I knew it was time for Terri to join us.

I worked exclusively with Dani and was almost disappointed when my time was up. Maybe I could do that extra hour today and visit Lana another day. And if I didn't get to cruise around on a yacht, worse things could happen.

"You connected with her," Terri noted with pride as she walked me out to my Jeep.

I told her how Dani and I knew each other. "The longer I sat with her, the more my hope grew."

"Careful," Terri cautioned. "We've discussed how long it can take before victims are ready to make a move."

"I meant hope for me."

She blinked at me, surprised. "For you?"

"From the start of freshman year, I planned to go into psychiatric health. It's a long story that we don't have time for, but I figured growing up with a narcissistic mother must have been preparing me for that sort of career. I'm a sixth-year senior now, and that decision doesn't feel like such a good fit anymore. I told you about my attack."

"When you were thirteen. I remember."

"That's where my passion is. Helping victims of violence. Whether domestic or otherwise. The thought of empowering women and children to take control of their lives empowers me. What a fulfilling career that would be."

The thought of not becoming a nurse had been playing around in my brain since last school year. After all these years, I was ready to move past my mother issues. That would be harder done than said, however, because contrary to what people believed, Mom wasn't dead. Every six or eight months, she'd email or call. I knew her phone number so never answered. She'd leave a voicemail. One where she talked about how wonderful her life was. How her nightclub was the most successful around. That her employees adored working for her, blah blah blah.

One time, she called from a number I didn't recognize. I shouldn't have answered and wouldn't make that mistake again. I let her talk for about five minutes then asked where she was. She refused to tell me. When I pushed her, she said she had to go. I realized then that she'd never said the name of this nightclub or where it was. Not during that call or in any of her voicemails. She never asked to come visit or for us to come to her. Never asked how Ashlyn or I were doing. Never asked me to call her back. The only reason for her call was to give a glowing report about herself.

That was fine. The woman hadn't contributed a thing to our lives in thirteen years, and I had no intention of inviting her back into it. Had she been contacting Ashlyn too? Probably, but Ash and I were determined to protect each other. That meant never talking about our mother.

"You can still use your degree," Terri told me.

I blinked. "Sorry, got lost in a thought. I what?"

"Once you have your bachelor's degree, you can shift your focus to becoming a domestic violence nurse."

"A what?" My heart raced. "Why haven't I ever heard of this before?"

"It would require specialized training and certifications, and you'd need three years of experience before you can get certified." She opened the driver's door for me. "If you want to hear more about this, let's set up a time to talk. We could go for a run on the beach." She reconsidered that. "Make it a walk. Not sure I could keep up with you."

I settled into the driver's seat. "I'd like that."

She closed my door and waved as I drove off. Being a domestic violence nurse sounded intriguing, but an additional three years of experience and training? I'd have to think on that. I wasn't sure I had the patience to wait that long.

CHAPTER NINETEEN

I pulled into the small parking lot next to a bright-turquoise apartment building a few minutes before two o'clock. It quickly became apparent that the cheery color and relatively easy access to the beach were the two best things about the place. I'd seen worse accommodations, though. Like the house Ashlyn and I had lived in until eighteen months ago. For what Lana was likely paying for this apartment, she didn't appear to be getting much. The turquoise paint was peeling. The only landscaping was a sad-looking palm tree and a row of scraggly shrubs running between her building and its bright-pink sibling. At least the parking lots had been resurfaced recently.

"Hey, Gemi. Come on in." Lana must have been watching for me because she opened the door as I reached to knock. "I don't have much to offer you. Can I get you a glass of water?"

I didn't really want anything, but Lana seemed eager to be hospitable and I needed to stay hydrated. "Water would be great, thanks."

The living room area of the tiny one-bedroom apartment held only a battered coffee table, an ancient television sitting on an equally battered end table, and a brand-new beige sofa. It took all my self-control to not snap a picture of that sofa to show Mrs. Carrere. She'd surely be pleased to know Heleena had used the money she gave her the way she'd said she would.

The couple had done all they could to brighten the space and make it feel homey. The lack of paint chips or dirty marks on the buttery-yellow walls told me they must have been painted recently and was probably Leena and Lana's doing. Surrounding a vintage poster of a hula dancer on the wall across from the sofa, they'd hung dozens of framed pictures of themselves. In each photo, the couple was smiling with their arms around each other. It broke my heart to think of how devastated Lana had to be.

"Wasn't she beautiful?" Lana stood next to me and gazed at the wall of pictures. Almost as an afterthought, she handed me the glass of water with ice.

"She sure was. It's easy to see how much the two of you cared for each other. How are you doing?"

"Surprisingly well." I was impressed by how strong her voice sounded. Then she added, "Which tells me I'm probably not dealing with reality yet." She gestured to the small, shaded balcony off the living room. "Let's sit outside. It's beautiful today." She laughed. "We live in paradise. It's beautiful every day, right?"

I heard a slightly sarcastic emphasis on the word paradise. That was what everyone thought of Maui. There was no denying its beauty. But it had to be hard to think of the island, or anyplace for that matter, as a paradise when the person you loved had been taken from you so brutally.

We settled into matching white plastic patio chairs with a small white plastic table between them.

"We spent lots of nights out here together," Lana mused. "We were both indoors at the salon all day. Since Leena was inside at the gym most nights, she wanted to be outside whenever possible. If we were home together and weren't relaxing here, we went for walks along the ocean." She gestured south toward the beach that was only two blocks away. "We didn't get to do that often enough. Between our work schedules and her training, we only got time together a night or two a week." She smiled, but this time her voice caught as she said, "Now and then, if we knew we wouldn't see each other until bedtime, we'd get up early and walk along the beach at dawn. I loved doing that."

"That's nice. I love early mornings on the beach too. And I understand the desire to be outside as much as possible. Sometimes I wish the gym were open air. How amazing would that be?"

"Amazing," she agreed, "but impractical considering the number of passing showers we get."

An awkward, momentary silence settled between us. I drank from the glass of water as Lana eyed a blue-and-black piece of clothing in the corner of the balcony.

"That's Leena's suit. We went swimming the night before she died and hung our suits and towels over the railing out here to dry. I brought mine in the next morning, but she was in a hurry and promised to get it later." She laughed. "Leena always turned into a slob the week before a fight, leaving her stuff all over the apartment . . ." She let the comment fade as she gestured at the swimsuit. "The wind blew it off the railing and that's where it landed. Haven't been able to touch it yet."

"Would you like me to pick it up for you?"

Lana shook her head before I'd finished the question. "No, I'll get to it. I'm not ready yet. It's like, if I leave it there, maybe she'll come home and pick it up herself. You know?"

Thoughts of Mom's things lying all over the bathroom sink flashed in my mind. Neither Ashlyn nor I touched any of it, sure she'd be coming back. After two weeks, we pushed it all to one corner. When a month had passed, Ashlyn swept everything into a box. Funny, after six months we donated everything of hers to the Goodwill store except for that box with her toothbrush, comb, and toiletries. She left almost everything behind, which was why we were so sure she'd be back. Guess she really wanted a fresh start.

Ashlyn tossed the box out when we moved to the condo, saying our mother wasn't allowed in there, none of her things either.

"Keep all memories of her to yourself, Peep," she'd demanded. "I don't even want to think about her."

Regarding Heleena's swimsuit, I told Lana, "I understand completely."

"I assume you came here for a reason," she said after another few minutes of silence.

"We were concerned about you. Salomon and I, I mean."

"Thank you. I appreciate that. That's not all, though, is it? Not that I'm not grateful, but a phone call would've eased your concern."

Time for the hard stuff. "You know I was the one to find Heleena's body?"

Lana nodded, the ice in her glass clinking against the side as she took a sip. "Detective Kalani told me that someone from the gym had been at the scene. I didn't know who it was until I got your text this morning. Then I knew right away. You're here playing detective, aren't you?"

"I can't stop thinking about her, Lana. I can't explain why, but it's become a personal mission to find out what happened." I could explain, but Lana didn't want to hear about my complicated feelings. "The people at No Mercy are like family to me. Heleena and I may not have known each other as well as I would've liked, but she was ohana as surely as my sister is my blood relative."

"That's so nice." Lana sat clutching her water glass in both hands. "Leena told me how supportive everyone at the gym was of each other. I have to say, I'm a little envious. I have two stylists that rent chairs in my salon. We chat during the day and know things about each other, but I can't say we're friends. Running that place takes all my time, so days off are for household errands or spending time with Leena. I don't have any hobbies that put me in touch with people. My family lives on the mainland. In Idaho. Other than Leena, I don't have anyone here."

For the first time, Lana showed emotion that was more than numb shock or a quiver in her voice. It seemed anger was the next stage of grief coming for her.

"Your life sounds a lot like mine. If you don't mind me asking, what did you and Detective Kalani discuss?"

"She came to tell me what happened and asked a few questions. She'd already been out to talk with Mr. and Mrs. Carrere and said one of them would be identifying her body." She laughed, a scoffing sound. "He hasn't seen her in five years. Her mother only saw her from a distance at the gym. I know every freckle on her body, but because I'm only the girlfriend, no one of any legal significance, people who were like strangers were called in."

It was a blessing, really. She wouldn't want that to be her final image of Heleena. I sure didn't.

She clenched her jaw and shook away her anger. "Anyway, because it was an 'ongoing investigation,' Detective Kalani couldn't say much. Mostly she wanted to know about Leena's daily life. Where did she go? Who did she see? Who might have wanted to hurt her? Things her parents couldn't answer because they had no clue who their daughter was."

I waited a bit to let her anger settle some before asking, "What did you tell her? I assume she asked about specific people. Anyone you felt might've been a danger to Heleena. There were people who weren't accepting of you two, right?"

Lana looked at me as though I was completely thick. "You mean like her father? Not that I think he did this to her. I don't think he ever gave a moment's thought to his daughter anymore. Definitely a hater, though. There are others too. We tried to steer clear of them."

"She mentioned trouble with people around the salon."

"Small-minded people are everywhere, but yes, there's this middle-aged husband and wife who walk past the shop a few times a week. They talk big and make threats, but they've been doing this for over a year. We're used to them so reply with nothing but a smile and a wave. Then they grumble louder and move on. Other than muttering fire and brimstone crap, they haven't done anything more than slide notes about us burning in Hell under the shop door. More bravado than bravery, a customer said." She shook her head. "They didn't do it. Besides, they're old. She's gimpy, and he doesn't have a firm muscle on his body. Leena would've had his face in the sand in two seconds."

I couldn't quite picture Heleena working over an elderly couple even if they were homophobic, but I understood her point. "You told Detective Kalani about them?"

"I told her. She said she'd stop by and have a chat with them."

"Anyone else in Kihei you can think of?"

Lana gave me an amused look. "You sound like a cop. Maybe you have a future in police work."

I laughed at that. "I don't think so."

"Other than working at the salon," Lana continued, "Leena spent most of her time at the gym. To me, it seems like a safe bet that someone from there did this to her. Callie Castro and Mona Randall are the two obvious ones, aren't they?"

"I'd hate for it to be one of our rats, but I have some suspicions about Callie. She's quick to anger but also quick to calm."

"That's what Leena used to say but thought it was usually Callie getting angry at herself. If she didn't perform well at practice or, God forbid, she screwed up during a fight. That didn't happen often, though."

"No, it didn't. Callie hasn't lost in a long time. You know she's the number one featherweight."

"Oh, I'm aware. Leena grumbled about it weekly. That puts her at the top of the suspect list, don't you think?"

I shrugged. "Sounds like a reasonable assumption, but I honestly don't know."

"Oh, come on, Gemi. As a top-ranked fighter, you must have a gut feeling on whether that possibility is worth pursuing or not."

"Are you asking if I'd ever consider taking out another fighter to keep my rank?"

Lana paused before answering. "Yeah, I guess I am."

Since it was a serious question, I took a second to think of an honest answer rather than an off the cuff *of course not*. "At this point in my life, no, I can't say I'd consider it. A few years ago, when I was so eager for that top spot, I might have. Not murder," I was quick to add, "but taking out a knee or dislocating a shoulder during practice? Maybe."

"Does Callie need money? It's fifteen hundred for first, right?"

"Right. A thousand for second, five hundred for third. And I have no idea what Callie's financial situation is."

"Leena was closing in on first prize. Probably not this fight, but maybe the next. If she'd done well this time, she'd rise in the overall ranks and have a good shot at number one in six months or whenever the next fight is."

"You think Callie may have killed Heleena so she would take her spot?"

Lana shrugged in reply.

"Murdering someone over a few hundred dollars?" I realized how stupid the question was as soon as I'd asked it. Two years ago, when Ash and I regularly got down to change in a coffee cup until payday, that much money would have meant the world to us. "I'm sure there are fighters out there desperate enough to do whatever they have to do. None of the fighters at No Mercy are like that, though."

Lana held my gaze. "You're sure?"

I slumped in the plastic chair. I had been until I started looking into Heleena's death. Now, maybe not. I felt almost foolish and like these people I cared so much about had duped me.

"You don't need to answer," Lana said. "It's written all over you."

"What about fighters from another gym or members who weren't fighters? Did Heleena ever say anything about them?"

"As in something negative?" She studied me again. If I were sitting there naked, I wouldn't have felt more exposed. "You're thinking of someone in particular. Who?"

Johnny Gambino. "I don't want to plant any thoughts in your head."

"She's never said anything about anyone from another gym. Unless she was about to fight one of them." Lana rested her head on the back of the chair as she thought. "A non-fighter member. Who else from the gym was she in contact with? Her coach, Ozzie,

168 | SHAWN MCGUIRE

obviously. Salomon. She really liked him. She said Kenny is a real character." We both chuckled at that. "She'd talk about random people. The selfie people both cracked her up and irritated her." Lana let her head flop to the side to look at me. "She spoke about you a lot. She was so impressed with you, Gemi."

Emotion overtook me for a few seconds. "We talked sometimes. She shared things about her family."

"Because she trusted you. But she also had great respect for you as a fighter. She came home one night raving about your warm-up routine. Something with kettlebells?"

I smiled. "It's a great one for the abs and obliques. And it works your balance too. You put your toes on a weight bench, hold on to the handles of the kettlebells, and get into plank position. From there, you lift the bell straight up or across your body."

"That's the one. She tried to demonstrate it for me here once. We don't have kettlebells, so she used my little five-pound hand weights instead. She got into position, lifted one of the weights, and crashed to the floor."

Lana started laughing at the memory. It grew stronger, her shoulders shaking, and then I realized she was crying not laughing. She covered her face with her hands. I reached over and placed my palm on her back, leaving it there until her sobbing slowed.

"That's the first time I've cried." Lana wiped her eyes on the hem of her shirt. "It hasn't felt real. I guess because they wouldn't let me see her, I have no proof she's dead. All I have are some words from a detective who showed up unannounced at my door without a shred of physical evidence. You know?"

I nodded. "I'm so sorry, Lana. This is why I'm here. I don't know if it helps you or not, but I know it was Leena." I touched my hair. "Mermaid."

The word set off Lana's tears again. "She was so excited about that hair color. We talked about it with the other stylists at the salon for a week. Planning which colors and in which order. Follow the rainbow or go random?"

This reminded me again of how little Heleena and I knew about each other. I wanted to gather all the rats together and have everybody talk for five minutes about themselves. What did they do when they weren't at the gym? It didn't matter if all they did was go home, drop onto the couch, and watch television all night long, I suddenly needed to know more about the people I claimed to care so much about. Did they ever consider mermaid hair? What color were their walls? Did they have a pet? How long had they lived on Maui? What was their day job? For God's sake, I didn't even know what my ohana members did for a living.

"Leena was really good at dyeing hair." Lana touched her own silver-gray locks, so stark against her dark skin, as a silent tear ran down her cheek. "I'm going to have to find a new stylist."

In my back pocket, my cell phone buzzed with a text. I didn't look, but it reminded me that I'd been here for a while. Lana had said she needed to be back to the salon by three o'clock. After such an emotional discussion, she'd likely need a little time to pull herself together before her next client. Time to move things along.

"Did Heleena ever talk about a guy named Johnny?"

Lana burst out with a laugh that surprised me. Then, in a strong New York accent, she said, "Gambino the Mobster. Oh, yes. She talked about Johnny a lot."

"What did she say about him?"

"That he was a nice but super stubborn guy who refused to take no for an answer. Johnny had a big crush on my girlfriend. Leena said he asked her out at least twice a week. She told him no every time, that she couldn't go out with him because she had a girlfriend. He didn't seem to understand why that meant they couldn't have dinner together. Leena decided it might be that he thought she meant a girl who was a friend. Finally, just last week, I believe, she told him she was in a 'serious romantic relationship' so she couldn't go out with him."

"Last week?" That was recent. Had that explanation and rejection been enough to push Johnny over the edge? "Did he ever come here? Or to the salon?"

"Here? I don't think— Wait. You think Johnny did this." Lana shook her head emphatically. "Leena never, not once, expressed any feeling of being unsafe around him. What makes you think he might have done it?"

I told her about the broom.

"That's upsetting," Lana agreed, "but I don't think it's related. He'd been asking her out and getting rejected for almost two years. Why would he finally explode about it now?"

"I don't know."

She went quiet for a minute, thinking. "You seem focused on the killer"—she stumbled over the word—"being someone from the gym. Or another gym. Why is that?"

I was about to break my promise to Detective Kalani, but Lana had the right to know. She had loved this woman, after all. I blew out a breath, psyching myself up to say the words.

"Maybe not someone from No Mercy, but yes, a fighter or a bodybuilder. Someone strong."

"Why?"

Another breath. "Did Detective Kalani say anything about how Heleena died?"

"No, and I asked a couple times." Lana paled. "You saw her body. Gemi, what happened to my Leena?"

As gently as I could, I explained that Heleena had been beaten and left on the beach. I left out the part about what the mynah birds and sand crabs had done to her.

"I know they're going to do an autopsy," I said. "I don't know exactly—"

"You're holding back. Don't do that. Something terrible happened to the love of my life. The least I can do for her memory is know what she went through."

How to say this? I didn't want to be gory about it. "The only way I knew for sure it was Heleena was by her mermaid hair and running shoes."

She shook her head, still not understanding.

"Her face was so swollen I couldn't recognize her." I remained silent for a minute while fresh tears streamed down Lana's face. "I'm so sorry."

Lana sucked in breaths like she was trying to control her anger. "Thank you for your honesty. This person being a fighter makes sense."

"It seems like a safe assumption."

She pushed her shoulders back. "There was one person at the gym she mentioned who didn't seem okay with us. A guy, muscular but more lean than bulky. Short hair. Around six feet tall."

"Ross Donnelly?"

"That sounds right."

"Asked her to go out with him 'just once'?"

Through a clenched jaw, she hissed, "Bastard."

I told her what he'd said earlier at The Juice Bar.

"So he used my girlfriend in one of the most disgusting ways I can think of in an attempt to make you jealous?"

"Right."

"That makes him repulsive and slimy on multiple levels."

Put that way, maybe I should reconsider being his friend. And maybe I shouldn't have believed his claim of that not being what he meant. Once again, I felt very naïve.

"He's clueless and self-centered," I offered "but I don't think he did it."

Lana grumbled something I couldn't make out and probably didn't want to.

Speaking of The Juice Bar, the tattooed woman came to mind. "I've got one other thing I wanted to ask you. Are you familiar with an organization called the yakuza?"

"Of course. Everyone knows about them." She paused. "Except you apparently."

"I don't watch a lot of news. It's depressing. Anyway, I heard that the group killed a man a few days ago."

Lana nodded and shifted positions. "I heard about the beheading."

Tattoo lady's buff arms could probably wield a sword too. "I guess they offer loans and *protection* to businesses."

"That's what I understand."

"There's no judgment behind this question, I swear. Did either you or Heleena go to them for help? I know the salon is struggling."

She glanced out at the ocean. "We are struggling. Leena and I talked about shutting down and renting chairs at another salon. To answer your question, no, we didn't go to the mob for help."

"I couldn't imagine you did, but I understand yakuza violence has been increasing lately . . ."

"And you're considering multiple options. I understand."

"I saw this woman today." I ran my hand up my arm and across my chest. "Tattoos everywhere. Long black hair, pretty face, intense eyes."

Lana waited for more, then asked, "What about her?"

I thought of the way Tattoo's stare practically bore into the back of my head. "The way she was staring at me, I felt like she was there to intimidate me."

"Why?"

"Maybe because I found Heleena."

Lana shook her head. "If whoever did this wanted to keep Leena's death quiet, they wouldn't have left her body on a public beach."

"That's what I thought too." So what was all that staring about? "Like you said, I'm considering multiple options."

She set her glass on the table. "I'm grateful for your help, Gemi. I know it would mean the world to Leena to know you were involved this way."

Not knowing how to respond, I nodded. "I know this just happened, but are you going to be okay? Moving forward, I mean, or do you need help?"

"I've got a lot of thinking to do. The rent is paid for this month, and I'll have enough for next month. After that, I'm in trouble. It took both of our paychecks to live here. And as you can tell by our minimalist decorating style, there isn't much left for anything else after paying for rent and necessities."

I remembered living that way. It sucked. And if it weren't for Ashlyn, I'd be in the same situation.

"We're having a small gathering in Heleena's honor after the fights tomorrow. Do you think you can come? I understand if it'll be too hard."

Lana took a moment before answering. "I think Leena would like for me to be there. Same place as always, right?"

"Right. We're kind of a superstitious group. If they ever held the fights someplace else, it would throw us all completely off our game."

"I hear you on that one. Leena was so routine about her preparations the night before a fight, I worried she suffered from a disorder of some kind."

I laughed at that. "If it eases your mind at all, I'm the same way. Once I'm done strategizing with Salomon tonight, I'll go home and perform the same ritual I follow every time."

Lana smiled as tears threatened again. "I don't know about easing my mind, but I like knowing she had a tribe."

She walked me to the door and said goodbye, promising again to come tomorrow night.

As I stepped out of the apartment building, my phone vibrated. Probably the same person from earlier. I pulled it out of my pocket and found two messages from two different numbers. The first was a voicemail from Detective Kalani, the second a text from a blocked number. Figuring it was spam, I opened the text first, and prepared to delete it right away. My blood ran cold as I stared at the message.

Stay out of things that don't involve you!

CHAPTER TWENTY

The timing of the text arriving just as I left Lana's place could have been coincidental, but I didn't think so. Feeling like I was being watched, I rushed to the Jeep, hopped in, and scanned my surroundings, looking for someone suspicious. But what would that mean? Someone blatantly staring at me the way Tattoo had earlier? Someone lurking behind a palm tree? Another member of the yakuza?

It could have been a wrong number, the little girl suggested.

True. That did happen. Some guy hits a wrong digit in his girlfriend's phone number and suddenly I'm looking at a picture of a visually unappealing body part.

I didn't think that was it, though. The killer sent it. But how did they know I'd been talking to people?

"Calm down and figure this out. Who knows?"

Risa, Ashlyn, Salomon, Ross, Lana. Detective Kalani.

The Carreres. Could the text have come from one of them? Neither Kalani nor Lana felt Mr. Carrere was involved with Leena's death, and they were probably right. But he could be trying to keep things quiet. He would want as little attention paid to Heleena's death as possible. Don't dig into it. Let the truth wash out to sea. Because too much attention could lead back to him and what he'd done to his daughter.

More angry than scared now, I opened the voicemail.

"Hi, Ms. Kittredge, this is Detective Kalani. I have a few questions regarding Heleena Carrere's murder when you have a few minutes. Please call me back at this number."

I tapped the little telephone icon, and Kalani answered on the second ring.

"Thank you for calling me back. I'd prefer to talk to you in person. It shouldn't take long. Can I meet you somewhere?"

The clock on the Jeep's dashboard read 2:50. It would take me twenty minutes to get back to Kahului. I'd told Risa I'd meet her at the harbor around 3:20, but if this had to do with Heleena's killer, that was more important than R&R.

"Sure. I'm just heading back to town. I should be there by ten after, give or take." If we met at the condo, I could dump my backpack and take the Indian. I was starting to feel claustrophobic inside the Jeep today. "Could you meet me at my condo?"

"Perfect," the detective said after I gave her the address. "This gives me a minute to stop at a food truck. I haven't had lunch yet. Can I bring you anything?"

That was awfully chummy of her. Why? Was she buttering me up for something?

Or was I getting paranoid? A much more likely option.

"Thanks, but I'm good." Besides, talking while eating would only slow us down. I really wanted to get to the harbor.

"All right. See you in a bit."

Before I could pull away, my phone buzzed again.

Half an hour until yacht time. Are you ready?

There were about twenty sun, swimsuit, and boat emojis tacked onto the end of Risa's question.

I'm ready. But I have to meet your detective friend at my condo first. I'll need a little more time.

A few seconds later: *Malia? What does she want?*

If I knew that, I would've already told her what she wanted to know. I'll get there as close to four as possible.

Thoughts swirled like palm fronds in a windstorm as I drove. What could the detective want to talk to me about? Hopefully, she had a lead on Heleena's killer. If she'd wrapped things up that quickly, Detective Malia Kalani might change my attitude about cops.

But why did she want to meet in person? If she'd solved the case, a phone call would be plenty. Would she even tell me? No, I'd find out on the evening news like everyone else.

Was I a suspect? I'd found the body after all. If she thought I was guilty, wouldn't she have hauled me into the station by now? Or was that what she was about to do?

Stop it, the little girl scolded. *You're being stupid again. You didn't do anything wrong.*

"Yeah, well, plenty of innocent people go to prison every year."

The detective hadn't arrived yet by the time I got there. That gave me time to change into my swimsuit and big T-shirt cover-up, grab a coconut water, and check on Hulu. He seemed happy for the company.

As I was scratching his head, which always made his eyes roll back, the doorbell rang. His eyeballs rotated back into place. "I'll get it."

"Silly bird." I set him on my left shoulder and went to the door.

"There's something you don't see every day," the detective said.

"This is Hulu. Hulu, can you say hi?"

The parrot looked at me as though to say, of course I can. He flapped his wings and squawked, "Hey, girl."

Detective Kalani chuckled. "Cute."

"Come on in." I led her to the living room and then echoing Lana's hospitality asked, "Can I get you something to drink? Water? Juice?"

"No, thank you." Detective Kalani gazed around the condo. "Nice place."

"Thanks."

She noticed my outfit next. "Going to the beach?"

"I'm actually late meeting Risa for a yacht ride."

"Sorry. This shouldn't take long."

I took a chair and gestured at the couch. As she sat, Hulu perched on the far end from her.

"I have some questions about MMA fighting." She eyed the bird and then flipped a few pages in her notebook. "You told me it was like 'boxing and wrestling and various martial arts all mixed together.' How long have you been involved with the sport?"

"I started MMA about a year and a half after we moved here. So almost fourteen years."

"You're considered an expert on the sport, then."

No one had ever asked that before. "I would say so, yes."

"I understand you've got a pretty good record."

"I'm doing well. Fourteen-and-two over my career. I'm hoping wins go to fifteen tomorrow night."

She nodded, eyes on her notebook. "The initial autopsy report showed that Heleena Carrere suffered massive head trauma, which was obvious. They also found that her airways, both nasal and tracheal, were so swollen it's possible she suffocated. They're still working on the final cause, but when so much trauma happens within the span of minutes, it can be hard to know which came first." She glanced up from her phone at me. "I'm sorry if this is upsetting. You look a little pale."

I shook my head, letting my medical brain handle this part of the conversation. "I'm a nursing student. The only thing upsetting to me is that someone did this to my friend. Feel free to speak clinically."

Detective Kalani gave a single nod. "Good. There were bruises around her throat that the examiner identified as coming from knuckles."

She curled her hand with her fingertips tucked down, forming the proximal interphalangeal joints, the middle knuckles, into a sort of weapon to jab with.

"You're saying," I clarified, "there were small, round bruises on Heleena's throat."

"Correct. All along here." She ran a finger from the center of her chin straight down her throat.

"The impact of a sharp blow to the trachea can do a great deal of damage." I felt like she already knew this. Why was she asking me?

Her brow arched as she wrote in her notebook. Hulu waddled closer, watched the ink appear on the page, and then grabbed her pen. Kalani snatched it back, and Hulu laughed at her. I transferred him to the back of my chair.

"Stay there or you're going in your cage," I warned.

"Based on the autopsy," Kalani began, scowling at the bird, "it appears the killer beat the victim to death with his or her fists. In your opinion, could a fighter do that kind of damage using just their fists?"

She suspected one of the gym rats. My heart felt like a twenty-pound weight in my chest.

"A fighter, a stranger on the street, a significant other. Given the right motivation and adrenaline level, anyone could beat someone to death."

The detective frowned. "Sad but true, unfortunately. MMA fighters typically wear gloves, don't they?"

"There are some fighters who like to work out with minimal protection. They feel punching a heavy bag without gloves toughens the skin by forming calluses over their knuckles. It can also help strengthen their wrists."

"*Some* fighters think that. What do you think?"

"I think that once past the 'new fighter' threshold, hand wraps can be enough. Personally, I feel that my hands are too important. I like to keep them protected even from scrapes and scratches, which can be distracting. Besides, wraps and gloves are required for the fights, so I wear them while training. That way they're invisible to me during the fight."

"If the attacker didn't wear gloves, what do you expect would have happened to their fists?"

My mind immediately started scanning the gym for a rat with

bruised or broken knuckles. Hard to spot if they wore wraps or gloves.

"If someone hit Heleena with bare fists hard enough to cause the kind of damage you described and I saw, their hands would be bruised and swollen at minimum. The skin on their knuckles might be split open from the repeated impact. He or she could have broken fingers. Possibly sprained or broken wrists. That's why wraps and gloves are required for the sport. They help protect both the opponent and the fighter."

"Heleena was the number two fighter in the featherweight class."

"In our gym, yes. She was number three overall."

"Overall meaning on the island?"

"Right."

"What can you tell me about the others in her class?"

I relaxed a little, grateful to be talking about something other than the effects of a beating on the human body. "I know the names of a few fighters at the other gyms, but I don't know them personally so can't speak to what kind of people they are."

She gave a crisp nod. "Understood."

"We already talked about Callie Castro. She's number one overall in Heleena's weight class. Has been for a few years. Mona Randall has been in the number three spot at our gym for more than a year."

"Where does Ms. Randall rank on Maui?"

"Fifth . . . no, fourth. Heleena was third overall. A fighter from another gym is number two."

"Was there a rivalry between them?"

"Sure, but I told you before, we get nothing but big egos and bragging rights for our ranks. And a small purse."

"Big egos," the detective echoed. "Big enough to lead to a beating on a secluded beach?"

"Heleena and Mona had a great relationship. They trained and practiced together. They even used the same coach, as did Callie.

They were each determined to be the one to bring Callie down. But that's true for everyone in their class. It's fun to knock the top rank off their pedestal."

"A great relationship, hey? How nice."

She was being sarcastic again. And I was being naïve. It wasn't realistic to believe there were no conflicts between the three. I thought things were great between Stacia, Aonani, and me. Then Aonani showed her true colors.

Seemingly out of nowhere, she asked, "What about their coach? Any reason you can think of that he might have done this?"

"Ozzie?" I burst out laughing. Hulu copied me, which made Kalani smile. "He's the most laidback dude I've ever met. We joke with him constantly about how we can't understand how he can train people to hit each other. One day he spent ten minutes capturing a fly that was buzzing around by the front desk bothering people and then released it outside. He literally wouldn't hurt a fly."

She made a note in her book. "What might it mean for him if Callie were to drop from the top rank?"

"I'm not sure," I replied. "Obviously, the more a fighter wins, the more people want to work with that person's coach. Ozzie works with Mona, too, and was also Leena's coach. I never saw that he had a favorite of the three. He was thrilled for Callie's success, but he was just as excited to see Heleena doing so well."

"Mona Randall runs a fishing boat, correct?"

"Right. Docks it at Lahaina Harbor."

"And Callie? Has your opinion changed at all?"

"You mean do I think she would hurt Heleena?" I winced and admitted, "Maybe. What's bothering me is I can't figure out why. Callie's pretty secure in that top spot. If she wanted to off her competition, why wouldn't she go for the number two overall fighter?"

"The person from another gym." She seemed to agree with that. "I spoke with Lana Madison. She said Heleena had been pushing hard lately."

"To improve?" I clarified and Kalani nodded. "Well, sure. We all strive to get better. With each fight, we learn things from other fighters and then try them during practice."

The detective stared at me, waiting for me to say more. Instead, I changed to a different topic. "Speaking of Lana, that's where I was when you called earlier."

Kalani dropped her head back and rotated it side to side. "Delivering flowers, I hope. I believe I told you to stay out of this investigation."

And yet, here she was involving me in it. "I wanted to ask if she knew of anyone who might have done this to Heleena."

She let out a long, slow sigh. "You didn't think I'd ask that question?"

"Detective Kalani, I care a lot about the members at our gym. I'm not doing anything that will interfere with your investigation."

"You have no idea what might interfere." Her eyes blazed.

Fair point. "As for Lana, I specifically went to ask her about Johnny Gambino." And the yakuza, but I wasn't about to open that topic.

"The guy who broke the broom? What did she tell you?"

"She said Heleena was irritated by him because he wouldn't back off, but it didn't seem she felt threatened by him. She also said Leena had mentioned Callie's temper, but felt it was directed more at herself than other fighters."

"It's worth taking a closer look at Callie, then," she mumbled more to herself than me.

"I guess so, but like I said, I can't come up with a solid reason for why she would have done this."

"Well, Ms. Kittredge, that's where I come in. I gather the facts and then figure out the connection between the suspects and the victim." Detective Kalani reviewed her notes and then shoved her pad and pen in her back pocket. "I think we're done. Thank you. This information about gloves and wraps could be helpful."

I stood, put Hulu on my shoulder again, and walked her to the door. "Have you narrowed down your suspect list yet?"

"I can't discuss those details with you."

She extended a hand to me for a goodbye handshake and glanced at my knuckles. I didn't flinch. Instead, I held both hands up for inspection. Hulu held out a foot.

"See? Wasn't me."

"I didn't think it was." She gave me a soft smile. "I know you're capable of defending yourself, but so was Ms. Carrere." At that, I did flinch. "Please, for your own safety, stay out of this, and let me and my team do our jobs. Okay?"

"Not sure I can stop asking questions."

"Maybe not, but you can keep yourself from purposely tracking people down to ask those questions."

Before she could open the door, I blurted, "I understand there's an uptick in yakuza activity on the island." Like I was an expert on the topic.

She paused, eying me closely. "Do you feel these two things might be related?"

"I don't know."

"Did Lana Madison suggest this possibility to you?"

I opened the topic, now I had to follow through. "Actually, that was the other reason I went down there. I don't know much about this group. Risa told me about them."

By the way Kalani's jaw tensed, I guessed she knew about Risa's eavesdropping habit.

"Heleena told me once that their salon was struggling. The banks wouldn't give them a loan, and they had no family or friends that could help. I asked Lana if they got a loan from the yakuza. She said no, but . . ."

"I'll make a note in the file," Kalani said after a short pause. "You're probably off on that one, but when seemingly solid leads result in nothing, we sometimes need to expand our scope. Good luck tomorrow night. I should check out a fight sometime. I've never been to one."

"It gets intense."

"I'm sure it does."

I opened the front door to find Risa sitting on the step.

"What are you doing here?" Detective Kalani asked.

"Eavesdropping."

Risa's expression remained steady. Kalani and I looked at each other, both seeming to wonder, *Is she? Wouldn't be a surprise.* Risa broke into a smile. "Joking. I want to get out on that yacht before the sun goes down."

"Let me put Hulu away and we can go," I agreed. "I've got to meet with Salomon later."

Kalani turned to leave but paused by Risa. "Staying out of trouble?"

She shrugged. "For now."

The detective shook her head and walked away, giving an over-the-shoulder wave as she did.

"What did she want?" Risa asked the second Kalani got into her unmarked car.

"She had a few questions. Let's get to that boat. We can talk about it more there."

As Kalani drove off, I remembered I'd wanted to mention that *stay out of things* text to her. No big deal. Her focus should be on Heleena anyway, not me.

CHAPTER TWENTY-ONE

I didn't know much about boats other than that they floated on water, varied in size, and were generally fun to be on. So when Risa referred to this boat as a yacht, I envisioned everything from a vessel the approximate size of a school bus to a small cruise ship. We ended up with an eighty-foot-long catamaran. At forty feet wide, the boat offered plenty of deck space where people could lounge about and soak in vitamin D. There was also a covered area below the deck with couches, tables, and chairs. Currently, nearly three dozen of the birthday boy's friends, family, and coworkers packed the space.

"Isn't this the life?" Risa waved at people on shore as we pulled away from the dock.

"I can't imagine living this way," I admitted, "but it's fun to play in this world for a while."

She made a face at me. "You need to dream bigger, my friend. We never know what we'll get if we ask for it."

We found a clear spot big enough to spread out our towels, slathered on a Salomon-approved amount of sunscreen, and lay down to enjoy the gentle rocking of the waves. Soft slack-key guitar music played in the background. For the next two hours, held captive on this boat, I'd let myself live the dream.

Risa sighed contently. "We haven't done anything like this in ages."

"Not since before you graduated last year," I agreed. "Life has gotten busy."

"True, but our restrictions are kind of self-imposed, don't you think?"

"What do you mean?"

"Neither of us has a boyfriend. We don't have kids. We live in condos that other people maintain for us. Well, the yardwork, not the cleaning."

I lowered my sunglasses to peek at her. "We have a cleaning lady."

She slapped her hand down on the deck in mock indignation. At least, I think it was mock. "When did that happen?"

I thought back to the Hawaiian woman's first visit to our condo. She stayed twice as long as planned and charged us triple, but it was worth it. Cleaning wasn't either my or Ashlyn's strong suit.

"About nine months ago, I guess. Ashlyn started traveling more and more. My schedule was getting busier too. She decided to pamper us with a fabulous woman named Anela who comes once a week to clean the bathrooms, dust, and mop the floors." I thought of the woman in her mid-forties with the round face and huge smile. "Her name means angel. She really is one."

"You're so spoiled."

"Hey, I didn't ask for her. I can scrub my own toilet." I adjusted my sunglasses. "Not a fan of dusting, though."

"The point I was trying to make was that if we wanted to start dating, we'd find the time. If we wanted to have kids, we'd figure out how to fit them into our lives. If we were married and wanted to have an affair, we'd find ways to sneak away."

"Risa!"

"Am I wrong?"

I swear, her mouth had no filter. And no, she wasn't wrong. "You're saying we need to get together for more than just dinner now and then?"

"Exactly."

Take a scalpel to your schedule and let me know, Professor Sato had said yesterday. Professor Hastings wanted me to do the internship. Now Risa wanted more of me. How finely could I dice myself with that scalpel?

"You're right. We need to make girls' nights or afternoons a priority. Not that I want to put all the responsibility on you, but your schedule changes. Mine is set." Stagnant. Stale. Repetitive. "You tell me when you'll have days off, and I'll adjust so we can do something together."

Besides, Risa liked being in charge.

"Deal. I'm going to hold you to this."

Smiling, I let myself relax until I felt like I was sinking into the deck. I dozed off for what seemed like a few minutes, but was apparently closer to half an hour, and woke to Risa poking my shoulder.

"Roll over. You're going to be all brown on front and pale on your back."

I folded my cover-up into a pillow and flipped onto my stomach as directed.

"What did Malia want?" At my confused, half-asleep expression, Risa clarified. "Detective Kalani? Why did she come to your place?"

"Oh, she had questions about how MMA works. She was interested in our gloves in particular." I paused as nausea that had nothing to do with the rocking boat hit me. "It seems that whoever killed Heleena did it with their bare fists. Which I could have told her the second I saw Leena's face."

And of course, saying the words signaled my brain to present me with the image.

"Now you're going to look for someone at the gym with bruised knuckles?" Risa asked.

I closed my eyes as the sun warmed my back. "You'd make a good detective."

"Does Malia have any leads?"

"I don't know what she's got. She can't talk about it. I have some ideas, though."

"About suspects? How many are on your list?"

Callie, Johnny, Mr. Carrere, a hater, another fighter, the yakuza. "I don't know, six or eight, I guess."

"You really can't leave this alone, can you?"

"Could you?"

She propped herself up on her elbows. "This is a perfect segue to something I've wanted to ask. Why are you so obsessed with this?"

"I'm not obsessed."

"You run your life on a schedule planned down to the minute sometimes. Within an hour or two, you went from finding a body on the beach to hunting down the killer. Makawao yesterday. Kihei today. Both required you to rearrange your days. You don't rearrange."

"I would for you." I glanced over my sunglasses and batted my eyelashes at her. "In fact, I did. Look where we are."

"Very sweet. Quit avoiding the topic."

I slid my glasses back into place. "A woman died, Risa. Isn't that reason enough?"

She sat up and faced me. "No disrespect to Heleena intended, but bad stuff must have happened to other gym members at some point, and you didn't get like this. You and Salomon are close, so I could see you dropping things for him. Maybe Stacia because you spend a lot of time together. Why Heleena?"

Risa was mothering me again. I had a mother before. It wasn't great. She sometimes forgot that I wasn't one of her younger siblings. I was almost thirty, six years older than her, and didn't need help running my life.

"This wasn't just *a* body on the beach, Risa. It was Heleena. And it wasn't 'bad stuff.' She *died*. No one from the gym has died before. Heleena and I might not have been besties, but we were friends. We worked out together and talked a lot about personal things that I wasn't at liberty to tell you about. And her little sister, Halle, is one of my students. That poor kid is putting on a brave face, but she has to be going through hell."

Risa didn't reply, which was the same as pushing me hard to say more.

"What if the killer is one of our gym members? I mean, what if the monster capable of doing that to another person is right there with us every day?"

What if there's a killer in your safe place? the little girl clarified. A cold shiver snaked up my back. What if?

"I agree," Risa said with little empathy, "that's concerning. But how did it become your job to hunt them down? Malia is working on that. If you want to help Halle or Heleena's parents, why don't you simply offer a caring shoulder or ask what you can do for them?"

I turned away and watched a sailboat in the distance. "Didn't you ask me to come on this boat to relax?"

"Partly. Mostly I asked you to come so I didn't have to make small talk with my coworkers. But since I've got you captive here, I think we should identify what's really bothering you."

"You should consider transferring to the psych department. Your talents aren't being fully utilized in the ED."

"You're the one studying to be a psych nurse. Which means you should know this. Come on, talk it out."

Do it or you'll never get to relax. The little girl sounded as irritated as I felt.

I rolled to my side and rested my head on my hand. "For as much as I thought I knew Heleena, I'm seeing now that I didn't know her at all. I'm feeling guilty that I listened and asked questions when she talked but never followed up."

"That's good," Risa praised. "But it's an answer you'd give someone interviewing you for an article. It's not the answer you give to someone who knows you better than you know yourself."

She intended for that to be comforting. Both for me and her motherly side. To have someone that far in my head, though, made me feel violated.

"Dig deeper," she pushed. "What was the first thing you thought when you realized it was Heleena on the beach?"

I sighed hard. The little girl was right, no sense fighting this. So I envisioned standing guard by Heleena's corpse while waiting for the cops Wednesday morning.

"My first thought was about Halle. She idolized Heleena. All I could think when I realized it was Leena lying there was that Halle would be devastated. I mean, her parents are scum. Well, her dad is scum. Her mom is clueless. Halle already lost five years with her big sister because they kicked her out." I blinked and waited for my emotions to settle. "It's just not fair, you know? Halle's got no one now."

"You don't know that." Her voice softened. "I agree, her parents were pretty awful to Heleena, but that doesn't mean they're awful to Halle too."

True. "I hope you're right."

"So," Risa flipped onto her back, "you find Heleena on the beach and claim the first thing you think of was Halle."

"I'm not claiming it. That's what happened."

Wasn't it?

"Go back there." Risa tapped my head. "Walk me through the timeline."

"Fine." I closed my eyes behind my sunglasses. "I was running along the beach, like I do multiple times per week, and saw feet sticking out of the heliotropes. When I got closer, I realized the woman was dead, pulled out my phone, and called 911."

"Did you already know it was Heleena?" Risa's voice had taken on a soothing, hypnotic quality.

"No. The dispatcher had contacted the police and was still on the line with me when I recognized the mermaid dye job."

"And then you called me?"

"Not yet. The dispatcher said the cops were on the way and asked if I felt safe staying there with the body."

"Did you?"

I stared past her at the blue ocean water and visualized the scene. The 911 call connected. The dispatcher was typing, letting the nearest squad know to go to the scene.

"Right after he asked if I was okay staying with the body, I realized it was Leena. I didn't want to be there but couldn't leave her alone. I figured I'd be able to defend myself if the attacker returned so told the dispatcher I'd be fine. Then he asked if I wanted him to stay on the line."

"And you said yes. Because you were scared."

"Sure I was scared." My throat tightened as though trying to prevent the words from leaving my mouth. I pushed my shoulders back to get a deeper breath and forced them out. "I got into martial arts and MMA to learn self-defense. It's empowering to know you're skilled enough to defend yourself in any situation. But Heleena knew everything I did and look—" My voice cut out on me.

"And look at what happened to her," Risa supplied softly.

"Right," I croaked.

"What else? This was upsetting, I understand that, but it's still not justification for obsessing this way over the killer." When I didn't reply after half a minute, Risa pushed, "You're standing on the beach, looking at the unidentifiable face of a woman you know. What else were you thinking?"

Letting myself stay in the scene, I looked down at Leena and murmured, "I was thinking that it could have been me. I started martial arts sixteen years ago after I was attacked in that parking lot. After earning my black belt, I took it to another level by taking MMA classes. I've dedicated a huge portion of my life to learning how to make sure no one ever lays an unwelcome finger on me again. Same training Heleena had." I took a deep breath and blew it out sharply. "Then, when we were sitting on the beach, you made that comment about the killer being someone from the gym. If that's true, it means the bad guy has infiltrated my safe place."

The question one of my warriors had asked echoed in my head. *This stuff doesn't really work, then, does it?*

Risa's brows rose. "You're really feeling vulnerable, aren't you?"

I nodded. That was too hard to admit out loud.

"And you're trying to take back control by hunting down the

killer and bringing them to justice."

I considered that. "I guess so."

"That's deep."

"It is." Risa was right. I needed to understand this. Since I was getting analyzed, I might as well put it all out there. "That's not as deep as this goes, though."

"No?" Risa stretched her legs out in front of her. "What else?"

"I'm wondering if this is all just smoke and mirrors. I mean, along with this being a sport that we enjoy, some of us train and fight so we can protect ourselves and others. What happened to Heleena is the exact kind of situation I teach my students to be prepared for."

"You're wondering if you're really helping."

"Right. Am I? Or am I just providing a false sense of security?"

"Of course you're helping. You've given dozens of women and children the confidence and skills they need to feel and be safe. That's no small thing."

"But will it really help when they need it? Heleena had tons of confidence and skill. I do, too, but while standing on the beach looking at her beaten body, I was terrified. I needed a stranger's voice on the other end of the telephone to make me feel safe enough to stay there." I inhaled sharply and then blew the breath out hard. "I'm going to be thirty years old next week. If everything I've dedicated myself to for the last sixteen years ultimately means nothing, I've wasted my life."

Risa gave me a soft smile. "I don't think that's the case. You're traumatized right now, which is understandable. You experienced something pretty awful."

I didn't respond. I had no more words.

"You're a fighter," Risa continued. "Literally, figuratively, and morally. You'll bounce back from this and find a way to use it for a greater good. You're trying to plow through this trauma like you do everything else. Give yourself time. It's only been two days."

I sat with that for a minute. Maybe she knew me better than I gave her credit for. I needed to follow the advice I gave women who came to me and be gentle with myself.

My voice quivered as I said, "I wish I knew what happened to her. Did her training fail her, or was she in an unwinnable situation?"

"Hopefully, Malia will figure that out for you."

We sat in silence for a few minutes, soaking in the sunshine and listening to the people laughing and talking around us.

"I've got to admit," I offered, "it feels good to get all of this out in the open. I'm less mentally cluttered now. Thanks for the therapy."

Graciously, she replied, "Anytime."

Out of nowhere, a shadow fell over us, and we turned to see a man and woman dressed in tan shorts, white polo shirts, and deck shoes.

"Sorry to interrupt." The woman gestured to the large metal tub they'd set on the deck. "Would you like a drink? We've got Mai Tais, Piña Coladas, Lava Flows, Margaritas, and Blue Hawaiis."

Risa sat up. "Lava Flow for me, please."

I flipped over and sat up too. "Have you got water in there?"

"Water?" the woman asked. "That's all?"

"I've got a title fight tomorrow, and alcohol will dehydrate me."

"Can't let that happen." Risa reached for the clear plastic cup with the red and white pre-mixed beverage the woman held out to her. "Give me a Piña Colada too. I'll drink it for her."

"What's your sport?" the man asked.

"MMA. I train at No Mercy."

He tilted his head. "You look familiar. What's your name?"

"Gemi Kittredge."

"I've heard of you. Bantamweight, right? You've got a perfect record." He shoved his hand through the ice to the bottom of the tub and pulled out two bottles of water. "We've got plenty more. There's also a table of food in the salon below deck. Help yourself or give a shout if I can get anything for you."

The pair moved on to the next guests.

"If he wasn't working," Risa began, "he totally would've asked you out."

"Not interested." I grinned and then chugged half of one bottle of water.

"Excuse me." A forty-something woman in a soft-pink tank suit knelt in front of us, looking at Risa. "I've seen you around the hospital. Which department are you in?"

"I'm a nurse in Emergency." She held her hand out. "Risa Ohno."

"Allie Thomas, neurologist. Nice to meet you." She released Risa's hand and turned to me. "I couldn't help overhearing what you just said. About fighting MMA."

"Are you a fan?" I asked.

Allie shook her head crisply. "Have you heard of CTE?"

"Sounds vaguely familiar. What is it?"

"Allie," a woman standing a few feet behind her interrupted. "This is a party. It's not the time."

She swatted at her. "It stands for Chronic Traumatic Encephalopathy. It's a brain condition that occurs after repeated blows to the head."

I shifted positions on my towel, turning slightly away from Allie. If I got a dollar every time someone asked me why I *let* myself get punched in the head, I'd have a year of tuition paid for.

"The condition is common in football, hockey, and soccer players. Also in boxers and MMA fighters. They used to call it being 'punch drunk.'" Noting my discomfort, she held her hands up in surrender. "I'm not trying to lecture you, but you know how once you know something you can't ignore it?"

Risa nodded. I gave a half shrug, half nod

"I chose neurology because my dad played football in college and professionally. After years on the field and numerous concussions, he started having trouble remembering things. Then his personality started to change, and he went from being fairly mild-mannered to having fits of rage where he'd yell at my mother and break things. I've devoted my career to the study of brain injuries. Now that I understand the disease, I feel it's my responsibility to inform those who need to know." She paused and gave a small, sad smile. "I'll go now. All I ask is that you be careful. The brain is so fragile. Once it's damaged, it can't be repaired." To Risa, she added, "See you around the hospital."

The woman standing behind her held a hand up in apology and led Allie to a different spot on the boat.

"She's right, you know," Risa said a minute later. "You need to think about that."

"I know." I finished my first bottle of water and reached for the second. "That's why I keep my head protected and let them punch me in the stomach. I'm proud of the fact that I've never had a concussion."

Risa blinked at me, unamused. "What's your signature kill shot?"

I swung my right hand toward Risa's head and made a *pop* sound. "Right cross to the left temple."

"You knock your opponents out." She slapped the deck hard, making those nearby jump and look. "Bam! Down they go. Out for the count. You claim to care for these people because of this bond you all have but are okay with possibly giving them brain damage?" She paused before adding, "You're a nursing student. It's a little hypocritical."

A squirmy feeling filled my gut. "You make me sound like a serial killer."

Risa echoed Allie's words. "Once you know about something, you can't ignore it."

"You think I should quit? Walk away from the thing I'm best at?"

"I know you love this sport, but you just told me why you initially got into it. To learn to protect yourself. You train your students to protect themselves with no expectation that they'll fight

MMA. All I'm saying is, if you're suddenly questioning the last sixteen years, maybe you need to shift your focus for the next sixteen. Does giving someone permanent brain damage fit with your mission? And as for MMA being what you're best at? I call BS on that."

I scowled at her, feeling like a naughty little girl who just got chewed out. "Been holding on to that speech for a while, have you?"

Risa shook her head. "Not that long. It's one thing to learn about stuff in the classroom and another to see it up close and personal. I've worked in the ED for almost a year and have seen some really nasty things." She patted random spots on her body. "This container of ours is remarkable. It's able to withstand all kinds of trauma and bounce back to full speed. And then"—she ran her finger down her inner arm from wrist to elbow—"one cut in the wrong place and we're gone."

My scowl deepened as I swallowed a mouthful of water. "Remind me to not hang out with you and your coworkers anymore. What a bunch of downers."

"We're medical people. As you will be soon." She'd turned her mother persona back on. "It's our job to sometimes save people from themselves."

"Sounds like I'm headed for the wrong profession. If I'm such a hypocrite, maybe I shouldn't go into nursing."

Her mouth fell open. "You don't mean that. If your grades are any indication, you've got a natural talent for this."

Or maybe I was just an excellent student.

Tired of being analyzed, I jumped up. "I'm going to get more water."

I chatted for a minute with the guy with the tub of beverages, grabbed another bottle from him, then went below deck for some food. As I loaded a plate with fruit, vegetables, and cheese cubes, I spotted Allie the neurologist on the other side of the salon, her back to me. Her warning about not being able to fix a damaged brain had gotten to me. I remembered Uncle Lonnie talking about some of his favorite boxers—Joe Louis, Sugar Ray Robinson, Leon Spinks, Micky Ward, and Muhammed Ali. He never said specifically what was wrong with them, just that they "weren't the same anymore." Being only ten or twelve at the time, I'd dismissed it. Brain damage was likely. The thought sobered me now.

Brain damage. Weight cutting. Why did I do this sport? Because it gave me an adrenaline rush. The sense of power, of being in control, was addicting.

Maybe you should just ride your motorcycle, the little girl suggested. *With a helmet.*

"Sorry to be a downer," Risa apologized when I returned. "I promise not to talk about head trauma or analyze you any further today."

We devoured the food and went back to get two more plates. A few minutes later, the captain announced that we'd be heading back into the harbor to pick up more partygoers and drop off anyone who needed to go ashore.

"Bummer," I said. "Despite the lectures, I'm not ready to go in yet."

"Stay, then. You don't have to disembark."

I checked the time. Five thirty. They circled back to the harbor every two or three hours. The next stop would be eight o'clock at the earliest. Too late. "I do. I need to get over to the gym to meet with Salomon."

"And then it's ritual night?"

I was already looking forward to my evening. "You got it."

Startling everyone on board, the catamaran's horn blasted. The crew members and others familiar with boating pointed at a boat that had zipped past us too closely and was pulling into the harbor way too fast.

I glanced at the name on the fishing trawler. Did it say what I thought it did?

CHAPTER TWENTY-TWO

I squinted, trying to see the name on the trawler's stern.

"Does that say *MON Ami*?"

Risa held a hand over her eyes as a sun shield. "I think so."

"That's Mona's boat."

"It's kind of a silly name," Mona had told us once. "Of course lots of boats have silly names. Mon Ami means *my friend* in French. I liked the idea of being with my friend. And capitalizing the M, O, N, and A means my friend is me." She blushed. "Or something like that."

As we watched, the *MON Ami* did the boat version of screeching to a halt by the dock. A woman that appeared to be Mona, I couldn't tell for sure from this distance, leapt off the boat and got into a waiting vehicle. Once she'd closed the car door, the trawler pulled away from the dock, obeying the speed limit this time, and headed back out to open water.

Mona kept her boat at Lahaina Harbor on the northwest side of the island. So what was it doing over here? The only reason I could think of was she needed to get to No Mercy fast. It was after five thirty. If she wasn't there before six, she'd forfeit tomorrow's fight. Talk about cutting it close.

Hadn't Salomon said she was waiting for her boat to get hauled into shore for repairs? Maybe it was something they could take care of on open water. Or maybe they hauled it in, fixed it, and instead of driving, she took the boat to the harbor here.

"Is it faster," I mused, mostly to myself, "to drive a car or take a boat from Lahaina to Kahului?"

"What?" Risa asked.

I brushed it off. "Nothing."

Risa and I went back to our spot to pack up our stuff and get ready to go ashore.

"Have you ever wondered," Risa asked, "about Ashlyn's job?"

I blinked at her, confused. "That's random. Where did that question come from?"

"It was one of those things where one thought leads to another and another." Risa lost her balance and almost fell. That had more to do with the free beverages than the catamaran rocking. "I was thinking about Mona forfeiting the fight because she missed weigh-in. That led to Ashlyn missing the fight because of her job. Then I wondered what she does when she's gone. I mean, she claims to be doing corporate training—"

"Hang on," I interrupted. "You think she's lying?"

"I don't know." Losing her balance again, she dropped down to sit. "Do you have any idea what the value of your condo is?"

Another random thought? "No. Ash bought it."

"Well, I know because I looked at one a few months ago. I figured I'm making an okay paycheck. I should be able to upgrade. Figured a two-bedroom condo would be nice in case my family can ever get here. One like yours goes for more than seven hundred thousand."

"Dollars?" I asked stupidly. "Are you sure?"

"The condo plus the new cars, the clothes, and all the other extras?"

Like the housekeeper, spray tans, and bi-weekly manicures. It all added up. I knew where Risa was going with this. "You're thinking there's no way she's making that kind of money."

"Not as a corporate trainer. Or whatever her job is."

Honestly, I'd had the same thought a time or two. I dismissed it as soon as it entered my mind, though. Ashlyn would never lie to me.

"It might be gullible, but I believe her. People stumble into great opportunities all the time. Why not Ashlyn?"

"Super gullible," Risa said without hesitation. "She's thirty-three years old. Her best position before this was restaurant hostess for that high-end place."

The catamaran eased to a stop at the dock, and the captain came over the speaker. "Attention, passengers. You're all welcome to stay on board. Our final stop will be at eight o'clock tonight. If it's time for you to go, thank you for cruising with us today. We hope you've enjoyed your time."

"I did," I grumbled to Risa, "except for the lectures and insinuation that my sister is doing something illegal."

"I didn't say illegal," Risa objected, reaching out a hand for me to help her up. "I'm just wondering what she does when she leaves."

Between Heleena's death, the semi-threatening text, and tomorrow's fight, I didn't need to be thinking about this too. An expert compartmentalizer, I tucked thoughts of my sister's job into a box in the back of my brain.

"I'll ask her sometime," I promised. "Right now, it's time to switch to fight mode. Or, more accurately, pre-fight mode."

"Right. Sorry. I didn't mean to upset you. It's just, we never see each other for more than a half hour, so I don't get to talk to you about the things bumping around in my brain."

"Careful about those brain bumps. Don't want to damage it."

"That's not funny." Risa pointed a finger at me and then draped herself over me in a hug. "You know how much I love you."

"I do, and I love you too. Which is why I'm driving you home. You're sloshed."

Risa had driven me to the harbor, which meant I had to drive her home in her beat-up Mazda and help her up to her apartment. Risa was a lightweight. A drink and a half was her limit. She'd had three.

"You're not going to puke, are you?" I handed her a big glass of water. "Here. Dilute the alcohol."

"I shouldn't have had that Blue Hawaii." She held the glass and swayed in place on the threadbare sofa, her eyes blank and staring.

"I actually might feel better if—"

Risa thrust the glass at me and darted for the bathroom.

Guess purging the alcohol from her system would work too.

Thinking of her wish to upgrade, I glanced around her apartment. It reminded me a little of Heleena and Lana's place. Like with theirs, any charm here was Risa's doing. She opted for plenty of rattan, bamboo, and textiles from the Philippines. That helped but didn't disguise the overall poor condition.

"The original listing," she had told me once, laughing, "claimed it had 'a remodeled kitchen and bathroom and upgraded tiling throughout.' Remodeled meant a new range in the kitchen, faucets in the bathroom, and a coat of white paint. Upgraded meant they'd replaced any broken or badly stained tiles. Everything works, so that's really all that matters."

Most important to her was to have enough money left after paying rent to send some to her mother.

She made do, but a second bedroom would be great. I agreed, it was time for something better, but even if she could afford it, going from this place to a condo like ours would be like culture shock. It had been for me.

"It's really nice," I told my sister when she took me for a walkthrough. "Almost too nice. Are you sure we can afford it?"

"I've got it all under control, Peep," she insisted and dragged me upstairs to see my bedroom.

Eighteen months later, we hadn't seen a single late payment warning. Risa was right, though. No way could Ashlyn's paycheck cover everything. Where was the money coming from, then? Why hadn't I ever pushed her more on this? Because I wanted to believe her. I couldn't deal with the possibility that my sister might be keeping secrets from me.

After tucking Risa into bed to sleep off her drinks, with a bucket at her side, I needed to get over to the gym.

"I'll check on you later," I called from the front door.

She snored in reply.

I walked the few blocks from Risa's apartment to No Mercy. By the time I got there, the official was just leaving. Aonani followed him, holding the door for me and then letting it go as I reached for it.

"Have a great night," I called after her, using enough kindness to make Auntie Amelia proud.

Inside, Mona was on her way to the locker room, looking more stressed than I'd ever seen her.

"All checked in?" I asked.

"Barely. Ozzie's furious."

"You missed a lot over the last few days. Did you hear what happened?"

She nodded, her eyes glistening. "I called Ozzie last night to let him know I'd be cutting it close. He told me about Heleena." A few tears spilled. "I'm dedicating my fight to her."

"Me too. A lot of us are. They told you about the gathering for her after the fights?"

"I'll be there. Maybe we can find a quiet corner. I'd love to catch up with you. Right now, I need to grab my gloves and meet with my coach."

As I watched Mona walk away, Callie Castro appeared at my side. "Too bad."

I glanced at her, confused. "What's too bad?"

"I was sure I'd be the only featherweight from No Mercy for this fight. Then she comes flying in the door at the last minute."

I stiffened, shocked by the callous attitude hidden behind the just-kidding smile. "Sounds like you're trying to use Heleena's death to your benefit."

Callie laughed. "Leena's death doesn't affect me that way. Talia's my only real threat."

Suddenly, I had the urge to contact the other gym or Detective Kalani and ask for someone to keep an eye on Talia.

"Leena was coming on strong," Callie continued, "and Mona's skills are improving, but I don't have anything to worry about. You know, there's a remote chance that Mona and I will fight each other tomorrow. If Talia doesn't make it for some reason, Mona will step up to her spot."

Maybe Mona needed to be watched too. "You worried about her?"

"About Mona? No. She gets in a lucky blow now and then, but I could take her."

Like people tended to resort to anger to mask fear or other uncomfortable emotions, was Callie using arrogance to mask anxiety?

"Funny," I taunted, "you seem a little worried."

She turned to face me. Her nostrils flared. Her jaw clenched and unclenched. Before she could say anything more, Ozzie was next to us.

"Looks like things are getting a little tense over here," he noted. "You two getting ready to go at it?"

With eyes on mine, Callie said, "Gemi's giving me a hard time. Nothing I can't handle."

Maybe I'd hit a little too close to something.

Ozzie pointed to the back corner. "You and Mona on the mat in five minutes."

Callie grunted and bumped my shoulder with hers as she walked away.

"She's edgy," Ozzie offered.

"We all are. It'll be nice to have this fight done. I'm glad Mona made it."

"By the skin of her teeth." He rubbed the back of his neck. "I thought for sure we were forfeiting this one."

"That would've destroyed her ranking."

"Yes, it would have. And it wouldn't look good for the gym either. I told her no more fishing trips so close to a fight. It's not possible to give a hundred percent to two things."

Not sure I agreed with that. It was doable but exhausting. "Good luck tomorrow, Oz. I have to change and meet with Salomon."

A few minutes later, my coach was snapping at me.

"Hope you had a good time lounging in the sun today," he said with full sarcasm. "The rest of us have been getting ready for a fight. Aonani and Stacia were done an hour ago."

When Salomon got tense, he got crabby.

"I told you I'd be a little late. It's only twenty after six." When that didn't ease his case of the grumpies, I wrapped him in a hug. "You're the bestest coach in the whole world. I love you, man."

"Get off me." He pushed me away, but there was a small smile on his lips now. "Strategy time. Mele's kill shot is a round kick to the head or a leg sweep and pin. You know how to avoid both, but I want to go over them a few times. Have that be the last thing in your mind."

Mele was like a moray eel. Her approach was to wait, wait, strike. And her round kick was just as effective as my right cross. Stacia was the best round kicker of all the women at No Mercy. That meant when we practiced together, I tried to avoid her kick while she did her best not to get trapped in my armbar. Tonight we only tapped each other. Our goal was to deliver or block, not to knock each other out. Neither of us wanted to risk injury at this point.

"Stop!" Salomon barked when Stacia connected with my jaw for the fifth time. "Too much sun today, Kittredge? You want to win tomorrow or not?"

After Stacia tapped me the first time, I got distracted by thoughts of CTE and my brain bouncing around inside my skull.

"Sorry, coach. Give me two minutes to get my mind in the game?"

Salomon scowled at me and turned to Stacia. "Princess needs two minutes."

"No worries," Stacia said. "I need to use the bathroom."

"You thinking about Heleena?" Salomon asked when Stacia walked away.

Best to be honest. I told him what Allie the neurologist said about brain injuries.

"I can't lie, mahi," Salomon said, less aggressive now, "I've seen fighters get real messed up. You're good at protecting your head, though." Without warning, he swung his massive forearm at me. I reacted immediately, blocking without thinking. "See? That's why we practice this over and over."

"And over." I laughed. I did the same thing with my warriors.

"You've had a lot going on this week. Will Ashlyn still be here for the fight?"

"She says she will. She's only over in Honolulu."

"That's a good thing." He put a hand on my shoulder and spun me toward the wall. "Go sit. Close your eyes."

That meant meditate. Get my head on straight. I'd taken a few minutes to warm up before stepping into the ring with Stacia, but I hadn't done any mental prep. Those couple minutes of quiet focus helped. When we faced off again, I blocked all but one kick. We shook hands, and Stacia was free to leave.

"Donnelley!" Salomon called, his voice echoing across the gym. "Get over here."

"Why?" I asked. "What are you doing?"

"I've been watching him. He's got a pretty good leg sweep. If he ever decided to get serious about this, he could do okay."

"You want me to go easy?" Ross joked after Salomon explained what he wanted.

Salomon sighed. "Gemi needs to be ready for a title fight tomorrow. Going easy won't help her. And your full out is maybe half of what Mele can do."

Ross scowled and gave a crisp nod. "Got it. Don't hold back."

This move was the easier one for me to avoid. Along with protecting my head, my feet never stayed still. I bounced around like one of those tiny rubber balls. Side to side, back and forth, and to the diagonal, constantly mixing it up which made it hard for my opponent to know where I'd go next. After fifteen minutes of repeating the same move, Ross was gasping for breath and had only come close to sweeping my legs twice. When Salomon finally said we could stop, Ross caught me off guard and dropped me to the mat by sweeping both of my feet out from under me. He caught me as I fell, so the impact wasn't hard, and straddled me.

"Sorry." He grinned, his face inches from mine. "For my own ego, I needed one win."

My breath caught, and my stomach clenched.

A boy is touching you, the little girl warned.

"Fair enough," I told Ross and shoved his shoulders. "Now get off me."

He helped me up, and we tapped gloves to end the practice.

"Go hit the shower," Salomon ordered, "and meet me in my office."

"Can't. A shower will ruin my ritual."

"Sorry, I forgot. Keep your distance, then. You smell."

In his office, we reviewed videos of Mele's two most recent fights, noting how she moved and her body language just before striking. After watching both videos three times each at slow speed, Salomon declared us done for the night.

"Visualize those fights tonight and tomorrow morning. What did you eat today?"

I explained my huge breakfast and the spread on the boat.

"Finger food? You're filling your tank on hors d'oeuvres?" He shook his head. "Go get your stuff. We'll get dinner before I drop you at home."

"I'll throw on my cover-up. That smells like sunscreen and ocean air instead of sweaty Gemi."

Laughing, I stepped out of the office and almost collided with a glowering Johnny Gambino.

CHAPTER TWENTY-THREE

Johnny was standing outside the office, waiting for the fighters to finish so he could clean the locker rooms.

"You startled me, Johnny," I told him with a nervous laugh. "I didn't see you before. When did you get here?"

"A few minutes ago." He let out a long, sad-sounding sigh. "I don't want to work tonight. I want to go lay on the beach and listen to the waves and look up at the stars."

I'd never heard Johnny talk about the beach before. He mentioned sitting on the docks or in his backyard, but never the beach.

"Which beach do you go to?" I asked him. The one that ran past Kahului Airport?

He shrugged. "I usually go to the one by Sprecklesville. I live over there."

"I didn't know that." I did a quick calculation. Sprecklesville was about a six-mile drive from Kahului. If he walked or ran along the beach instead of taking the road, it was approximately three miles from Sprecklesville to the spot where I'd found Heleena's body. "Do you still like to run, Johnny?"

He gave an eager nod and perked up a bit. "I love to run."

"Me too. I especially like running on the beach because there's no traffic. And sometimes no people." Which meant no witnesses. "Do you ever run on the beach?"

"I do." He grinned and held a bare foot out in front of him. "I like the sand between my toes."

"Have you ever run with any of the other fighters?"

"A few times." He grew quiet again, his hands clenching his new broom so tightly his knuckles paled.

"What's wrong?"

"It's my fault Leena's dead."

My mouth went dry. "Your fault? What do you mean?"

His head dropped forward, and he stared at the ground. "I should've run with her that night."

But he didn't? My suspicions about him deflated. "Did she ask you to go with her?"

"No, but sometimes I followed her to make sure she was safe. If I did that on Tuesday, she'd still be alive."

He threw his broom to the floor and stormed away, leaving me with my mouth hanging open. Was it comforting or creepy that he followed her?

"You're still here," Salomon noted as he pulled the office door shut. "You okay, mahi?"

"Yeah. I was just chatting with Johnny." Great news that he wasn't the killer. A little concerning, however, that he might be a stalker.

"That reminds me, I talked with him about going to the Carreres' house. He admitted that he stole the address from the computer."

"How?"

"He came into the office to empty the trash one day. I stepped out while he was in there and forgot to close the student master file. It was right there on the screen. He grabbed the address from the first 'Carrere' listing."

"Halle comes before Heleena." At least I had the answer to one question. "Did he say why he went to their house?"

"He wanted to talk with Heleena and decided it would be more romantic to surprise her at home. Apparently, he heard one of the guys talking about surprising this girl he wanted to ask out by showing up at her apartment. I pushed him a little more, and he said

208 | SHAWN MCGUIRE

he kept asking out Heleena because Ross keeps asking you. Johnny learns by watching and copying. He figured that was how it was done."

I shook my head. "Ross told me he was trying to impress me by being flirty and macho. Little did he know he was passing his idiotic ways on to Johnny."

Salomon chuckled. The older wiser man amused by the younger stupider ones. "Anyway, I chewed Johnny out. He was pretty embarrassed and promised to never look in the files again."

"You trust him?"

"I'll give him another chance. I should've locked the computer."

I couldn't say much. I was giving Ross a chance. "You can be a real softy sometimes, you know that, coach?"

He scowled and pointed at me. "Don't cross me, Kittredge. I'll make you do burpees. Don't think I won't."

I laughed and went to the locker room to grab my stuff.

* * *

The aromas coming from the food truck made my stomach growl. Salomon ordered two plates of chicken hekka with vegetables and cellophane noodles, and we sat on the beach to eat. No more discussion of tomorrow's fight or Heleena or anything remotely negative. Once we left No Mercy, we were done with that kind of talk.

"Nice night." I stared up at the stars and shoved a forkful of hekka into my mouth.

"We live in paradise." Salomon gave a contented sigh. "Every night is nice."

"Don't know about that, but most are."

He filled me in on the happenings with his wife, Nettie, and their daughter. "April says the baby is moving like crazy. Keeps her up at night."

I bumped his shoulder with mine. "Grandpa Salomon. And I

thought you were a softy now. You're going to turn into a complete marshmallow."

"Never."

"Right. The crustier men are before, the squishier they become with babies. Especially if it's a girl."

I remembered Auntie Amelia telling me that about my grandfather. "Snarly old bastard until Ashlyn came along. He was like an overstuffed cream puff by the time you were born."

Salomon made a face but didn't disagree. "She's having a baby shower in a couple weeks. You and Ashlyn should come."

"I'll be there. If Ash is around, she'll come too. Tell Nettie to send me the details."

Salomon wiped his mouth with a paper napkin and laid it on our stack of empty plates. "You okay by yourself all the time? You know you can call me if you ever have a problem."

I appreciated that more than I could say. "So far, so good. The condo people are good about coming when we call. Or so I've heard. We haven't had any troubles yet."

"Okay. You've got my number. Don't be afraid to use it."

"I know. Thank you, maku." *Makuakāne* was Hawaiian for father. Like he'd shortened my nickname, I shortened his as well.

We hung out and watched the waves washing up on shore for another few minutes. Finally, he stood and said, "Let's get you home." Fifteen minutes later, he pulled up to the condo and instructed, "Take it easy tomorrow. Light run to stay loose. Eat a good breakfast, then take it easy the rest of the day. Be in the Paia locker room by five o'clock."

"I know, coach. All of that goes for you too."

"Except I need to be there by noon." He winked. "And I can run as far as I want."

"Which is about two miles." Laughing, I darted out of the car before he could respond. The second I entered the front door, Hulu greeted me. "Aloha. Food?"

"Poor bird." I tossed my rubber slippers in the closet and

dropped my bags by the kitchen island. Hulu's water dishes were still full, but he'd devoured every last food pellet. I put more in his dish and left his cage door open so he could wander the condo.

Upstairs in my bathroom, I shifted into ritual mode and turned the tub water on as hot as I could stand and dropped in a few handfuls of Epsom salt. From the basket on the counter, I took two bottles of bubble bath and sniffed them. The pineapple-mango was a little too invigorating for this time of night. I returned it and squeezed a generous amount of the vanilla-coconut-gardenia into the water stream. While the tub filled, I lit vanilla-scented candles and placed them around the room. Finally, I turned on soft guitar music, played over a portable speaker, and then sank into the bubbles. I exhaled as the Epsom salt helped my muscles relax. The workout tonight wasn't all that intense, so it had to be the stress from the rest of the week making me so tight. Had it really only been three days since I'd found Heleena's body?

As I lay there, I thought of the yacht cruise this afternoon. Allie the neurologist in particular. I believed that certain people came into our lives for a reason. Sometimes, like with Risa, it was to form a lasting friendship. Other times, like with Allie, people came through to deliver a message. Thirty wasn't old. In fact, I was in the best physical condition of my life, but I wasn't a kid anymore either. Maybe it was time to step away from fighting MMA. I could become a coach instead. I'd make it my mission to teach my fighters to block those head shots at all costs.

You're supposed to be relaxing, the little girl reminded me.

"You're right. No thinking about this right now. Negative thoughts are not allowed in the ritual space."

That was an epic challenge tonight. Instead, I forced myself to listen to the music and envisioned standing in the center of the octagon tomorrow night, holding that women's bantamweight first place medal high overhead.

How many hours did I devote to fighting every week? I'd never bothered to calculate. It had to be the equivalent of a part-time job.

And this wasn't even UFC official. How much time would going pro require? Salomon had suggested it more than once. That would mean even more training, going to the mainland to fight on the national stage, and eventually other countries. I'd have to give up school for sure. And teaching my warriors. School, no problem. Walk away from my warriors? I couldn't do that. I'd be miserable without those kids. No, my plan all along had been to finish my degree and get a good nursing job. Maybe become certified in domestic violence nursing. I'd have three years of experience in no time. After that, I could go on to graduate school. It was a lot of schooling, but I'd surely have a great-paying job in the end.

Is that what I wanted, though? Would a job with a decent paycheck be enough? Only if that job also allowed me to make a difference. Was that asking too much?

Ashlyn had blushed when I teased her about seeing a man on this trip. What if that was true? Her getting serious about someone would turn my world upside down. The day was coming, possibly soon, when I would need to stop relying on her so much and support myself. And I sure didn't want to rely on anyone else.

"Except we don't care about any of this tonight." I sank lower into the bubbles. "Tonight, all we care about is relaxing. We're not even going to meditate on Mele's fights tonight. We'll do that in the morning."

I slid my favorite cherry-pink with bright-yellow Easter Peeps scrubby bath mitt onto my hand. Ashlyn bought it for me years ago. She also gave me the gardenia body gel I loaded onto the mitt. No one knew pampering like Ashlyn, and she'd taught me well. I scrubbed away the layers of sunscreen, sweat, and grime that had accumulated during the day. Then I let out most of the cooled-off dirty water, added fresh hot water to the tub along with more bubbles, and washed my hair—using the bubble bath as shampoo, I wasn't picky that way. A few more minutes of soaking and I'd be ready to let everything from the day rinse down the drain with the water and suds.

Hulu hopped onto the edge of the tub, startling me. "Bubbles, Kenichi." He leaned forward and popped a few with his beak.

I laughed at him. "What does Kenichi mean?"

He squawked but didn't answer. Not that I'd expected him to.

By the time I was ready to get out of the tub, I felt mellow and a little sleepy. I switched the music from the speaker to earbuds so I could maintain my dome of serenity. After drying off and toweling my hair until it was nearly dry, I slathered on a layer of vanilla body lotion. Finally, I put on the one silky nightgown I owned, sat outside on the lanai with a cup of tea, and thought of our elderly neighbor in California. Old Mrs. Oberholzer would sit on her front porch and wave me over. That meant it was teatime. We'd drink whatever blend she'd pulled out of her tea bin, nibble small sugar cookies, and talk about our days. When Mom announced we were leaving, Mrs. Oberholzer gave me the beautiful china teapot and matching cup, blue with white edelweiss flowers and gold trim, that I used on every ritual night.

"Never put these in a dishwasher or microwave," Mrs. Oberholzer cautioned in her strong Austrian accent, tears threatening to spill. "Remember to have tea and cookies once a week and think of old Mrs. O when you do."

I didn't have tea often, but I always thought of the woman with the sparkling medium-blue eyes and scarf tied around her head whenever I did. Risa said we made time for things that were important. Both of my dear friends—one old and wise, the other young and wise—were right. I made a silent promise to make more time for tea as I dipped a tiny sugar cookie into the cup.

I refilled my tea from the beautiful blue china pot, and as I gazed at the skyful of stars hanging over the ocean, my phone rang.

"What are you doing?" Ashlyn asked.

"Drinking tea."

"And thinking about Mrs. Oberholzer? I wonder how she is."

"We should send her a letter." There were voices in the background on Ashlyn's end of the call. "Where are you?"

"Oh, it's this big open room. It's very echo-y, isn't it?"

"A big open room? Like the hotel lobby." Ashlyn had the strangest way of identifying things sometimes.

"Sure. Are you ready for tomorrow?"

The hesitant, dismissive tone in that "sure" made me pause. Risa's comments earlier had me wondering if Ashlyn was lying to me. But why would she? We could say anything to each other. What could she be hiding? Not a talk to have right now, but one we'd for sure have soon.

"All ready," I agreed. "I did my bath and had my two-bite cookie."

"Are you going to watch a movie?"

She meant something sappy.

"That might be too much girly for me."

"Just try it. You know you love watching Hallmark with me."

"I don't mind it at Christmastime." And Cassie the good witch was kind of fun.

"They might have a Christmas flick on tonight."

"It's March."

"You can never have too much Christmas in your life."

"You can, actually." When Ashlyn didn't reply, I added, "I'll think about it. When will you be home?"

"Flight gets in tomorrow at 4:20. Then I'll run my stuff home, change into something fight appropriate, and rush out to Paia. Don't worry. I'll be there." Someone in the background spoke to Ashlyn. "Tell him two minutes." To me, she said, "They're waiting for me."

"Who is?"

"The conference people," she replied with a sigh. "I swear, they can't even fix their own drinks without me."

"You need a new job."

"Nah, I love my job. How's Hulu? Let me say goodnight to him."

Taking a sip of tea while it was still hot, I slid the screen door aside and went in search of the parrot. I found him sitting on the edge of a large potted plant about to pluck one of the leaves.

"Hulu, stop!"

He hung his head and put a foot over his face.

I switched on the speakerphone, then held it out to him. "Ashlyn wants to say goodnight."

Telephone calls confused the bird. Hearing Ashlyn's voice but not seeing her didn't compute. As Ashlyn spoke baby talk to him, he tilted his head to one side and then the other. He looked behind him as though she might be there.

"How's my bird?" Ash crooned. "Who's a good parrot?"

Finally, he bounced, recognizing her voice. "I love you, Kenichi."

"Do you know what that means?" I asked with a laugh. "It's the third time he said it."

If not for the background noise coming over the speaker, I'd think the call dropped. "Ash?"

"What? Sorry, Jeannie was signaling to me."

She was distracted. Time to cut this short. "Say goodnight, Hulu."

He ruffled his feathers and echoed, "Goodnight, Hulu."

Ashlyn laughed and I shook my head. Goofy bird.

"I'll see you both tomorrow night," she promised. "Sleep well, Peep."

After hand washing the teapot and cup in warm soapy water, part of the ritual, I tucked Hulu in for the night. "Sleep well, bird."

"Nighty-night. Sleep tight."

I got into bed and decided, just this once, to try a movie instead of falling asleep to guitar music like usual. As Ashlyn had predicted, there was, unbelievably, a Christmas movie on the Hallmark Channel. A woman's car ran off the road as she was making her way to a small Colorado mountain town. The hunky town handyman rescued her, but a storm was coming, and it would be days before they could get the right parts to fix her car. Fortunately, he had a guest house she could stay in.

By the first commercial break, I was yawning big enough to make my jaw pop.

"If nothing else, this will put me to sleep."

I set the timer on the television to turn off in an hour. The last thing I remembered before my eyes slammed shut for good was the stranded woman, the hunky handyman, and hunky's two kids from his deceased wife were snowshoeing through the woods, looking for the perfect Christmas tree for his mountain house.

CHAPTER TWENTY-FOUR

I woke the next morning in full Bull mode. That was the goal with all the pampering and preening, after all. One night of that much girly-girl and I was ready to pound on someone. I always wondered what would happen to Ashlyn if she spent one day Gemi-style with no makeup and letting her hair air dry. She was fine wearing shorts and a T-shirt, but the closest she ever got to the rest was going a day without washing her hair or wearing only mascara and no eyeliner. We were as different from each other as possible in every way except one: we'd do absolutely anything for each other. Absolutely anything.

Since it was Saturday, I didn't have school, and with it being a fight day, there were no classes to teach at No Mercy. I could sleep in, but my body was so programmed to rising early, it was a challenge to sleep until seven.

"Good morning, Hulu," I greeted and pulled the cover off his cage.

"Rise and shine."

I added water to his bowl. "Ashlyn comes home today."

He did a little side-to-side head-bopping dance at this announcement. Most of what the bird said or did was a conditioned response—when you hear or see this, say or do that—but some things could only be explained as him being able to analyze and form a conclusion. Like his excitement over Ashlyn's return. I let him out of the cage, and he flew to the floor to walk around.

I stood on the lanai with a glass of water, breathing in the ocean- and flower-scented breeze, and thought about the day ahead. Salomon wanted me to meditate on those two Mele fights we'd watched, inserting myself as her opponent. I closed my eyes and imagined the octagon rising around me. Envisioning the island's number two fighter in front of me was just as easy. I ducked away from the punches she threw and danced back from her leg sweeps. But then Mele became Heleena and a punch landed squarely on my jaw.

"I think it's time for a little deprogramming," I told myself and stared out at the ocean. Maybe a run on the beach where I found Heleena would help me process what had happened. It's not like I could get much more distracted by her memory. Detective Kalani finding the killer would help most, but I needed to confront my demons surrounding this.

I changed into my running gear and, in the spirit of being safe and avoiding traffic in my distracted state, decided to ride the Indian over to Kanaha Beach Park instead of running there. Salomon's voice immediately filled my head. *A run on the beach is fine but there's nothing safe about that motorcycle. Take the Jeep!*

At the garage door, I remembered Hulu was out, turned back, and found him in the foyer playing with a piece of paper.

"What is that?" I took it from him. It was a sealed envelope with *Ms. Kittredge* written on the front in swirly handwriting. "Where'd you find this?"

Whether he really understood me, I had no idea, but he waddled to the front door and tapped the floor.

Someone shoved this under my door? Warning bells went off throughout my body. I held the envelope by the edge to not smudge any possible fingerprints. Wasn't that how they did it on TV? I took it to the kitchen and carefully slid the letter opener across the top. That was not what they did on TV. The recipient would immediately call the police. This might be nothing, though. How embarrassing would it be to call Kalani over only for it to be a flyer for a landscaper or something?

Inside was a single piece of beautiful writing paper. At the center of the paper were two words written in the same swirly handwriting: *Back off.*

After a few seconds of trying to understand what this meant, my confusion turned to fear, and my hands started shaking. Was this from the same person who sent that text? Was it Heleena's killer? Back off from what? The text said *stay out of things that don't involve you.* Did they know I'd been conducting my own investigation? And more importantly than any of that, how did they know where I lived?

I should let Detective Kalani know about this, but my thoughts were all over the place. I needed to pull myself together first and think logically. After tucking the note back inside the envelope, I shoved it in a kitchen drawer. Then I put Hulu in his cage and headed for the beach.

* * *

In an out of the way spot near Kahului Harbor, I parked the bike and stretched lightly, loosening my legs for the run. While doing so, I gazed down the beach to the spot near the heliotropes. I planned to run past the spot where I'd found Heleena and complete the route I hadn't gotten to complete on Wednesday. Maybe I'd pause by the shrubs on the way back for a moment of silence.

As I closed in on *the spot*, I noticed someone sitting near the shrubs. My heart stuttered. I slowed to a walk, inhaling deeply to calm my breathing. It was Homeless Harry.

I raised a hand in a friendly wave, walking even slower to not spook him. He waved in return. Good start.

"You're Homeless Harry."

He tilted his head to the side and squinted, deep weathered lines forming around his eyes. "I know you too. Don't know your name, though."

"I'm Gemi. Gemi Kittredge. I found the dead girl here a few days ago."

"I found her first," Harry stated, pushing his shoulders back. "Don't got a phone." He slapped the sand with an open palm. "Waited right here and kept an eye on her 'til someone came along."

Right. You waited right there and watched the mynahs and crabs have their way with her. "That was very noble of you, Harry." I took a step closer. "Can I ask you something about the girl?"

"Did you know her?"

"I did. Her name was Heleena Carrere." My voice broke as I added, "She was my friend."

He placed a hand respectfully over his heart and then gave me a go-ahead nod to ask my questions.

"Were you here when she died? Did you see what happened?"

He looked away. "The detective lady already asked me that."

"I'm not a cop. Heleena and I fought together at the same gym."

Harry snorted. "Looked to me like she needed more lessons. Let that other lady work her over good."

Every hair on my body stood at attention. "You saw her? The other lady?"

"Like I told the detective, I couldn't see faces. It was too dark. I heard their voices, though. It started out calm enough. One told the other, 'I need you to forfeit the fight.'"

Forfeit? It had to be Callie. Anger flooded me. "What else did she say?"

"The other one laughed and said, 'Never going to happen. I've worked too hard.' Then the first said, 'I'll square up next time, I swear.' That's when things got heated. One, I don't know which, said something about needing the prize money."

Needing the money? My anger turned into dread as a new thought occurred to me. As Kalani and I had discussed, there wouldn't be any benefit to Callie for Heleena to drop out. Leena wasn't a threat to her. What if Heleena had been trying to get Callie to back out? Leena and Lana needed money for the salon. Heleena was pretty much guaranteed to take third place which meant five hundred dollars. The standings flashed in my head. If Callie dropped out, Heleena would fight Talia. Even if Talia won, Leena would get the second place thousand-dollar prize. Had Heleena been desperate enough to ask Callie to forfeit?

If she had, it might have set off Callie's explosive temper. I'd seen Callie go nuts in the octagon more than once. One time, the ref needed to pull her off her opponent before she did severe damage. Then, seconds later when the fight was over, Callie was once again her sweet pink-teddy-bear self.

This didn't feel right, though. Not Heleena asking and not Callie beating her that way. There was no doubt, Callie was physically capable. But her losing complete control and beating Leena to death for asking a question was unimaginable. And terrifying.

"I swear," Harry was saying when I tuned back in, "with all the punches being thrown, it sounded like two or three of them were working that girl over."

Two or three? That's what I'd thought after seeing all the bruises on Leena's body and how she obviously hadn't protected her face. Was it the yakuza and not another fighter? Had Lana lied to me about them getting involved with the group? That would mean the yakuza asked Heleena to throw the fight. Why would they do that? I stared out at the ocean, as though I'd find the answer there. The yakuza were involved with gambling, weren't they? Wasn't that what Risa said? People bet big time on these fights. Maybe the group was trying to rig the bets.

Was that what the "back off" message meant? Were they directing me to throw my fight too?

Not sure bad guys leave notes, the little girl said.

True. And Harry said it was two women.

"You're sure there were two women?" I asked Harry. "Only Heleena and the woman who beat her?"

He nodded his shaggy-haired head. "Two women, I'm sure. It only sounded like more than two."

Was the tattooed woman the killer?

"The one doing the hitting," Harry continued, "was like a cyclone. Never seen anyone wail on another person like that. That Heleena girl, at least I guess it was her, she was on the ground and the other one kept hitting. I'll never forget the sound. It was awful." He winced and turned a little green.

Sort of inefficient for people who prefered blades and bullets, as Risa said.

"I'm sorry you witnessed all that, Harry."

He shrugged and looked down at the sand. "I'm sorry I couldn't stop it."

I headed back to my bike, running at full speed. Harry said he'd told Detective Kalani all this, but I needed to make sure.

CHAPTER TWENTY-FIVE

Instead of going home and calling Kalani, I went straight to the police station.

"I was running on the beach again, and Homeless Harry was there." I settled into the chair next to her desk, told her what he said, and then explained my admittedly weak theory of Heleena asking Callie to forfeit the fight. "If she did, that could have triggered Callie's temper and made her lose control."

"What would Heleena's motive have been?" Kalani asked, scribbling a note on a pad on her desk.

"Money. Their salon was struggling to the point that they considered shutting it down and going to work for someone else. By eliminating a top rank, Leena had a good shot at a larger prize."

She considered it before saying, "There might be a little merit to that, but it makes more sense that a lower-ranked fighter wanted to eliminate Heleena as competition. We're already looking into the other featherweight fighters. For the record, I'm about ninety-nine percent sure Callie Castro had nothing to do with this."

"Why?"

"Because she was attacked last night."

I nearly sprang out of the chair. "What?"

"Same M.O. She was out for a run later at night and got jumped. Fortunately for her, other people showed up just as she was knocked to the ground and her attacker ran off. The people went to Ms. Castro's aid and called 911, but they could only identify the attacker as a woman."

Too dark to see her face. "Is Callie okay?"

"She's fine. Shook up but not even a bruise. The people showed up so quickly the attacker didn't even have time to speak." Kalani shook her head. "Ms. Castro must have an angel watching over her. She could've ended up like Ms. Carrere."

Was it possible someone was specifically targeting the featherweight women?

"What about the yakuza?" I blurted.

She paused then asked, "What about them?"

"Risa told me that they're into gambling and various forms of entertainment. What if they're trying to get Heleena and others to throw their fights?"

Kalani stared at me while tapping her pen on the notepad. "Is this some random guess or do you have proof to back this up?"

I thought of Risa's one thought leading to another thought comment on the boat. "I don't have anything solid, but there was this woman at The Juice Bar."

She sighed. "Tell me."

I described Tattoo to her. "There's a rumor going around that she's yakuza. She was staring at me then sat behind me and was listening to my conversation with one of the other fighters."

"What were you talking about? You and the other fighter."

"Various things. At one point, he asked if I'd been digging around in Heleena's death. I told him I found her body and had a few thoughts on who might have done this. Right after that, the woman got up and left."

"And naturally you went from this woman being a patron at a local establishment to a murderer because she took a little too much interest in your conversation?"

It was a stretch, but not out of the realm of possibility. "A few hours after that, I received a text that said, 'stay out of things that don't involve you.' And someone slid a note under my front door last night that said, 'back off.'"

"Both sound like excellent advice, if you ask me."

"What if," I pushed, "the tattooed woman was sent to find out if I knew anything?"

Kalani folded her hands on top of her desk. "The text and note do sound like threats. You think this woman sent them?"

"I don't know who else would have done it."

"All right. How did she get your phone number?"

I couldn't answer that.

"Who does have your number? Who knows where you live?"

"Not many people. I've got a pretty small social circle."

"Who?"

I listed professors at the college. Nurse Terri. I'd exchanged phone numbers and email addresses with a few students but not street addresses. Risa, of course.

"You're missing an entire group." When I didn't reply, she prompted, "Where do you spend a large portion of your day?"

"The gym? I didn't mention any of them because Salomon is the only one there who has my information."

"But Johnny Gambino found out where Heleena's parents live."

"Turns out he saw a file left open on the office computer when he was cleaning one day and grabbed their address. It was a fluke."

"All right." She seemed satisfied with that answer. "Who else?"

My small circle was getting bigger. "My sister has a friend, Jeannie, who comes over. I suppose Ashlyn could have told some of her coworkers, but why would they have a beef with me? We never have people over, though." I paused. "Well, there's our cleaning lady."

"You have a cleaning lady?"

"My sister hired her." I racked my brain. "No one else. Seriously. Salomon and Risa are it for me. That makes four people who have come to our condo."

"What about your neighbors?"

"We know some of them, but it's not like we have barbecues on the lanai." I frowned. "That makes me a little sad."

"Repair people?"

I shook my head. "The condo is new. We haven't had any problems with it. We get a few deliveries, but they know nothing about us."

"You'd be surprised what they might know. Same with your neighbors."

Thinking too long on that comment would make me completely paranoid. "What if someone followed me? I'm not sure how the person got my phone number for that text, but whoever slid that note under my door could have followed me home."

"Your eavesdropping tattooed woman?" She obviously wasn't taking me seriously.

"Maybe it was. If the yakuza are involved, they might know I've been asking questions. Tattoo could have been sent to silence me."

Kalani laughed softly. "I think you're so sure there's a connection with her, you've bent the facts to fit that vision."

I frowned. "You make me sound like a nutjob."

"Not a nutjob. It's very common with rookies."

"Rookies? I'm not a cop."

She pointed her pen at me. "Exactly what I've been telling you all along. Stop trying to investigate this case."

I looked away and crossed my arms over my chest. "Why do I think you've done that before? Set people up to scold them."

"Because you're far from the first person to think they can do my job better than I can." Kalani tapped her pen again. "Look, I agree with what you said about them being involved with fixing the fights. That *could* be possible. The chance of them coming after you because you found Heleena's body is very thin. I'm going to back burner the whole yakuza option for now and focus on other fighters first."

Her demeanor had changed with the yakuza discussion. She straightened things on her desk, didn't hold my gaze for quite as long, and kept playing with that pen. "You're afraid of them, aren't you?"

"Of the yakuza? I think a small degree of fear is a good thing when it comes to them. Gemi, the best thing you can do is follow the advice on those messages. Back off and stay out of this. I think if you do, they'll leave you alone. In the meantime, be aware of your surroundings." Before I could reply, she added, "I know you can defend yourself, but both Heleena and Callie were jumped, presumably by the same person. Go home and stop playing amateur detective. Focus on something else and let me worry about catching the killer. Speaking of which, don't you have a fight you should be preparing for?"

She was being very logical. It was hard to argue with logic. "Salomon wants me to take it easy on fight days. I was going for a short run on the beach when I came across Harry."

Her eyes narrowed and a smirk turned her mouth. "Define short. On Wednesday you told me you were halfway through a fourteen-mile run."

"I planned on about eight miles today. Kahului Harbor to Sprecklesville. Didn't get that far. I'll take a few laps around the neighborhood when I get home and do some stretching. I need to hydrate too." I looked forlornly out the window. "Left my water in the saddlebag."

"You brought your bike?" Kalani perked up. "Show me."

We passed by a refrigerator on our way out and she grabbed water bottles for both of us.

"Sweet." She walked slowly around the Indian, taking it in. While she knelt to inspect it closer, she pointed across the lot to an all-black bike. "Mine's over there."

"Also, sweet." I went to check out her Harley. Similar lines to mine. Looked like the detective and I had some things in common.

"We should go for a ride sometime," she offered when we met halfway between the bikes.

A friend? Other than Risa? Or Ross? "I'd like that."

"For now, focus on your fight. I assure you, I'm on top of things with this case." I must've made a face because she added, "You don't trust cops, do you?"

"No. Long story."

"I promise, Gemi, I will find who did this to your friend."

I stared for a few seconds then relented with a nod. "You coming to the fight tonight?"

"I planned on it. That could be the best place for me to catch our bad girl."

CHAPTER TWENTY-SIX

I pulled into the driveway, feeling excited to go for a ride with Malia someday, and found Risa sitting on my front steps. My spirits sank a bit. I loved Risa, I truly did, but she was going to be in mothering mode today as she was on every fight day. The last thing I wanted right now was to be mothered.

My suspicion was confirmed the second I removed my helmet and turned off the bike.

"You rode your motorcycle today?" she asked, appearing at my side in the garage. "Doesn't Salomon forbid the bike on fight day?"

"And the day before." I held out my arms and looked them over, then twisted left and right to inspect my legs. "No road rash. I appear to have survived."

"Not funny."

I closed the garage door, and she followed me into the condo.

"What's the matter?" she asked. "You're in a mood. Didn't you do your ritual last night?"

I rubbed my hands over my face and sighed hard. Maybe it was that note and the text, but I felt on display. Like I was being watched. Or maybe it was all the fight day rules. Do this. Don't do that. Sometimes it seemed my life was in control of me instead of me being in control of it.

"Give me five minutes to take a shower. I went for a run along the beach and feel like I have sand everywhere."

"The beach? Let me guess. The one where you found Heleena? Are you a glutton for punishment?"

"Clearly I am because I let you follow me into the condo."
She scowled. "Go take a shower. Did you eat?"

I tossed my running shoes in the closet. "Not yet."

"You're fighting in eight hours, and you haven't eaten? You know you can't eat within two hours of the fight. It makes you sick."

"God, Risa, lay off for one minute, will you?"

She jolted like I'd slapped her and clamped her lips shut. I immediately felt bad, but her nagging was too much.

While standing in the stream of steaming water, the tensions of the past three days reached the overflow mark. As much as I wanted to hold it all in and save my frustration for when I was in front of Mele in a few hours, I couldn't stop the tears. I cried for Heleena's death and for Callie getting attacked. For my unrelenting schedule that I wasn't sure I could or even wanted to maintain anymore. For the niggling feeling that my sister was hiding something from me. Even for Risa who meant well but was adding more frustration than friendship to my life lately.

The cry helped. I toweled off, pulled on some clothes, and went to face my naggy friend.

"Feeling better?" Risa asked with an edge to her voice.

"I am. Sorry I snapped." I should talk to her about the mothering thing. It was ingrained in her as the oldest child to take care of her siblings, but I wasn't her little sister. And now wasn't the time. "I've got some things to tell you about."

This turned on her gossip radar and diffused her irritation. "Uh-oh. What happened?"

"Let's go get food. You're right, I need to eat something."

I wanted to go somewhere different. Both to try something new and to be someplace where no one knew us. But I couldn't risk food that would disagree with me this close to the fight. The Juice Bar had super healthy, super tasty options, and they'd customize anything for me. I ordered a lightly seasoned grilled chicken breast with sliced avocado and a side of steamed veggies. Then I added a bowl of plain Greek yogurt with a handful of berries, a sprinkle of chia seeds, and a drizzle of agave nectar for dessert. I usually saved dessert for after the fight, but at the moment, I wanted more comfort than chicken and veggies could provide.

Once we were done here, I'd go home and stretch. Maybe get in a couple easy laps around the subdivision because my run on the beach had been cut short. I preferred to take a twenty-minute power nap before a fight, but I wasn't sure I'd have time for that. Besides, the adrenaline would kick in when I entered the octagon, like it always did. I'd sleep tomorrow. With a bantamweight first-place medal on the pillow next to me.

"Okay," Risa blurted when she couldn't wait any longer, "what's got you so on edge?"

Her tone implied that somehow I'd brought on whatever this was. Either she was super judgmental today, or I was super critical.

"Where to start?" Today wasn't the day to mention my lack of passion for nursing. I didn't want to discuss Ashlyn either. "I did go to the beach where Leena died. I wanted to deal with what happened to her and hopefully stop the visions of her beaten face from showing up at the exact wrong times."

I explained my conversation with Homeless Harry and then stopping to talk with Malia.

"Malia? Since when do you call her by her first name?" Risa could be a little territorial as well as parental.

I ignored the question. "I was almost positive Callie killed Heleena. Harry confirmed that the attacker was a woman, but then Callie got jumped last night."

"So who's the killer?" Risa concluded.

"Exactly." I sighed and dropped my head forward to stretch my neck. "The good news about that is Johnny Gambino is off the list. That makes me feel better."

"Ross Donnelly is too."

"He was never on my list." Except for those few moments when I thought he might have retaliated for Leena humiliating him.

Risa responded with arched eyebrows.

"What's that look for?" I asked.

"You like him."

Today? She had to address my nonexistent love life today? "I'm starting to like him but not in the way you're implying."

"Mm-hmm." She wasn't buying it.

Risa knew about the attack when I was thirteen. She knew that was why I was so passionate about helping women and kids. She didn't, however, seem to grasp how much the attack had messed with my head when it came to getting close to men. Even Salomon had been kept at arm's length for months.

"Did I ever tell you about my last date?" I asked, knowing full well I hadn't.

Her eyes lit up. "No. When was this?"

I thought back. "Would've been the fall of my senior year in high school. So thirteen years ago."

"Thirteen years?"

"I'd told two girls that I'd had a bad experience with a guy but not the full details about the attack. They wanted to help ease me out of my fear of dating so set me up with this really nice guy. He didn't understand why but agreed to only doing group activities. One Friday night we all went to a football game. We chose a spot in the highest corner of the bleachers. At one point during the fourth quarter, we were all laughing hard over something someone had said. He leaned over and kissed me on the cheek. It was quick, very sweet, and I didn't freak out. A few minutes later, when he innocently placed his hand on my knee, I did freak. I'd been studying taekwondo for almost three years by then, and my self-defense instincts took over." I covered my face with my hands and through my fingers admitted, "I elbowed him in the Adam's apple."

"No!" Risa gasped.

I lowered my hands. "The poor guy. I felt so bad. Still do. He coughed for like ten minutes, tears streaming down his face.

Needless to say, that was our last date."

"And you haven't been on one since." She frowned, confused by this.

"That incident, innocent as it was, set me back." She still didn't seem to understand, but as long as she respected my wishes, I wouldn't push the issue. "I'm not interested in dating. At this point, I can't see where a man is going to enhance my life. I'm not saying never, but not now. And not Ross Donnelly. He and I are going to try being friends because I realize I need to push myself to start trusting again. My walls are up, though, and I'll put an end to the whole thing in a heartbeat if he doesn't follow the rules I gave him."

"What about that guy on the yacht yesterday? The one who seemed so enamored with you?"

Was she serious? "I don't even know him. Neither do you. He's an MMA fan, not a Gemi fan."

"Don't be so sure. I can do a little digging and get his name and number. Let me ask a few questions."

I stared at her until she started squirming. "Why would you do that? I just told you I'm not interested."

"Because you're so wrapped up in your limited world of school and the gym. You need to expand a bit."

"I'm working on that. What about you? When was your last date?"

"I can't remember. But I know when my next one is. Saturday with a guy from orthopedics."

"Ah, so you're feeling guilty? Trying to set me up for a double date?"

"A double date would be so much fun."

"No, it wouldn't. Dead serious, Risa, not interested."

"Gemi—"

"Stop. I need to switch modes now. I have to quit thinking about everything else or I won't be ready for Mele."

"Nice." She pouted. "Try to be a friend—"

Was she always this passive-aggressive, or was I extra sensitive right now? I reached across the table and lay a hand on her arm. "You're a great friend. I promise, if the desire to go out with someone strikes, you can set me up."

She rolled her eyes but didn't respond otherwise.

"If you really want to help me right now, take me home and go for a run with me. Just a short one. Then strap on the sparring pads."

"Fine. But don't hurt me. Last time I let you beat on me, I ached for two days."

"I'll go easy." I winked. "Promise."

We had gone half a block to Risa's car when out of the corner of my eye, movement across the street caught my attention. I could've sworn it was the tattooed woman. But in the split-second it took me to turn my head, she had vanished. Or maybe she hadn't been there at all. From the way the back of my neck prickled, like it had when she was staring at me in the café, it had to be her. Why was she watching me? And how many more encounters did I have to have with her before I could convince Kalani something was going on with this woman?

CHAPTER TWENTY-SEVEN

We got to Paia a few minutes before five o'clock. Risa parked in the lot behind the bright ocean-blue restaurant and saloon that always hosted the fights. The restaurant's menu was satisfying in a comfort-food way, and the bartender mixed well and stronger as the night went on. The saloon was no-frills but had a history of spontaneously attracting big-name bands that had come to the islands to perform. Tonight, however, the action was in the building out back.

Risa popped the hatchback and grabbed my duffle bag.

"You ready?" she asked.

"I am. Let's do this."

Inside the building, the crowd was already large and loud and would double in size over the next hour. They always did the fights between the third and fourth ranked fighters first, saving the top ranks for later in the day. The energy from the crowd worked like a shot of adrenaline for me. The further into the mix we went, the more pumped up I got.

"Gemi!" someone shouted. "The Bull is here!"

"My bet's on you tonight, Bull. Don't let me down."

"Twelve straight tonight, Gemi."

Past the point of getting embarrassed by this attention anymore, I was flattered that I'd developed a fan base. I held up a hand in a wave as I walked through the throng to the back of the building. There, the event promoter had hung a heavy curtain, forming a locker room of sorts for the fighters. Freestanding screens further divided the area, giving the illusion of privacy where we could prep. "Right on time," Salomon praised when he saw me. "That's a good start. You ready?"

I glanced at Risa and grinned. "You two keep asking me that like I might not be." I held up my hands. "Wrap me up, coach."

Sitting on the hospital-style table put me at the perfect height for him to wrap my hands with the five-meter-long cotton strip. I let my mind clear as I watched the process.

Starting with my left hand, he folded the soft gauze back-and-forth four times to create a pad that he placed over my knuckles. Then he wrapped the strip around the pad twice and crossed it over the top of my hand to my wrist. Because it was vulnerable, he wrapped the gauze around my wrist three times then up between my pinkie and ring finger. Back around my wrist and up between my ring and middle fingers. Around my wrist again and then between my middle and index fingers. Around my wrist, around my thumb, and then he wrapped the remaining strap around my wrist. Finally, he used surgeon's tape to hold the gauze in place. Then he repeated the process with my right hand.

The wrapping process was part of our pre-fight ritual and was meditative for me. For my first fight ever, Salomon took care of it, so we were sure the wraps were right. He did it again for the second fight because I didn't remember what he'd done. It became his job after that. A sort of final connection between my coach and me before the fight started.

"Feel good?" Salomon asked after finishing my right hand.

I stretched my fingers wide and then clenched them into fists. "Perfect as always."

"Good. I'm going to check in with Stacia and Aonani."

"Who won?" I asked.

Unable to hold back the grin, he said, "Stacia."

"Fantastic!" A cheer went off in my head for her.

"I'll come back before it's time for you to go out." He turned to Risa. "Positive, motivating talk only. Pump her up."

She gave a salute. "Yes, coach."

After the fight coordinator stopped by to inspect my wraps, I pulled off my loose-fitting running shorts revealing my snug black yoga shorts beneath. I wore a matching black sports bra under my oversized T-shirt. Once I'd removed the shirt, Risa pushed my fingerless gloves onto my hands. My hair was already pulled back in a ponytail, so all I needed was my mouth guard and then I'd be ready to go.

"You got this." Risa followed Salomon's orders and was almost as intense as I was. "You're rock solid. This chick ain't got nothing on you."

"Nice grammar," I teased as I did neck rolls and shoulder shrugs to loosen my muscles. "Oh, I forgot about my necklace. Will you take it off me and keep it safe?"

"You always forget the necklace."

Risa removed it and held it in her palm so I could see the little leaf with the 'A' and the clear crystal charm. Guess this was part of the process too. I sent a quick thought of love to my sister, then gave a nod. I reached up to touch the now empty spot between my collarbones and got a flash of Tattoo staring at me from across The Juice Bar. Had she been looking at my necklace? Was that what caught her attention? Why would it?

Risa tucked it into her pocket and gave it a pat. "Safe and sound. What's wrong? What are you thinking?"

I shook my head. Didn't matter what the woman had been looking at. Not right now, at least. "Nothing. I wonder if Ash is here."

"Let's go see."

Risa walked with me to the curtain, and we looked out at the crowd.

I smiled and waved. "Lots of my students are here. Oh, Aria and her dad. She's new. Halle and Mrs. Carrere too. That's nice. Hope they stay for the gathering after." I scanned right to left again. "I don't see Ashlyn."

"She'll make it. She would have called or texted otherwise."
Risa had her phone in her hand. "Speaking of texts, just got a
message from Malia. She's tied up with something but wishes you
good luck."

I nodded. A little disappointed but not exactly surprised.

One of the fight volunteers, a big Hawaiian dude named Keola,
came up behind us. "You've got about thirty minutes, Gemi."

"Thanks, Keola."

"Good luck tonight." He blushed and added, "Don't tell Mele,
but I put my money on you."

"You're betting against your girlfriend?" Risa asked.

"Shh." He looked behind him, probably for Mele. "This is
money, not love. Gemi's better."

Mele had lost only one fight. A simple match with an unknown
fighter no one had expected anything from. Mele's mistake was
underestimating the girl. I wouldn't do that. I might be the better
fighter, but Mele was focused and determined.

"You better get out of here before she sees you talking to the
enemy," I ordered, shooing Keola away.

Risa and I went back to my spot behind the curtain. A guy in a
black T-shirt with *Volunteer* in blood-red lettering that matched the
one Keola wore stopped by. He was scrappy and might qualify for
flyweight if he ate a triple cheeseburger just before weigh-in.

"I wanted to congratulate you now. You got this, Bull. No
doubt, that medal is yours."

I laughed at his intensity and then looked at Risa. "No pressure.
No pressure at all."

"You worried?" she asked.

"Not really."

"Let's turn that into a not at all."

She plugged my earbuds into my ears and turned on the mix of
classic rock songs I'd created just for fight nights. While I listened, I
stretched and bounced around, loosening up. Risa squirted water
into my mouth every few minutes. Enough to keep me hydrated, but

not enough to make me need the restroom.

The closer the time came for my turn in the octagon, the more I danced around. Not because I was nervous, at least no more so than I ever was, but to pump myself up even more. I focused and shut out everything except what was right in front of me.

When Salomon stopped to get me, I pulled the earbuds out and stated, "Let's go get that medal."

Risa pulled back the curtain and my coach and I stepped through. The crowd's excitement rose to a fever pitch as Mele and I entered the cage. I knew from watching videos of my matches that I looked like a physically different person when I fought. My face changed. Gone was any resemblance to the baby-faced blond everyone knew. My mouth guard gave me a tough pout. Adrenaline coursed through my body, making my energy level skyrocket. I squinted and my vision tunneled. Right now, the only thing I was focused on was Mele. The roar of the crowd became white noise, further blocking any distractions.

And then Ashlyn appeared at the side of the octagon, Jeannie at her side. She jumped up and down and waved at me with both hands. I was overjoyed that she made it, but why was she wearing sunglasses? Must have forgotten to take them off.

I raised my hand in a wave of acknowledgment and returned my focus to the woman across from me. As I stood on my side of the cage, glowering at Mele while the event promoter introduced us, my feet began to paw at the mat. The Bull was ready to fight. We came together, touched gloves, and the fight was underway.

We danced around for a few seconds, getting a read on each other and trying to establish dominance. I knew Mele's style would be to try and land a series of body blows right away in the hopes of wearing me down. Ready for them, I either backed away from the jabs or blocked them easily.

I preferred to go right for the head, and Mele knew that. She taunted me, leaning in with her chin or holding her arms out wide in a come-get-me stance. I had learned that patience was the best defense. I would wait for the perfect moment to let loose rather than tire out my arms with strikes that wouldn't connect or have an impact.

As expected, Mele was focused, laser sharp. She landed a couple body blows and got me with a knee to the stomach once. I felt it, but the knee didn't have the impact on me it might on another fighter thanks to my kettlebell planks and adrenaline level. I landed a right cross to her jaw that had her seeing stars. While she tried to regain her bearings, I swept her legs and was going for an armbar. The bell rang, signaling the end of the first five-minute round, so I had to let her go.

I went to Salomon who squirted water in my mouth and mopped my forehead.

"You're doing great, mahi. Keep it up. She's tiring herself out."

He was right. By the mid-point of the second round, Mele had thrown a flurry of kicks, knees, and punches that only grazed me and, more importantly, spent her energy. Now was the time for me to ramp up the intensity. My punches landed squarely where I aimed them. Side kicks connected with Mele's ribs. I swept her feet once and almost dropped her, but she had great balance and recovered. She kept her hands up, denying me access to her left temple.

Like a bull cornering its victim, I backed Mele against the fence and was about to pelt her with a flurry of blows. My adrenaline spiked, ready for the attack. The roar of the crowd said they knew what was coming too. I'd land one strike after another until Mele was so worn down her hands would drop. That was when I'd go in with the kill shot. Right cross. Match over. Medal mine.

Except, just as I got Mele where I wanted her and raised my fist to strike, I heard Ashlyn's voice in my head. *Just leave me alone!* It was so real she could have been standing there next to me instead of Mele. Something was wrong.

I looked down at her for a second. Half a second. In that half-second, I saw that Ashlyn had taken the sunglasses off, revealing a huge dark-purple bruise over her right eye. And Tattoo was standing next to her. What was she doing here? Whatever she was saying to Ashlyn, my sister was looking her square in the face, not at me and my impending kill-shot right cross. Ash was staring down the tattooed woman with a defiant set to her jaw. But I knew my sister better than anyone and recognized the look behind the glare. Ashlyn was scared.

In the next half-second, Mele stomped on my foot and spun away from me. Then she released a powerful round kick that caught me squarely on the jaw.

Then my vision faded to black, and I dropped to the mat.

CHAPTER TWENTY-EIGHT

All I wanted to do was leave. I wanted to slink out of the building in shame and go home to lick my wounds. My record was ruined. Those who came to cheer me on would be so disappointed. Those who had placed bets on me would be furious. Like anywhere, the payout was bigger for the underdog. The odds had heavily favored me, so those who had put their money on Mele were ecstatic and would shout their thanks to me as they collected their winnings.

One of the fight volunteers came to my area in the temporary locker room. "Your sister is at the curtain insisting she needs to come in and see you. I told her no one other than fight people were allowed back here. She keeps demanding."

Of course she did. She'd gush all over me and want to talk about what happened. I couldn't deal with that right now. "Tell her I'm fine and I'll find her in the saloon later."

"What happened?" Salomon was equally devastated, more than a little upset with me, and not willing to accept my *don't want to deal with it right now* brush off.

"Ashlyn," I finally said as though that explained it all. It didn't. "I looked away for a second. Someone hit her. She's got a black eye, and this woman who's been following me —"

I stopped there. I had no proof that Tattoo had been following me.

Salomon's expression changed to one of pity, then he wrapped me in a hug. "You can't keep sacrificing yourself for your sister.

Ashlyn wasn't in danger. Her problem could have been dealt with two minutes later. You had Mele right there. The title was yours."

How could I get him to understand that Ashlyn and I had this connection? I swear, I heard her thoughts. *Just leave me alone!* She was trying to be tough, but I heard her fear as loudly as if she'd hollered in my ear. Who the hell was this tattooed woman, and why was she hanging around us?

He was right, though. Ashlyn was scared but not in danger at that moment. Jeannie was at her side. She didn't need me. Instead of admitting that to Salomon, I asked, "That's all you have to say? I figured you'd chew me out good."

He gave me a tight smile. "I'll have plenty more to say tomorrow. How's the jaw?"

I pulled the icepack away and moved my jaw from side to side. "Not horrible right now. Ask me later. And by 'tomorrow,' does that mean you want me to come to the gym?"

"Don't know about you, but I wouldn't want to have that discussion just before teaching the kids."

My spirits sunk even lower. My warriors. How many of them just watched me fail?

"See you at the gathering." His tone made it clear, me not attending wasn't an option. No matter how badly I wanted to hide, I had to stay for Heleena.

"How's your foot?" Risa asked.

"I can walk, but it hurts."

She asked me repeatedly if I wanted to go out and watch the rest of the fights. I said no every time, using first my foot as an excuse, then my jaw, then my bruised ego.

When the last fight was over, she grumbled, "We can go now. Everyone left the building. You can sneak out to the car and no one will see you."

"No," I said, "this is about Heleena, not me."

"Then pull yourself together and quit pouting. You're acting like such a sore loser."

The nag was back. "Can't I have a minute to feel sorry for myself?"

"Sure you can. That minute was up an hour ago."

My foot hurt too much to wear a shoe, so Risa strapped a fresh icepack to it with an elastic bandage and found a crutch for me to borrow. She brought my stuff to the car and then walked me into the saloon. I did my best to ignore the comments flying around. Fighting boosted my confidence. Winning made me feel safe. The ribbing reminders that I blew it tonight made me feel weak and helpless, like that girl in the parking lot who needed her friends to save her.

I looked down, avoiding eye contact with people, and ended up looking right into the face of one of my students.

"You did so good," Halle Carrere told me with a huge smile.

"I lost." I hadn't said those words out loud yet.

"But you were this close to winning." She held her thumb and forefinger about a millimeter apart. And then, as though it was a given, she added, "You'll do better next time. Heleena always told me doing your best matters more than winning. Did you do your best?"

I blinked, tears stinging my eyes. "I really did."

"That's all that matters," she repeated.

"Did it hurt when she kicked you?"

I turned to see a dozen more of my students gathered around. They all wore the same type of expression Halle did. They came to watch me fight and right up to the end, I was giving them what might have been the best fight of my life.

I smiled. "It did hurt. I don't recommend it."

"That kick to her ribs," Darren held his stomach as though in agony then threw his arms in the air. "That was so awesome. You think your jaw hurts? Her ribs are going to be killing her tomorrow."

"It's okay that you lost," Aria Vega told me. "You left your mark. And I don't mean just a physical one."

I stood there talking with them about the fight for another few minutes and realized it didn't matter what anyone else in the building thought. My warriors were proud of me. And they were looking to me to see how to handle a loss, so I needed to be a gracious loser.

"Gemi." A hand on my arm stopped me from moving on to Heleena's gathering. It was Mrs. Carrere. "I wanted to ask you about the self-defense classes." Her cheeks flushed pink as a hibiscus. "The ones for women."

I took her hand and squeezed it. "Tuesday nights at seven. Saturday mornings at nine."

She nodded as though committing the times to memory. "Can you teach me to do some of what you just did?"

Looking her dead in the eye, I asked, "Any reason in particular?"

She seemed to understand my meaning. "No. But we never know, do we? Regardless of needing to protect myself, it sure would be nice to have your kind of confidence."

The last few minutes with my students had helped me regain some of what Mele had taken from me. "Come talk to me after Halle's class on Monday."

She explained that they weren't going to stay for the gathering. It would be too painful, and she didn't want any of the attention on them when it should be on Heleena. I understood that.

After they left, Risa gave me a gentle shoulder bump. "Looks like you don't need a medal to prove you're a winner."

"Thanks." I returned the bump. "That was quite possibly the cheesiest thing you've ever said."

She shrugged. "I like cheese." Her eyes went wide. "Incoming."

Before I could ask what she meant, Ashlyn's arms were around my neck.

"Oh, God, Peep. She got you right in the face. Are you okay? Do you need to go to the hospital?"

Gasping with pain, I croaked, "You're squeezing my face, Ashlyn."

She let go instantly. "Sorry."

"My jaw hurts, my foot hurts, and I've got a bit of a headache." Brain damage? The first signs of CTE? "I'll be okay, though." I brushed my fingertips over her black eye. "What happened?"

Ashlyn gave a dismissive flick of her perfectly manicured hand. "The guy in the row in front of us on the plane. He was taking his bag out of the overhead and got me right in the eye with his elbow."

She was lying. She didn't look at me as she spoke. Instead, her attention was on Jeannie who nodded in agreement with everything she said.

"Who was that woman you were talking to?" I asked. "The one with the tattoos? Looked like she was yelling at you."

She frowned, unsure of what I meant, then her face brightened with understanding. "Is that what distracted you?" She looked past me as she explained, "I made a comment about her tattoos and apparently offended her. No clue who she is."

Another lie. Ashlyn always looked me square in the face when she spoke. "Interesting, because I've seen her before. A few times, actually. I got the impression she knew me."

Ash's hesitation before responding was very brief but long enough that I caught it. "Well, there aren't many people left on the island who don't know you."

"Especially after tonight," Risa quipped and put her hand over her mouth. "Did I say that out loud?"

I made a face at her. "Brat."

"Jeannie's going to take me home," Ashlyn said. "I know there's a gathering for Heleena, but that's for you all."

She hugged me gently, and I put my hands on her shoulders, stopping her from walking away. "We need to talk when I get home. All right?"

Her megawatt smile faded. "Sure. We can talk."

It hurt my heart worse than my jaw, foot, and head combined to think that my sister was lying to me. How long had that been going on? Was it just since this job of hers started or had it been longer than that?

Or was I imagining things? Over the last few days, I'd accused numerous people of being Leena's killer. Thankfully, not to their faces. I decided the tattooed woman was a member of the yakuza and was sent to intimidate me. And now I was sure my sister was lying to me even though she had immediate and legitimate-sounding explanations for everything. Maybe I'd finally pushed myself past the breaking point.

"Let it go." Risa turned me toward the group. "Gathering now, sister later. One thing at a time."

If tonight hadn't taught me the importance of that, I'd never learn it.

CHAPTER TWENTY-NINE

Everyone was clustered around the bar in the corner of the saloon. They were subdued but not morose. Leena wouldn't have wanted people to be morose. There were a lot of "remember when" memories being shared along with a good deal of laughter and more than a few tears.

Once it appeared everyone had arrived, the bartender prepared Heleena's latest favorite power drink, a blend of fruits and veggies and kelp. She poured out dozens of shot glasses of the thick concoction and set them out on the bar for everyone to take.

Coach Ozzie stood at the center of the group and wiped his eyes with the back of his hand. He put an arm around Lana, and they held their shot glasses high. His voice broke as he loudly proclaimed, "You'll always be number one in our hearts. To Leena!"

The crowd repeated, "To Leena," and everyone tossed back their shots. In her honor, we tried to ignore the fact that the gloppy drink was horrible. Someone finally said, "Glad she could fight better than mix a smoothie."

Mona, wallowing from her own loss tonight, stood silently at Salomon's side. She held a box prettily decorated in mermaid shades with *Donations for Heleena Carrere* written on every side. I dug a couple twenties out of my pocket and hobbled through the crowd with my crutch to add them to the collection.

"Who made the box?" I asked the stocky, weather-beaten brunette. "It's very pretty."

"Callie did," Mona replied with a smile. "Looks like Heleena's hair."

It was either an aftereffect of getting kicked in the jaw and my head hitting the mat or something was off about that statement. Whatever it was, I froze momentarily, the bills halfway in the slot on the top of the box. I blinked, let them slide in, and returned Mona's smile.

"Sorry about your fight tonight," I told her.

"Yeah." She let out a shaky sigh. "Yours too. Guess that's what happens when we try to serve too many masters, right?"

"You may be right. How was your trip, by the way?"

"The fish were biting good. My customers were real happy. Don't think I'll schedule so many one after another that way again. It was kind of intense. And never so close to a fight. Ozzie's not happy with me."

"How many bookings did you have?"

Mona held the box out to a guy with a stack of bills. "Went around the saloon. Everyone pitched in."

I waited while he fed half of the stack into the slot and then the other half.

"That's so nice," Mona praised. "Thank you. Lana's going to use this money for the salon. She said something about advertising and a new sign out front."

I nodded my approval. "That should help."

"What did you ask me before?" Mona wondered. "Oh, how many trips. One every day starting Monday."

Tingles shot through me again. "Monday? I thought you left on Tuesday."

"Nope." She repositioned her hands from the bottom of the box to the sides and reached it out to more people with bills in hand.

My mouth went dry. "What happened to your hands?"

I gestured at the purple-green bruises and crusty scabs on her knuckles. It took about a week for bruises to go from pink red to blue purple to purple green. A week from now, they'd be yellow brown.

Mona glanced down at them and replied, "Hazard of working on a fishing boat. Slipped and fell on the wet deck, landed hard."

"Sorry to hear that." I willed myself to stay composed. "Must've made fighting tonight really painful."

"Yeah," Mona laughed. "Funny how adrenaline and enough gauze can ease the impact. Not enough to help me pull off a win, unfortunately." A shadow darkened her face for a split second, and then she started talking faster. "Of course being gone all week, I wasn't in the right mindset. And while I got plenty of exercise on the boat, I didn't get any practice. I figure if I can do as well as I did tonight in this condition, I'm on my way to that top spot."

I swallowed the dry lump in my throat, pulled my phone out of my back pocket, and held it up as though it was ringing. "Sorry, I have to take this."

"Where are you going?" Risa asked, following me out of the saloon.

"Gotta make a call. Do me a favor?"

"What's going on?"

"Go keep an eye on Mona. Don't let her leave. If she tries to, enlist Salomon and any other fighter you can grab."

Her eyes narrowed, then went wide with understanding. She darted back to the gathering while I hit redial on a recent call and shuffled out to the parking lot.

The voice on the other end of the call greeted, "Detective Kalani."

"It was Mona Randall. We're still at the venue in Paia. You need to get out here."

"Gemi? Slow down. Give me a detail or two."

I told her about Mona's hands. "She said she slipped and fell on her fishing boat. The thing is, when a person falls, they put their hands out to soften the impact and land on their palms, not their knuckles."

"That may or may not be true depending on circumstances. What else have you got?"

"She knew about Heleena's hair."

Kalani paused before saying, "What about her hair? You mean all the colors?"

"Right. Heleena got that done on Tuesday morning. She showed it off to all of us at No Mercy that night. Mona just told me she left on her first fishing trip on Monday. How did she know about Leena's hair?"

A white sedan with "Maui Police" on the side pulled into the parking lot in front of me. An unmarked sedan was behind them. The detective stepped out of the unmarked car. I signed off the call and held my hands out as though to ask, "Why didn't you tell me you were seconds away?"

"What happened to you?" Kalani gestured at the crutch. The icepack on my foot turned warm long ago and had been removed.

"My fight didn't go as planned. What's going on? Why are you here?"

"To arrest Mona Randall. She was one of the fighters on our list who would benefit from Heleena not fighting. Salomon told us she was running fishing trips, so we went out to Lahaina Harbor and talked to some folks about her boat. A few people stated they'd seen it docked there during the day Tuesday. Others said they'd seen it Tuesday night. We got a warrant to check the GPS and it showed that the MON Ami didn't leave Lahaina Harbor until early Wednesday morning."

The truth sank in, and my knees went weak. "Mona killed Heleena. Why?"

"That's what I'm going to find out."

* * *

Risa and I stood outside the saloon, along with everyone from No Mercy, as the uniformed officer led Mona to his vehicle.

Loudly enough for everyone within a block radius to hear, Mona hollered at Kalani, "I had nothing to do with this."

With far less drama, the detective replied, "Then you shouldn't have an issue helping us out by coming in and answering a few questions."

"Mona?" Salomon asked once both cars had driven off. "Really?"

His shock turned to anger after I told him about Mona's knuckles and the details surrounding Leena's mermaid hair.

"She also tried to take the collection for Lana," Risa told us. "She headed for the side door with the box in her hands. When I asked where she was going, she looked down like she didn't realize she was still holding this huge box and made some lame 'silly me' excuse. Then the cops walked in."

Salomon shook his head, looking like he couldn't deal with anything more tonight. "I'm going home." As he walked away, he called, "I still want to talk with you tomorrow, mahi."

"You ready to go?" Risa asked.

I yawned in reply, suddenly exhausted. "Very ready. I need to put more ice on my foot and take an ibuprofen."

She took the crutch from me and put it in the back of the Mazda. After a few minutes of silence as we drove west along the Hana Highway toward my condo in Wailuku, Risa quietly asked, "What happened? With the fight."

I rolled down my window to let in the night air. "No big mystery. I let myself get distracted."

"That wasn't just distraction." Risa's gaze shifted between the road and me. "I never took my eyes off you during the entire fight. Not once. I've never seen you in better form. You were patient, appeared to know what Mele was going to do before she did it, and set her up perfectly for that right cross. And then, you froze. It was like someone pressed a pause button on you. It wasn't for even a second, but it was enough for Mele to act."

"You got the name right."

"What?"

"Right cross."

Risa didn't find my deflection of the conversation funny. She turned right onto the road to Baldwin Beach Park, pulled to a stop in the empty parking lot, and turned off the engine.

"Tell me what's going on, Gemi. You were so focused, what distracted you like that mid-fight? Was it Ashlyn? I saw her standing nearby."

I took in another deep breath of ocean air and turned in my seat to face my friend. "Have I ever told you about the connection Ash and I have?"

Risa frowned. "You're super close. Everyone who knows the two of you knows that."

"It's more than being close. It started when I got attacked that night when I was thirteen. My friends immediately called my mom. She couldn't be bothered with coming to pick me up. I have no clue what was more important than her terrified daughter, but they called Ashlyn next."

"And she didn't hesitate." Risa's stern expression softened.

"She was on a date with this boy she was crazy about. All she'd talked about for months was going out with him but was too afraid to ask him. Finally, he got the hint and asked her."

"And in the middle of her date, she came to your aid."

"Wasn't even the middle. They hadn't even gotten to the restaurant yet. The boy was cool about it. He went and got takeout for them instead, but they only had one or two other dates after that."

Risa pushed her seat back as far as it would go and pulled her legs up. "That's when the sister superpower started?"

"Yeah, it's weird. We just know things about each other. That happens a lot with twins. You know how one twin will get hurt and the other twin, miles and miles away, will feel it?"

She nodded. "I've heard of that."

"It's that kind of thing. Right there, in the middle of the fight, I swear I heard Ashlyn's voice. Not just a feeling but her actual voice inside my head. It sounded like she was in danger or afraid. So I looked down, saw the black eye, then saw that woman standing next to her."

"What woman?"

"The one covered in tattoos. You didn't see her?"

"Tattoos? That could mean—"

"Yakuza. I first saw her at The Juice Bar. Kym said this woman comes in now and then and thought she might be one of them. I noticed her looking at me. Not just a casual glance, but intense staring. She even walked up to get a closer look."

I reached protectively for my throat, the spot she had focused on, and for a split second a beheaded body on the beach flashed in my mind.

"Oh yeah." Risa pulled my necklace out of her pocket and handed it to me.

I blinked away the awful image and dangled the necklace by the chain, the parking lot light glinting off the infinity symbol. "I think this is what she was staring at. If she knows Ashlyn, she's seen her necklace and must have connected us. Why, though? What are the chances that someone who knows my sister would just happen to show up when I was there?"

"It's a public place," Risa dismissed. "You said she goes there sometimes."

"But don't you think it's a little strange for her to show up at The Juice Bar and then my fight where she stands right next to Ashlyn?"

She remained quiet before admitting, "Okay, it's a little suspicious, but you don't know that she was looking at your necklace or that there's a connection to Ashlyn. Maybe she's an MMA fan and recognized you."

"I don't think so. She sat at the table right behind me at the café. I didn't know she was there, but Ross said she never took her eyes off me."

"One weird encounter and you're freaking out?"

"It wasn't just one. I swear I saw her again this morning. We were leaving The Juice Bar, and I was sure I saw her out of the corner of my eye. When I turned to look, she wasn't there."

"That's because you're stressed out and seeing things."

"She was definitely at the fight."

Risa didn't reply to that.

"And then there was the note shoved under my door last night."

"At the condo? What did it say?"

"It said 'back off.' I thought it was for me since I was the only one home. I figured it was someone upset that I was nosing around in the investigation. But now that I think about it, it said 'Ms. Kittredge' on the envelope, so it could have been for Ashlyn. What if someone is telling *her* to back off? What if she's involved with something or someone dangerous?"

"Someone dangerous? You think Ashlyn is mixed up with the yakuza?" She laughed like she didn't believe me, but it wasn't very convincing. "I'm sorry I ever mentioned them to you."

"After seeing Ash with that tattooed woman tonight, I'm telling you, she's afraid of her." I listened to the waves washing up on shore and thought of my sister trying to defend herself from an organization that beheaded people. "How do I dig into them?"

"The yakuza? You don't. You do as that note said and back off."

"You know me better than that. If Ashlyn is in danger, there's no way I'll stand down."

She jumped out of the car, paced a circle around it twice, and stopped in front of it. She stared at me through the windshield, her breathing fast and ragged.

"Seriously, Gemi, I've seen what they do to people they're upset with. Poking around in Heleena's murder was one thing. You *do not* want to mess around with these folks." She paused to catch her breath then asked, "You haven't talked to anyone else about this Ashlyn/yakuza thing, have you?"

I got out and leaned on the car door, keeping my weight off my bruised foot. "Only you."

"Good. Okay, let's back up a minute. I can tell you're serious about this, but I think it's a real stretch. You have no proof that Ashlyn is in trouble. She's had a valid explanation for everything you've asked her. You're only assuming the tattooed woman and that note are connected. As for Ashlyn being afraid of her, do you remember the day she found that centipede in her bathroom?"

I nodded and chuckled. "I thought she was going to need therapy."

"The point being, it doesn't take much to scare her." Risa stepped closer to me. "I'm begging you, don't go looking for trouble. The yakuza are total badasses. Talk to your sister. Find out if you're right about her being in danger. If she is, you have to get help. As in, talk to Malia."

For the first time in thirteen years, I felt like the cops might not be as inept as I'd thought. They caught Heleena's killer. Maybe I'd been wrong about their search for my mother. She clearly didn't want to be found. No sense wasting time and resources on someone like her when there were people like Leena and Mona to focus on.

"All right, I'll talk to Ash," I agreed, and Risa slumped with relief. "But if I'm right and she's in danger, I will dig into this."

"With Malia's help. Right?"

I nodded. And if the detective wouldn't help, I had no qualms about handling this myself.

CHAPTER THIRTY

Risa pulled to a stop in front of the condo and asked if I wanted her to come in. I thanked her, but all I really wanted was a shower, ibuprofen, and some time with my sister.

Inside, Ashlyn was in her bedroom unpacking. If I stopped and said anything, we'd start talking and I wouldn't get into the shower for another couple hours. I desperately wanted to wash this night off me before doing another thing, so I tiptoed past her bedroom and slipped into mine. This meant the moment I turned the shower on, she was outside my bathroom pounding on the door.

"Are you sure you're all right? What happened after I left? Do you need to see a doctor?"

"Ashlyn!" I hollered back. "I'm fine. I'll be out in a few minutes."

As I was toweling off, she knocked on the door again. "Detective Kalani is here to see you."

What was she doing here?

I pulled on a pair of boxer shorts and a T-shirt and hurried downstairs to find Malia sitting in our living room. Hulu stared at her from his perch on the arm of her chair. My sister sat on the couch across from them.

"How did it go?" I asked the detective.

"How did what go?" Ashlyn asked and then gasped. "Did you catch Heleena's killer?"

Malia looked pointedly from me to my sister and back. Message received.

"Why don't we go out on the lanai to talk?" I suggested

There, she settled onto the loveseat. "Not sure this is any more private."

"Maybe not, but at least we won't get interrupted by questions every thirty seconds." I took the chair next to her, pulling it close so we could keep our voices low, and propped my foot on the coffee table. "What did Mona say?"

"First, let me clarify that I wouldn't normally talk to a civilian this way. But in your case there's the Risa factor. She'd harass me to the end of days until I spilled."

I chuckled. "She would. Thanks for breaking protocol."

"Mona confessed to everything. It was all about money. Her fishing boat needed repairs and upgrades if she wanted to stay competitive with the other charters, so she took out a loan from some questionable people, and the payment was due."

"The yakuza?" I joked.

She hesitated, then nodded.

My jaw dropped. "Really?"

"You had a lot of the pieces, just the wrong players. Yes, Mona got a loan from one of the yakuza factions. The loan came due, and she didn't have the money. They agreed to give her an extension if she helped fix the outcome of the fights in her weight class. They basically wanted the top three fighters taken out. Not necessarily dead, but not fighting. Or willing to throw their fight."

"According to Homeless Harry, that's what Mona told Heleena. 'I need you to forfeit the fight.'"

Malia nodded. "Mona said she honestly thought Heleena would help her out. When she refused, Mona panicked, and things got out of control quickly."

"Then she attempted to attack Callie to stop her from fighting?"

"Right. They said if Mona could take out the number one fighter, Callie, they'd knock five percent off the interest and give her another week to pay her loan. Turns out, that was a decent amount of money for Mona, so she was willing to try. Lots of bets had already been placed on Callie's fight. If she didn't win, the yakuza stood to make a small fortune. If Callie didn't fight, Mona would step in to face Callie's opponent. If Mona could then pull off a win, that fortune would double. Now Mona's in big trouble, and I don't just mean for killing Heleena."

"The yakuza," I supplied. "I assume Mona gave up and confessed to all this figuring they can't reach her in prison?"

"That's what she thinks. She owes them quite a bit of money. If they want to get at her, I'm not sure any place is safe."

I shuddered. Desperation made people do stupid things. "Did you ask her about the text and envelope I received?"

She nodded. "I did. She didn't know anything about either of them."

My mind spun. "Then who could have sent them?"

"You could try tracing the phone number."

"It was blocked."

"If anything else comes from it, let me know. There's nothing more I can do right now."

Still shocked that Mona went to mobsters for help, I asked, "Are the yakuza mixed up with the island's MMA gyms?"

She wiggled her hand in a maybe-maybe not gesture. "I don't think they are directly, but I'm not completely sure. It seems more that they're messing with the outcome of the fights. And I know you think that tattooed woman was following you, but we couldn't find any connection between her and tonight's fights."

"That's because she was there to intimidate my sister."

"She was at the fight?"

"She was." I gave the recap of how Tattoo caused me to lose my fight. "Ashlyn says she doesn't know her. She claims she made a comment about her tattoos that made the woman mad and that's why she was staring Ashlyn down. I think Ash is hiding something."

Malia hesitated then said, "Regarding this mystery woman, I did a little digging. Her name is Kiyoko Tachibana. That's literally all we know about her." She ran her hands over her arms, indicating the tattoos. "She does appear to be yakuza, but we haven't been able to tie her to any factions. We can't find records of any kind on her. No record of birth. Nothing. She's like a ghost. We want to talk with her regarding yakuza activity, but every time we spot her, she disappears before we can get close."

"It must have been her watching me from across the street. I swear she was there, and a blink later, she wasn't."

"Like I said, she's a ghost." Malia stood. "That's all I've got for you. I'll get out of here so you can rest. How are you feeling?"

"Foot aches. Jaw aches. Head feels a little better after drinking some water."

"Go drink some more, then."

I limped along with her to the front door and grabbed the crutch I'd left propped there. "I'll walk you out."

"You don't need to."

I glanced at Ashlyn, who'd moved to the kitchen, and whispered, "I want to ask you about something else."

The Harley was parked in our driveway, the shiny parts gleaming from the streetlights. Her matching black helmet rested on the seat.

"What's up?"

"What's involved in becoming a cop?"

Malia was struck momentarily speechless. "Are you asking for yourself or a friend?"

"Myself," I admitted. "Tonight's fight wasn't as satisfying as others have been. And not just because I lost."

"What's going on?"

I sighed and leaned hard on the crutch. "I'm going to be thirty in a few days. To date, my best paying job has only paid slightly better than minimum wage."

"You're not going to get rich being a cop," Malia cautioned with a laugh.

"But it would be satisfying."

"I agree with that. My job is hard and can be frustrating, but it can also be very satisfying. Like tonight, getting justice for Heleena."

She frowned. "You're attending college, right?"

"Have been for the last six years. When I started, I really wanted to get into nursing for personal reasons. The passion isn't there anymore, though. I've only got a semester to go, and I'll finish because at least I'll have a degree, but I don't want to be a nurse."

"Where's your passion now?"

"Helping abused women and kids become strong and independent both physically and mentally."

Her eyebrows rose. "Wow. That's practically a mission statement."

I smiled. "I've thought a lot about it lately."

"Tell me why you're thinking about police work."

A good question that I didn't have a solid answer for. Ashlyn would be shocked. So would Risa. I'd done nothing but spout distrust for cops for the last decade.

As I struggled to form a reply, Malia stated, "Your hesitation in answering that question says you need to think about it some more. It should come as naturally as your women and kids comment."

"I do need to think more. But that's why I wanted to talk with you first." Then I put my other concern out there. "I'm worried that something's going on with Ashlyn."

"Something illegal?"

"Maybe. I don't know for sure."

"I've been a cop for fifteen years. You don't just graduate from the academy and become a detective. If you're thinking you'll be able to go get a little training and then investigate whatever she might be messed up with, think again."

I investigated Heleena's case without being a cop. Sort of.

The detective seemed to read my mind. "No vigilante justice, Ms. Kittredge. Don't go nosing around in anything else. If you really think your sister is in trouble, talk to me. I'll look into it."

I put a hand over my heart. "Vigilante justice? Nosing around? You wound me, Detective Kalani."

She rolled her eyes. "Promise me you won't go off on your own again."

"Okay."

She grabbed her helmet. "I'm leaving before I hear something that will get you in trouble." She pulled on her helmet, threw a leg over the bike, and started the engine. "Go rest that foot. You promised we'd go for a ride soon."

I saluted. That was a promise I would keep.

Two steps inside the condo, I was assaulted by the smell of chocolate. I found Ashlyn in the kitchen ladling waffle batter onto the maker.

"How long was I outside?" I asked.

"I made the batter earlier." She took a bowl of berries, a can of whipped cream, and a container of chocolate syrup out of the refrigerator. "I figured you'd want your post-fight crappy food."

My stomach growled. "More tonight than ever."

She handed me an icepack from the freezer. "Go sit and prop up that foot."

Grabbing the mysterious envelope from the drawer as I passed by, I hobbled over to the dinette table. It was nice to have Ashlyn home. As she prepared the waffles, I looked a little longer at her black eye. It *could* have been from an accidental elbow. And she might have been telling me the truth about unintentionally insulting Kiyoko Tachibana. If Tattoo was a member of the yakuza, she could have been at the fight tonight to keep an eye on Mona and any other fighters who were supposed to be rigging the outcomes.

Ashlyn set a plate in front of me and plopped down with her own smaller plateful. She squirted a way too small amount of whipped cream onto my waffles. I motioned for her to keep going, laughing as she covered every square inch then added syrup.

The first bite was heaven. I'd pay for it tomorrow with a very unhappy tummy, as I always did, but tonight it was worth it.

Ash pointed at the envelope. "What's that?"

I turned it over to show her "Ms. Kittredge" on the front. "I thought it was for me but have no idea what it means. Maybe it was meant for you."

She slid the note out, read the "back off" directive, and frowned deeply.

As she stared at the paper, I noticed something I hadn't before. I grabbed it from her and held it up to the light. "There's a watermark."

"A what?" she asked, blinking.

I held it so she could see it too. "It's really faint. Looks like a hibiscus."

She didn't reply, other than to frown again.

"Any idea what this means?"

"Not a clue," she murmured and shook her head slowly.

Don't get all suspicious again, the little girl ordered.

She was right. We lived on a tropical island. Flowers were everywhere. Anyone could have paper like this. Maybe a neighbor delivered it. Maybe they were upset with something we'd done or didn't like the noise from my motorcycle at night.

At what point, though, was the recurring hibiscus not coincidental?

"If I ask you something," I began between bites, "you'll tell me the truth, won't you?"

Confused by the question, she replied, "Of course I will. What's up?"

I took a breath and put my worries out there. "I have concerns about your employment. I don't doubt your ability, but I don't understand how your background qualifies you to get a job that pays enough to afford this condo. And the cars, clothes, and other luxuries."

She didn't respond. I hadn't asked her a question, though.

I chewed and swallowed another forkful of waffle. "Risa told me she was ready to upgrade and looked at one of these models. They're listed at over seven hundred thousand dollars, Ash."

"That sounds about right." There was no hesitation, nothing in her voice that indicated she'd paid for this place with anything other than a legitimate paycheck.

"Do I need to be worried? Are you involved with something illegal?"

She laughed. "What, like the yakuza?" She said it with four Us. *Yakuuuuza.*

"Were you listening to my discussion with Detective Kalani?"

She cleared her throat. "For a minute. Then I felt guilty so came in here and worked on your waffles." She held her left hand in the air, placed her right over her heart, and looked me dead in the eye. "I swear to you, I'm not doing anything wrong." She laughed when I didn't ease up. "Seriously, Peep, you've got crime on the brain. Speaking of which"—she reached out and lightly tapped my head—"how's yours?"

I wasn't sure that I'd gotten the whole truth from her, but at least the topic was open now. If there was more she needed to tell me about, she would.

I told her about the cruise and Allie the neurologist's warning about CTE. "Everyone's going to think it's because I lost, but tonight might have been my last fight."

Ash's eyes went wide, and she choked on her waffle. "Oh my God."

"I haven't decided for sure so don't get too excited, but I know I don't want to mess up my brain."

"I know how much you love this, Peep, but nothing would make me happier." She gave a happy little wiggle and loaded her fork with whipped cream and berries. "That will really open your schedule. How will you fill all that time?"

"I'll still workout, my body won't let me quit that. And I could never walk away from my students. I'll still teach. Maybe I'll coach other fighters."

"It was a joke. You don't need to fill every minute of your day." She paused, giving me her most serious expression. "You know why you do that, don't you?"

"Fill my days? So I can do all that I want to do."

She shook her head. "You do it to keep yourself so busy you can't think of anything else. When you're quiet and still, that's when the demons can enter. You have never fully dealt with your demons, Peep. You've kept yourself in a constant defensive mode for seventeen years. It got better for a while when we first moved here, then Mom left, and you ramped right back up." She wiped a drop of chocolate sauce from my chin. "You need to deal with what happened before you completely break down."

I snorted. "You mean grow up, get a real job, and start supporting myself?"

All things that were lacking in my life. As I'd become vividly aware over the past four days . . . as I was trying hard to not have that breakdown.

"There you go again. Defensive. No, that's not what I meant. I'm so proud of you for all that you've accomplished. Your ability to protect yourself, and me, is beyond impressive. Not to mention comforting. The 'real' job is right around the corner. You'll be a nurse soon."

Not going there. Not tonight.

"My point is," she concluded, "you need to stop running at full speed all the time and let the demon in so you can finally slay it."

I pouted over yet another lecture, then grabbed her hand and placed a kiss on it. "And Risa thinks she's the one who knows me best. She's got nothing on my Ashy."

She kissed my hand in return, her eyes glistening.

"I might need help," I admitted, my throat tightening with emotion. "I've been 'running at full speed,' as you say, for so long I'm not sure I know how to slow down."

"That's what I'm here for. You give a whistle, and I'll be at your side. Now and always."

Just like she was that night seventeen years ago.

My heart swelled, and not for the first time, I realized how blessed I was. We settled into comfortable silence, and I let myself enjoy the rest of my crappy food. When my plate was almost clean, I said, "I was thinking about getting a tattoo."

"Really?" Ashlyn gasped and clapped excitedly. "I know a great place. What do you want to get?"

"I'm thinking a mermaid. In honor of Heleena." And the *first* crime I helped solve.

Suspense and fantasy author Shawn McGuire loves creating characters and places her fans want to return to again and again. She started writing after seeing the first Star Wars movie (that's episode IV) as a kid. She couldn't wait for the next installment to come out so wrote her own. Sadly, those notebooks are long lost, but her desire to tell a tale is as strong now as it was then. She lives in Wisconsin near the beautiful Mississippi River and when not writing or reading, she might be baking, crafting, going for a long walk, or nibbling really dark chocolate. You can learn more about her work on her website www.Shawn-McGuire.com

Made in the USA
Las Vegas, NV
01 November 2021

33484830R10148